SHIP OF THE DEAD

ALSO BY JAMES JENNEWEIN
AND TOM S. PARKER

RUNEWARRIORS
SHIELD OF ODIN

RUNEWARRIORS
SWORD OF DOOM

SHIP OF THE DEAD

JAMES JENNEWEIN AND TOM S. PARKER

HARPER

An Imprint of HarperCollins*Publishers*

Library of Congress Cataloging-in-Publication Data
Jennewein, Jim
    Ship of the dead/ James Jennewein and Tom S. Parker. — 1st ed.
        p.   cm. — (RuneWarriors.)
    Summary: In order to save his one true love and prevent the destruction of the earth,
Dane the Defiant must defeat an old—and undead—enemy.
    ISBN 978-0-06-144942-0 (trade bdg.)
    1. Vikings—Juvenile fiction. [1. Vikings—Fiction. 2. Dead—Fiction. 3. Fate and
fatalism—Fiction. 4. Adventure and adventurers—Fiction. 5. Humorous stories.]
I. Parker, Tom S. II. Title.
PZ7.J4297Sh 2011   2010013687
[Fic]—dc22   CIP
                                                                                AC

Typography by Carla Weise
11   12   13   14   15   CG/RRDB   10   9   8   7   6   5   4   3   2   1
❖
First Edition

Hail, Corpse Maidens

High we fly on magic steeds
O'er battlegrounds of blood
Choosing heroes brave in deeds
Soldiers old and yet to bud.
In death they find an afterlife
In Valhalla's halls they spree
Odin smiles upon their honor
And on us, the Valkyrie.
—Ancient Norse kenning attributed to
Drudd the Scribe

~ ~ ~

"I find I worry less about my weight now
that I'm dead."
—Thidrek the Terrifying

~ ~ ~

PROLOGUE

THE EVIL PLAN IS BORN

The goddess of the underworld had kept Thidrek the Terrifying waiting for days. At least it seemed like days; he couldn't be sure. Here in the underworld, outside the massive doors to her inner sanctum, there was no sun, moon, or stars above, nothing but a void of continual darkness, which made keeping exact time rather difficult.

Thidrek hated waiting for anyone or anything. In the past, as a lordly prince, *he* had made people wait. He'd made people scream in agony, too; such was his love of torture. But he was a prince no more. Just a rotting bag of bones, another wretched subject of the almighty priestess of sin and evil, the goddess Hel. Worse, to his despair, it had been a long, long time since he had terrified anyone.

At last the doors creaked open and he was ordered forth

for an audience with She Who Made the Darkness. The hall was enormous and after a long walk he came to a flickering pool of light where sat a colossal throne, sheathed in shadow. He knelt and bowed his head.

"Your majesty," he intoned, "a faithful servant awaits your command."

From out of the darkness came a deep, throaty hiss that sounded like a death rattle. "My dear Thidrek," the voice rasped, "would you like to be terrifying once more?"

"Indeed, your majesty! Pray tell me how I can bring this to pass."

"You will lead my army of the dead to make war on the living," she said. "You will kill every soul on earth who worships my hated father and brother, Odin and Thor. And then I will reign as queen of the earthly realm, loosing upon the world all that is filthy and foul."

It was a tall order, Thidrek knew, but he just couldn't pass up a chance to conquer the world. Ever since his childhood, this had been his dearest wish.

"I will do it, m'lady. When can I start? Now? I was thinking I could start now."

"Before you lead my army, Thidrek, you must prove yourself worthy."

A test. He hated tests. Even more than he hated to wait. But he would do *anything* to become terrifying again. "Say it, your majesty. Tell me what I must do."

She leaned forward, her sinewy arm moving into the

light. He saw it was dark and scaly, more beast than beauty, her hand not a hand at all but a three-pronged claw. He felt the cold caress of her claw against his cheek and her very breath upon his face, and he was utterly her prisoner as into his ear she whispered:

"Bring me . . . the Ship of the Dead."

1

DANE YEARNS
FOR BLOOD

D ane the Defiant peered out on the fog-shrouded meadow, knowing that screams of pain would soon shatter the predawn stillness. With two armies soon to meet here in battle, by mid-morning this lush field of wildflowers was sure to be spattered with blood and strewn with body parts. But he cared nothing about who lived and died; only *how* they died. Because when the Valkyries came for those who met death bravely—to take their souls to Valhalla—Dane would then have a chance to see his beloved Astrid again.

It had been two months since she had been compelled to leave earth and join the ranks of Odin's corpse maidens. Two months of agony for Dane. He tried his best to accept his fate of being without her forever. But every morning when he awoke and grasped the awful truth that her absence was real and not just a terrible nightmare, his heart ached anew. He prayed and prayed to Odin to release her so she could become human again and return to his side. When that didn't work, he loudly damned the gods for their callous, unmerciful ways.

His angry passions spent, he began to think more clearly. There *had* to be a way to break Odin's hold on Astrid. Perhaps a bargain could be struck with the gods. He would offer to perform any brave feat they wished *if* his reward was Astrid's return. Would they listen, or would they casually incinerate him with a lightning bolt? No matter; nothing would stop him from trying to get her back.

But he had to have someone take his offer to Asgard, the heavenly place where Odin and his kind resided, and he reasoned that a Valkyrie who regularly flew between heaven and earth could serve as messenger.

His plan was this: He would watch the battle from his place of hiding, and once the butchery had ended, he would creep in among the bodies in hopes of intercepting a Valkyrie. He knew it wouldn't be easy—Valkyries were usually invisible to the living. But if *he* was seen by a Valkyrie—especially by Astrid or Mist, a corpse maiden who'd previously saved his life—perhaps they might make themselves visible to him. Or so he hoped.

"When's this supposed to start?" asked Jarl the Fair. "There's no one here but mourning doves." Indeed, the ghostly cooing of the doves was the only sound heard across the fog-cloaked field.

"Don't worry, Jarl," Dane assured him, "you'll see blood soon enough."

"*See* it? I'll be in the thick of it!" Jarl proclaimed, sharpening his knife blade. "When the fighting starts, Demon Claw will show no mercy." Demon Claw was Jarl's knife; Jarl was the kind of fellow whose weapons were more dear to him than his friends. Tall and well built, with a striking mane of blond hair, Jarl thought himself the perfect specimen of Norse manhood: an intimidating physique made all the more daunting by an obsession to die courageously in battle so as to gain entrance into Valhalla.

The other two beside him, Dane's best friends Drott the Dim and Fulnir the Stinking, were not, Dane would readily admit, prime models of Viking masculinity. Short and chubby—"stocky" his mother called him—Drott always had the vacant look of a man a couple arrows short of a full quiver. Fulnir was taller, more muscular, and much keener of mind, but sadly he suffered from intestinal maladies. It was said that, if farts were gold, Fulnir would be the richest man in the world.

"We didn't come here to *join* the battle," Fulnir said. "We're here to help Dane find a Valkyrie."

"That was my understanding," Drott said. "Besides, I wouldn't even know whose side to fight on. By the way, who *is* fighting?"

"Olaf Bloodaxe versus Guthorn Wormtongue," Dane said.

"I'm joining Bloodaxe," Jarl said.

"Why? Because his name has *blood* in it?" Fulnir teased.

Hearing a sudden rush of footsteps, Dane and his cohorts whirled round to see five towering, wraithlike Berserkers. One of them held a long spear, the point of which he held against Dane's throat. Three carried swords, and the final one, the largest, held a doubleheaded war axe. Naked to the waist, their battle-scarred bodies and beards were painted a chalky white, giving them a horrific ghostlike appearance. They wore hollowed-out skulls of wolves and bears as helmets, and from within, their eyes resembled those of crazed beasts craving blood.

"Spies! For Bloodaxe!" hissed the one with the spear at Dane's neck.

"No!" Dane blurted out. "We're from Voldarstad, two days south! We came to—"

"They lie!" spat the one with the axe. "Kill them!"

"We're not your enemy," Dane insisted.

"We're here to join you." This from Jarl.

"Join *us*?" said the axeman. "We fight for Wormtongue. While approaching, did we not hear you say—and I quote— 'I'm joining Bloodaxe'?"

"Aye, I heard him say it," said the spearman. The others nodded their skull heads in agreement and raised their weapons to strike. Dane knew they'd be dead in an instant.

"You *meant* Wormtongue, right, Jarl?" Dane said. "We've *all* come to fight for him."

"Hail Wormtongue!" Drott yelled.

The spearman hesitated, then turned his skull head to the axeman. "Well, we *are* a bit short on men. Let's put them in the shield wall, see how fast they die."

Dane gulped.

A row of no fewer than a hundred men stood shoulder to shoulder, each with his shield thrust forward, overlapping the shield to his right. The effect was that of a veritable wall of shields, the first line of defense against the enemy. Behind this shield wall were two more equally strong lines of men. Wormtongue's cavalry—warriors mounted on massive war stallions, each man with long spear and sword—guarded both flanks. The army stood in place, inviting Bloodaxe's troops to come and meet their death.

"Well, isn't this a bite in the backside," said Drott.

Dane and his friends stood smack in the center of the shield wall, feeling decidedly less excited about things. Each held in one hand the sword he'd brought from Voldarstad and in the other hand the round limewood shield he had been issued. This was their only defense, for unlike the rest of Wormtongue's men, who wore chain mail and helmets fashioned of iron or leather, Dane and his friends stood bareheaded and armorless. Worse, the Berserkers had positioned them where the best of Bloodaxe's troops were sure to attack. The strategy, the spearman explained, was that while the enemy skewered Dane and his friends with their spears and swords, the Berserkers—positioned immediately behind them—would dive in and chop the attackers to pieces.

"I can understand if you feel a bit exposed there," said the spearman, "and it's true, the enemy *will* see you as easy prey. But while you're attracting their death blows, we'll swoop in and kill the men who've killed *you*."

Drott raised his hand. "Sugestion. How about you kill them *before* they kill us?"

The spearman mulled this for a moment. "I kind of like the original plan."

"It works for me," agreed the axeman.

A piercing war cry sounded from somewhere off in the fog. "Kill them!" the voice screamed. There was silence, and then what seemed a thousand voices answering in unison, "Kill them all!"

"Thanks for volunteering us for death, Jarl," Fulnir said, his voice quaking.

"Thank Dane—he's the reason we're here," Jarl snapped.

"Jarl is right," Dane said. "Sorry for dragging you into this."

"I have to pee," Drott said.

"I just did," Fulnir said, looking at a wet spot down his leg. "Are you as scared as I am?" They all nodded, even Jarl.

"I admit I wanted to see Valhalla," Jarl said, "but not today."

The axeman leaned over their shoulders and said, "Fight well and you'll all feast at Odin's table tonight!"

"I hope they're serving mutton," Drott said. "I like mutton."

Hearing a whooshing sound above, Dane looked and saw a swarm of sparks arcing through the mist. Flaming arrows, hundreds of them, headed directly at them. "Take cover!" he yelled.

Dane went down on one knee, holding the shield above him, trying to make himself as small as he could beneath it. *Whump!* A smoking arrow tip penetrated his shield, stopping an inch from his eye. He heard a scream of pain and behind him saw the axeman's beard was on fire. He had taken a flaming arrow in the chest. The Berserker furiously beat at his face with his hands, trying to put out the fire. Suddenly another arrow buried itself in his neck; a fountain of blood spurted out, dousing the flames. The axeman stood for a moment, relieved he was no longer on fire. Then fell over dead.

Ten or so other men had also been hit by the rain of arrows. A few were dead, others crying out in agony. Dane glanced left and right and saw his friends were unscathed. Jarl hacked away at an arrow that had been embedded in his shield. Dane decided he'd better do that, too.

That's when the enemy came out of the fog, running down the hill, shrieking like banshees and pushing a large wagon laden with flaming oil pots. The wagon was aimed at the center of the shield wall, the very spot where Dane and his friends stood.

"The cowards!" yelled the spearman. "Using fire wagons to scatter us! Hold the line, men!"

"Hold the line?" Fulnir said. "Is he serious?"

"Retreat!" Jarl shouted.

For an instant, Dane felt the impulse to charge forward into the fray—to put his strength to the test. But just as quickly, Jarl and Drott pulled him back away from the onrushing fire wagon. Jabbing with their weapons, the Berserkers pressed them forward again, hoping Dane and his friends would absorb the force of the wagon's collision.

Dane and friends braced for impact. But then the front wheels of the wagon hit a small boulder on the ground and, careening sideways, it tipped over, spilling its cargo of flaming oil onto the grass in front of Wormtongue's troops. Remarkably, not a man was even singed.

"Attaaaack!" screamed Dane.

The shield wall broke. Wormtongue's troops surged forward to meet the enemy—as did the Berserkers, who ran full speed past Dane and his friends to meet the best of Bloodaxe's warriors head-on. There was a furious clash of shield upon shield and clang of metal upon metal. Jarl too began to run into the battle. Dane grabbed the scruff of his coat, stopping him. "I meant for *them* to attack, not *us*," Dane said.

"Oh." Jarl watched, excited by the bloody combat. He was like a little boy with such a taste for honey that he'd stick his hand into a beehive to get it. This time, though, Jarl came to his senses, declining to join the fray.

"I say we leave before anyone notices," Dane said.

No one disagreed. They hurried away into the fog, escaping from a battle none of them wished to fight.

High in the skies above, two Valkyries sat astride their pearl-gray mounts, peering down at the battlefield. Each wore the standard-issue uniform of golden-winged helmet and swan-feathered cloak over bronze chest armor and lily-white gown.

"Can you see anything?" asked Mist, the one with coal-black hair. "I hear men fighting and screams but that's about it."

"How are we supposed to choose the brave dead if we can't even see them?" Astrid said. The breeze blew her long blond hair across her face, and she had to brush it away from her eyes. "Why won't they let us braid our hair? Or at least cut it so it's not constantly blowing in our face?"

"Just one more stupid rule we have to follow," Mist replied.

When Astrid had agreed to join the Valkyrie sisterhood, she'd had no notion the job would prove so demanding. First, there was the celestial steed that she'd been issued— Vali, named after the youngest of Odin's sons, a god of war. The aptly named horse had a combative, willful nature, and no Valkyrie had ever tamed him. Astrid had labored long and hard to gain command of the animal, learning that if Vali sensed any weakness or hesitation in her, the sky steed was quick to mischief.

Next there had been her new powers of invisibility. Though thrilling in its own way, she had learned it took skill and concentration, and she had not yet fully mastered it. And then there was the violence that she was forced to watch. How else would a Valkyrie be able to tell which warriors were the bravest and most worthy of being taken up to Valhalla?

But most difficult of all was trying to forget Dane.

Astrid had tried to convince herself that the pain of leaving Dane would fade with time, like a wound healing. But just as she began to believe the door to her past was closed for good, like a viper springing from the grass, a sudden memory would strike—Dane's valiant smile, his hearty laughter—and she'd realize that the pain had never left. It had taken root deep within her like a phantom heart, still beating, still calling to her. If she was ever to find peace, she knew she must cut this heart from her very core. She had one future now—as a corpse maiden in service to Odin—and had to devote herself to carrying out her sacred duty.

Now, poised above yet another melee of blood and gore, she was trying to do just that—scouting for mortals worthy of the great hall.

She spied the third sister who had been dispatched with them to the battlefield. It was Aurora with the fire-red hair and smug, competitive nature. Aurora gathered the heroic dead as if it were a contest, as if she believed that the more dead she brought to Valhalla, the better chance that Odin would look upon her with favor. She was not satisfied to stay an ordinary corpse maiden for long; no, she told her sisters that she had made plans for advancement, whatever that meant.

Aurora rose from the battlefield with *two* dead warriors slung over her horse like sacks of grain. She stopped her horse beside her sisters, grinning like a proud fisherwoman showing off her prized catch. "Oh, my," she said, smirking, "did I take the two *you* had your eyes on?"

"It's quality, not quantity," quipped Mist.

"That's why I chose *only* the bravest," Aurora said with a sniff.

"Really? The one on top has arrows in his back," Mist pointed out. "And *usually* that means, uh, retreat?"

The said warrior raised his head and sputtered, "I—I—I can explain—"

"Odin takes a dim view of cowards entering Valhalla," Mist said. "And a dimmer view of sisters who ferry them."

"But I fought ever so bravely," the warrior pleaded. "Then we were outnumbered and—*aaaggghhhh*!" Aurora pushed him off her sky horse, and he fell screaming to the ground below. Without so much as a "good day," Aurora kicked her steed's flanks and flew off.

"I should've let her take the coward and get demoted," Mist said. "Fun to see her mopping up puke in Odin's mead hall. I suppose we should have a look. I'll take the south side of the meadow, you take the north. Good hunting."

Mist flew down, disappearing into the fog. Astrid was about to follow when she heard the sharp call of a hawk. *Screeee!* The bird appeared from out of the fog, a bloody shred of flesh in its beak. As it flew by—so near she could have touched it—the bird's eyes met hers and Astrid felt a sharp pang of inexplicable sorrow. She gasped, trying to catch her breath, and when she did the bird was gone.

Was this an omen? With anguish so intense, Astrid feared that it was. Someone close to her, someone she loved, was soon to suffer a terrible fate.

2

CROSSING THE
RAINBOW BRIDGE

ane had never seen such grisly carnage. The battle was over, and hundreds lay dead or dying in the blood-soaked meadow. He, Jarl, Fulnir, and Drott went about the bodies, doing what they could, offering sips of water and placing the warriors' swords within their grasp so they could die like proud Vikings should, clutching their weapons.

"What did they all die for?" Fulnir asked, gazing across the battlefield, further disgusted to see the many birds of prey feasting upon the dead.

"Cheese . . . ," gasped one of the dying. It was the spearman, they saw, lying among a heap of nearby bodies. Kneeling beside him, Dane removed his Berserker wolf skull and gently propped the man up, giving him a sip from his goatskin.

"Cheese?" Dane asked.

"Wormtongue's son wanted to marry Bloodaxe's daughter," the spearman managed to say, his weak voice a whisper. "But Bloodaxe pronounced the boy unfit to join his clan. Wormtongue wanted revenge . . . wanted Bloodaxe to fight . . . so he insulted the thing Bloodaxe is most proud of . . . his cheese making." The Berserker took his last breath and died, his spear clutched firmly in his hand. Dane lowered his body to the ground.

"Cheese. They all died because of . . . *cheese*," Dane said, shaking his head.

"Men are *so* stupid," a female voice said.

He looked up. A Valkyrie on her horse hovered above them.

"Mist!"

Drott, Fulnir, and Jarl gazed upward, their mouths dropped open in wonderment as they beheld the raven-haired beauty in her Valkyrie regalia astride the massive celestial steed. "It's a . . . it's a . . . it's a . . . ," Drott sputtered.

"Valkyrie!" Fulnir yelped.

Jarl went down on his knees and muttered, "Take me . . . take me now to Valhalla."

Mist sighed. "You're not fit for the great hall."

Jarl gaped in shock, as if he'd been slapped. "Because I'm not brave enough?"

"Because you're not dead enough."

"But if I *was* dead—"

Mist lost patience. "When that happens, a decision will be made!" Her horse descended and off she hopped. "Dane, what are you doing here?"

Dane hesitated. "Is Astrid with you?" he said, scanning the sky for a sign of her.

"No . . . she is at another blood feud. Is that why you came? To see her?"

"I thought a fight like this would attract Valkyries." Then he stepped forward and took her by the hands. "I want you to take a message to Odin," he pleaded. "Tell him that I will do anything—anything he asks—to win Astrid's freedom."

Mist's mouth dropped open in shock. "Take a message to . . . Are you mad? Odin does not bargain with humans. He cares nothing for your concerns." Mist walked away, threading her way among the dead. "I saw a man with a red beard die bravely . . . now where is he?"

Dane caught up with her. "Are you saying you won't help me? You share blame for Astrid joining your sisterhood!"

"It was the Norns she dealt with, not me. Dane, I know you are hurting, but you must forget Astrid. She is Odin's maid now. You must not attempt to seek her . . . or Odin will banish you to Hel's realm forever."

Dane felt a buzzing in his head. "He told you this?"

"No, it's standard policy," she said. "If any mortal harasses a sister, he's sent to Niflheim." Dane knew that Niflheim was the underworld where the hideous goddess Hel reigned over the tortured souls of those denied entrance to Valhalla.

An eternal sentence of agony. Would that be his reward for wanting to reunite with Astrid? Too saddened to speak, Dane watched Mist search among the bodies for a soul to take to Valhalla. "I thought I saw him fall right around here somewhere," she said to herself. "Maybe he crawled away." As she turned to examine another pile of corpses, Drott and Jarl began to pelt her with questions about Valhalla. *Is the food good? How about the weather? What does Odin really look like?* and such.

"So you've personally met Odin?" Jarl asked in wonder.

"Yes, one time I had to refill his ale jar," Mist said.

"Really? What'd he say?"

"He said, 'Thanks.'"

"All he said was thanks? No tip?"

"No. He said he wasn't in the habit of tipping any of the serving wenches in Valhalla, because if he tipped one girl then he'd have to tip them all, and that would just lead to a lot of jealousy and confusion and it wasn't worth it."

"What's the best part of being a Valkyrie?"

"The travel."

"Are all Valkyries as pretty as you?" asked Drott.

"Yes."

"Can I kiss you?" he asked.

"No!"

Dane stood a short distance away, wretched and miserable, his hopes for Astrid's return all but crushed. He kicked himself for ever believing in his stupid plan, and gazing at the dead all around him, he began to wish he was one of them. Fulnir came over to offer his condolences.

"I know it's not like you to give up," said Fulnir, "but this time you better do what she says."

Dane was about to agree when a loud snort from Mist's celestial steed drew his attention. The horse was using his head to nudge a body off a prime tuft of grass. The animal rolled the body away and began to eat, avoiding spots stained with blood.

An idea came to Dane, one so audacious his heart began pounding in excitement. He knew it was the only way. "You're right, Fulny, it's *not* like me to give up."

Dane ran to Mist's horse and leaped onto his back. The horse whinnied and kicked, trying to unseat him—but Dane's heels gave a hard kick to the steed's flanks. Suddenly Dane was in the air and moving fast—*flying*! He held firm to the horse's reins as he heard Mist's cries of protest, and braving a look down, he saw his friends gazing upward, utter shock and delight on their faces. The last thing that went through his head was the worry that this might be the last he'd ever see of them.

Dane held tightly to the reins, trying to forget his fear of heights. He tried imagining that he was astride an ordinary horse, riding on the ground, but the wind in his face and the nearness of the clouds reminded him he wasn't. He shut his eyes and gave the celestial steed his head, knowing that most horses race for home and their oats if given the chance. All he had to do was hang on and chances were the horse would know where to go.

Higher and higher they rose, the air turning more frigid. When Dane next dared to open his eyes, he saw they were engulfed by clouds. With the ground below obscured, the churning in his stomach eased and he was able to think more clearly. What would happen when he reached Asgard, if indeed this was where the horse was taking him? A Valkyrie's steed returning without a corpse, *or* a corpse maiden for that matter! Even if by some miracle of chance he *did* find Astrid, what would he say? "I love you and I'll do anything to get you back"?

His plan was utter lunacy. He'd given in to impulse without a thought as to what might happen, and now here he was, a puny human arrogantly challenging the rule of the gods. If merely harassing a maiden was punishable by an eternity in Niflheim, he could imagine what kind of excruciating pain he was in for.

To say nothing of what his father, Voldar, would say. As a denizen of Valhalla, surely he would have a few foul words about his son's foolhardiness. What would Dane say to him if they happened to meet? He pushed all thoughts of his father from his mind. Dane pulled hard on the steed's reins, trying to stop his ascent, but the horse shook his head wildly and flew on, unperturbed.

When at last they broke free of the clouds, what Dane saw took his breath away. A vast and vivid rainbow such as he had never seen arced across the sky before him, its many bands of color shimmering in the sunlight. Mesmerized by the sight, he relaxed his hold on the reins and the horse flew on, traveling across the rainbow as if it were a bridge, and then Dane realized what the rainbow was: Bifrost, the legendary pathway to Asgard.

Looking down through the glowing bands of light, he saw he was flying over a wondrous valley of verdant fields and forests, a sparkling river curving around it all, and up ahead, soaring impossibly high over the valley, the craggy peaks of a magnificent mountain. Beyond that, rising even higher into the mist—Dane gasped as it came into view—Odin's enormous fortress, its massive, glowing roof shingled with golden war shields. Valhalla itself!

He had heard the fantastic tales of this place from Lut the Bent, the wise man of his village. He had said that Valhalla was so inconceivably big that, if you were inside, you could barely see the opposite wall. There were five hundred and forty doorways, each wide enough to allow eight hundred warriors to walk out abreast. Odin, it was said, had built Valhalla to house his thousands upon thousands of dead heroes who, on the day of doom known as Ragnarok, would be called to fight the dark forces of destruction in an epic, earth-shattering battle.

Dane gazed up at its vastness in amazement. How wondrous! To be in the presence of Valhalla itself, the paradise every Norseman dreamed of, a hero's reward for bravery and valor. He ached to fly straight to its gates and reside there forever with his father and Astrid.

His celestial steed had other ideas. The horse veered sharply downward and Dane had to grab his mane to keep from falling. Down they flew, past the end of the rainbow and over a treeless meadow where, he was shocked to see, ten Valkyries had landed their mounts and were unloading their slain cargo. His heart leaped when in the distance he saw a maiden, her blond hair streaming behind her. Was it Astrid?

He had to hide from the Valkyries. He jerked the reins to steer his steed toward a grove of trees beside the meadow. The horse gave in and swooped away, alighting at last in the high grass of the grove, well out of sight of the others. Dane slid off his steed, relieved to be on solid ground again. The leaves on the trees were brilliantly golden in color, and looking closer, he was amazed to see that each leaf was made of pure gold. A light breeze rattled through the trees, and each leaf shimmered and shone in the sun. Dane tied the horse's reins to a tree branch and went off to find Astrid.

He crawled through the high grass, moving toward the sound of voices. He parted some shrubbery and peered out onto the meadow. The Valkyries were gathered along with the slain warriors they had ferried. Most of the dead had gruesome wounds, missing limbs, split heads, slashed-open throats. One had even been impaled on a spear, its point sticking out through his back. Despite their injuries, no one seemed in pain—rather, they stood there calmly as a regal-looking Valkyrie addressed them.

"My name is Rain. I am queen of the Valkyries. On behalf of Odin and all the other gods and goddesses, I welcome you to Valhalla," she intoned in a soothing voice. "As you may know by now, you've just been slain." There were murmurs of alarm among the men. "I realize this can be rather a disappointing and disorienting experience. But remember, we're here to help you adapt to your new surroundings and ease your way into what most find to be a ridiculously pleasurable afterlife."

Dane searched the faces of the Valkyries, looking for Astrid, but many maidens were obscured by the hulking warriors. "Your corpse maiden will escort you up the sacred path to Valhalla," Rain continued. "Odin will rise to greet the bravest among you—but those who are not greeted should not feel slighted, for Odin has many duties and cannot personally welcome everyone. Questions?"

A warrior missing his right arm raised his left. "My right arm was hacked off. Will I get another?"

"Of course," she chirped. "Tonight you will feast and drink and then sleep the sleep of the dead. When you awake, all your wounds will have healed and your spirit-bodies will be made whole again."

The dead whose hands were still attached applauded. The others used their stumps to thump their chests.

As another question came, a handsome young warrior shifted his weight and Dane caught sight of the Valkyrie right beside him whose arm was entwined in his. Astrid! He couldn't breathe. The young warrior looked over and smiled at her. Astrid glanced up and gave him an affectionate smile of her own. *What?* That was the very smile she used to give Dane—that look of warmest sunshine that told him he was special. And now she was giving her smile to someone else!

He felt a stab of jealous indignation. Had Astrid already forgotten him? Had he come all this way, braving his fear of heights while risking eternal torment in Niflheim, only to see his beloved cozy up to a handsome corpse she'd just met? He fought the urge to leap over the bushes and confront her and the slain warrior. The Valkyrie queen now bade her sisters to escort the slain up the flower-lined path toward Valhalla. As the dead began to walk, Dane saw why Astrid had held the young warrior's arm. Half of his foot had been chopped off, and she was helping him walk by supporting his weight.

Relieved, Dane thought that perhaps her smile had just been to reassure the warrior that he would soon be whole again. Yes, that had to be it, Dane made himself believe. She was only doing her job as a corpse maiden, helping the slain to adjust to the afterlife, offering comfort where needed.

Dane waited until they had all disappeared up the path and then crept out of the golden grove, following a safe distance behind, keeping out of sight.

Shortly after leaving the meadow, the path led into the

mountains and cut through the granite rock, becoming a passage framed on both sides by soaring cliffs. After an arduous climb, Dane rounded a turn to find himself in view of the towering gates of Valhalla itself.

Taking refuge behind a boulder, he watched in silent fascination as the massive gates creaked open and five guards appeared. Dressed in shining coats of chain mail and leather armor, the guards were as large as white bears and twice as vicious looking, and as the Valkyries led the newly slain past them through the gates, the guards studied each passing warrior with the fiercest of stares, no doubt making sure that he deserved entrance to Odin's hallowed corpse hall. Astrid too had disappeared inside the gates, and having seen the size of the guards, Dane decided it was best that he stay hidden and await her return.

For what seemed hours he lay against the rock, listening to the ghostly echo of raucous songs and laughter coming from the hall. *The dead really know how to celebrate,* he thought. And why not? They no longer had to worry about earthly responsibilities like feeding their families, protecting their homesteads, or picking lice from their children's hair. Valhalla was one big holiday, with father Odin providing the never-ending food and drink.

Was Astrid joining in, enjoying herself too? Possibly lounging beside the handsome young warrior—or sitting on his lap!—quaffing hornfuls of mead?

At last he heard the gates squeak open, and peering out

from his hiding place, he saw a figure emerge alone. It was Astrid. The gate closed behind her and she started down the path. His heart pounding, he waited until she passed him by, then leaped out from behind, clamped a hand over her mouth, and pulled her into the shadows. She fought him, easily breaking free of his grasp and throwing him to the ground. She drew her knife, ready to plunge it into him.

"It's me! Dane!" he said.

She froze, struck speechless, gazing on him like he were some kind of horrifying apparition. He rose to embrace her. She recoiled, raising her hands as if to ward off evil.

"Astrid, what's wrong? I've come for you."

"You—how did you—"

"I stole Mist's horse."

"You what?"

"I was at a battle and she came—and I tried to get her to carry a message for me to Odin, but she refused and so the only way I could come here was—" This wasn't going the way Dane had imagined it would. Instead of the hugs and kisses he had expected, she was giving him looks of dread and backing away like he was a rabid weasel. "Astrid, aren't you glad to see me?"

A sharp look of pain leaped into her eyes and she quickly turned her back and hurried down the path away from him. Dane followed, calling her name, but on she went, and when he finally caught up to her and whirled her around to face him, he noticed tears in her eyes.

"Astrid! I have to see Odin. I'll do anything he asks to get you back. You have to take me to him."

"Oh, Dane," she said, putting her head in her hands. "That's impossible. You have to go back. You have to go back now!"

"Don't you want to be free—and be with me again?"

"*Be* with you?" she said. "I am no longer mortal! I have given my oath to serve Odin."

"Oaths can be broken!"

She slashed at the air in front of her, as if Dane had said the unspeakable. "Not this one. Not unless I wish to find myself in Niflheim. Do you wish that?"

Dane stared at her for a moment. "If you can't join me on earth, then there's another way we can be together. Here. If I die in battle—"

"No. You will *not*, Dane," she said.

"You have no control over that."

"None of my sisters will take you," she warned. "Nor will I."

Her words struck him like a hammer. "Are you saying . . . you don't *want* us to be together?"

"I am saying . . . dying bravely is one thing. But *choosing* to die is cowardly." She paused and Dane saw she was close to tears. He noticed that hanging on a chain around her neck was the Thor's Hammer locket that he had once given her to cement their devotion to each other. "If you love me, then go live your life . . . with courage and without self-pity. That is the only way we will meet again."

Then she left him, hurrying down the path. He stood and watched her go, the cold finality of her words like knives in his heart.

3

A FRIGHTFUL
APPEARANCE

How lucky I am! thought Grelf the Gratuitous as he sipped his warm brandy and put his feet to the fire, wiggling his toes. Oh, how kingly were his comforts! And to think, only months before he had been a fugitive on the run, barely escaping the executioner's axe. And now look at him! Ensconced in soft-furred luxury in the service of a fat, rich, and undemanding lord—a far, far cry from his last employer, Thidrek the Terrifying.

Not that life with Lord Thidrek had been unendurable. The man had had wit and a fair degree of charm, considering he was a ruthless, murdering tyrant. As his man-in-waiting, Grelf had served his every need, from picking out his wardrobe to making sure he had an unobstructed view at the weekly beheadings.

But if Grelf ever slipped up or forgot the tiniest detail, if

Thidrek's demands were not met promptly and to the maximum effect, punishment—as the lash scars on Grelf's back attested—could be severe.

Which was why Grelf had not mourned when—many months before, during his fight with Dane the Defiant—a Thor-sent whirlwind had sucked Thidrek off the face of the earth, never to be seen again. Realizing that the villagers who had hated Thidrek would be looking to kill him, too, Grelf had stolen a horse and ridden away as fast as he could. He hadn't stopped until he reached a faraway place where no one had ever heard of Thidrek the Terrifying. Just to be safe, he had changed his name to Gudrid the Servile, so that no one from his checkered past would ever find him.

And now, here he was, in his own spacious cottage on his new master's estate, warming himself before a great fire. In the main house, his generous lord had retired early and Grelf had his night free to do as he wished. And so, as was his habit, he sipped his brandy, dreaming of the many servant maids he would one day have, as he drifted off to sleep before the fire.

What was *that*? His eyes fluttered open. Again he had heard it. The *clip-clop* of something—someone—approaching. Was it his lordship? Unlikely. A log then collapsed into ash, and seeing that the fire needed tending, Grelf came down off his chair and knelt before the stone hearth. A chill swept through the room. He laid a birch log on the fire, stirring it ablaze once again, waving the woodsmoke from his eyes. He rose to return to his chair, shocked to find he had a visitor in his chamber.

Draped in shadow, a tall silhouetted figure, black as night itself, stood across the room just inside the doorway.

"W-who are you?" Grelf squeaked, backing away to the far side of the room. "What do you want?"

The figure gave an icy chuckle. "Not exactly the welcome I was expecting."

"If it's food you want, go on and take it. There's a stew on the fire and—and flatbread in the food box."

"Food?" came the voice from the shadows. "I've come for something far more nourishing than food."

"It's silver you're after, is it? Well, I'm afraid my coffers are bare. But if you take it up with my master—"

"Bah!" flared the ghostly figure. "I care nothing for food-stuffs or silver! I've come for you, Grelf. I'm here to renew our friendship."

At the sound of his own name spoken by the stranger, Grelf felt his vitals shrivel. Something about the voice. The figure stepped forward and the firelight caught the features of the visitor's face. Grelf was for a moment without breath. He tried to speak but found himself lacking a voice as well; all he could issue were pitiful little choking sounds.

"Ah. It *is* you," the figure said.

Impossible! Grelf could scarce believe his eyes. Before him stood the very image of his old master, Thidrek the Terrifying. The same haughty voice, the same chilling smile.

Every bit alive, or so it seemed. But how could it be? Grelf had seen his master sucked into the heavens in a god-sent windstorm. Surely he *had* to have died. Grelf rubbed his eyes, believing this a dream. Yes, of course, he must have drifted off while warming himself by the fire. That had to be it. But when again he opened his eyes, the figure was still there, leering from beneath his oilskin cloak.

"Come into the light and let me look at you, Grelf."

"G-Grelf? Who is Grelf? I—I am Gudrid the-the-the Servile—"

"Come, Grelf! I know it is you!" the voice commanded, and the apparition slid back its hood.

Grelf stepped forward, trying not to show how badly he was shaken. Drawing nearer, he saw Thidrek's face fully illuminated in the firelight—and oh, what a sickening sight he was. Gaunt and emaciated, his face was half eaten by rot. A maggot wiggled out of a hideous gash on his cheek. Part of his upper lip had been torn away, revealing blackened and decayed teeth.

"Lord Thidrek . . . is it really you?"

"Of course it's me, man! Are you not glad to see me?"

"Of course I am, my lord, I'm just—well, you surprised me."

"I see you've put on some weight since I last saw you."

"M-m-my lord," said Grelf, his voice quavering in fear. "You're l-l-looking a bit—how shall I put this—under the weather?"

"I should say so, Grelf. I've caught a nasty dose of being undead."

"Un . . . dead, sir?" said Grelf, not altogether grasping his meaning.

"Yes, Grelf, un*dead*! Need I explain everything?"

"Well, you being so much more knowing than me, sir," Grelf said wisely, "how can it be otherwise?"

A smile of supreme pleasure appeared on his master's face. "Ah, Grelf, how I have missed you."

"And I you, sire," said Grelf, laying it on ever thicker. "And I certainly would care to hear your explanation of your new—uh, undeadness."

"Well, you see, there's being alive, like you—laughing and singing and being in the pink of good health. There's dead, as in stiff as a stump. Long gone. Expired. Extinct. Bereft of any animating spirit. And then there is a curious state of being somewhere *between* those two. It is rather fascinating, actually. Though one's body is dried up and devoid of any vital fluids, it is able to move about rather well and perform most of the daily tasks necessary to carry on the work at hand. One feels powered by a strange kind of potency. A devilish pep, let's call it. One doesn't *feel*, exactly; the undead have no feelings. We have urges. Brute impulses. Which we can satisfy only by performing the deeds she who has sent me wishes performed."

Despite his fear, Grelf was aching to ask his master how it was that he had died and become undead. And who, he was curious to know, was this "she" he was referring to? But though he was ever curious, he was crafty as well, and said only what would appeal to Thidrek's selfish conceits.

"It's certainly wonderful to see you again, my lord. What is this 'work at hand' you are involved in? It certainly does sound interesting. It must be nice to have something to occupy your time with—in your condition."

But Thidrek was in no mood for small talk as Grelf felt the heat of his gaze.

"Get your things, Grelf. We've work to do."

A cold panic crept up Grelf's spine.

"W-work, sir? I'd be delighted to serve you again, your lordship, really I would—nothing would please me more. But you see, I have a new master now, a rather nice one at that. Not as nice as you, of course—who could ever replace you? What I mean is, I'm *his* now. It wouldn't be fair to just jump ship and leave. Besides, he has big plans for me, sire, big plans. I'm to write his memoirs, the story of his life, and he'd be lost without me, really he would. He's become quite attached to me, sir, quite attached, and so you see that's why I can't possibly go with you."

Thidrek's hand shot forth, seizing Grelf by the neck and, with inhuman strength, lifted him straight off the floor until they were face-to-face.

Grelf gulped. "I'll get my things."

4

A DARING
DECISION

D ane made his way down the mountain path in a daze of despair. All hope of reuniting with Astrid was dead. She could not break her oath to Odin, and he could not pass through the gates of Valhalla as a coward who chose to die. Only by accepting their fates to be apart would he ever see her again.

Astrid said that if he lived his life with courage, he would pass into Valhalla. Courage, he knew, was not just on battlefields. It was displayed daily by ordinary people who lived decent lives, facing hardship, providing for family and friends. His father, once a warrior, had become one of these people, finding true happiness in the simple pleasures of a peaceful village life. Until Thidrek the Terrifying had come and murdered him.

Dane awakened from these thoughts to find he had

returned to the meadow near the golden grove. The trees were engulfed in fog, and drawing near, he spied Mist's horse, still feeding on the high grass. But every time he came close, the horse trotted farther away, leaving the grove of golden-leafed trees and moving into an adjoining one. Dane followed the horse, calling to him as he gave chase, but the animal seemed not to hear him as he moved on, disappearing altogether in the fog. Quickly tiring of this game and anxious to get home, Dane cursed and ran after the horse, determined not to lose sight of him. He ran through brush and briar and down another long pathway, bound on either side by high thorny brambles, growing more irritable as he went.

At last, in a small clearing, he spied the horse again. From out of the white swirling mist he appeared to him as a pale apparition, his head bent to the ground, lapping water from a small pool.

Dane approached with caution, stepping slowly. This time the horse stayed put, seeming by his manner to have arrived at the place he had intended. Dane drew up beside him and patted his neck, trying not to show any spite to the animal. He heard the murmur of falling water and noticed fish darting in the pond and birds flitting about on the floating flowers. A white swan swam into view. The horse lifted his head and whinnied, and as he did so, the mists began to lift. Something then caught Dane's eye and, peering upward, he saw a waterfall appear and then behind that something that literally took his breath away.

Could it really be?

There, like some giant towering sentinel, stood a tree of indescribable size. The storied Tree of Life. Yggdrasil! Rooted just a short distance away. Dane stared dumbstruck at the majesty of it. Legend said it was the most massive living thing in all creation, that its uppermost branches encircled the heavens and that its roots stretched down into the very underworld of Niflheim itself. Dane's father had once claimed that ten thousand longships could be built from its trunk, with enough wood left over to build a roomy hut with attached outhouse for every man and woman on earth. Gazing in wonder at the tree, Dane was sure his father had not exaggerated, for he guessed its trunk was at least five hundred paces around—and its height could not even be measured, for it disappeared into the heavenly mists above.

Then Dane remembered something *else* about this tree . . . something of great significance. According to legend, this was the dwelling place of the Norns, the Goddesses of Time—the keepers of the Book of Fate. *Everyone's* fate.

Peering across the pond, his gaze fell upon a stone altar at the base of the tree, and atop the altar lay a large, squarish object. The largest book Dane had ever laid eyes on. As he looked through the thinning wisps of fog, the book appeared to be many centuries old, its ancient leather cover cracked and worn and cloaked in mystery. Dane stood for a time gazing at the enchanted thing, afraid to even touch it. Flicking a nervous look around, he wondered where the Norns might be. Were they watching him at this very moment, preparing to leap out and smite him with their godly powers?

Just as quickly he found himself cursing the Norns and the powers they had over humans. *Who are they to sit and write our fates, as if we were but clay figures to play with, only to crush us on a whim? The witches! They're probably off with the gods right now, planning more ways to torture us!*

Dane remembered what his father had said about the Norns and their fate making: "It's a bad system, but we humans are stuck with it."

"But are we?" Dane asked himself, struck with a new thought so daring it scared him to think it. He knew he had been fated to die months before—and that the Norns had changed his fate when Astrid agreed to serve Odin. That meant that, in some circumstances, fate could be changed. It was *negotiable*. If *that* was true, the only thing he lacked was bargaining power. Something to trade. If he could not strike a deal with Odin, perhaps he could bargain with the very goddesses who ruled fate. A surge of anger arose in him, quickly overtaken by an even more powerful feeling: the return of hope.

In the early morning chill, Lut the Bent and the boy William the Brave trudged up to Thor's Hill, the small tree-less hillock that lay between the village of Voldarstad and the woodland that ran up the side of the mountain nearby.

The ten-year-old boy had come to Lut's hut at dawn, terribly worried about the fate of Dane the Defiant. Four days before, Dane and his friends had set out on their foolish quest to find a battle where Valkyries swarmed. Lut had tried talking Dane out of going, saying that his plan to bargain with Odin was insane. "A bear will not haggle with a gnat," Lut had told him. "Astrid is gone. Be a man and accept it." But Dane, blinded by his love for her, had gone off on his absurd, dangerous errand.

He still had not returned and William was frantic with despair. Dane had rescued the boy from a life of thralldom in the service of the cruel Thidrek the Terrifying. He had defeated Thidrek with the boy's help, and thus William was freed from slavery and dubbed "William the Brave." Since then, he had come to idolize Dane like an older brother who could do no wrong.

"What if he never comes back, Lut?" William whimpered as they crested the hill.

The lad had suffered greatly during his brief life, Lut knew. When Thidrek's armies attacked his Saxon village looking for plunder and slaves, Thidrek himself had murdered William's mother and father, right in front of the boy's eyes. Now the prospect of losing Dane as well was too much to bear. Lut put his arm around William's shoulder, trying to calm his worries. "We will pray the gods bring him home safely," said Lut.

It was a short walk to the giant granite runestone that had been erected the season before to honor the exploits of Dane and his friends, including William. They had all been named Rune Warriors for the courage they had shown in defeating the foul Godrek Whitecloak.

Lut stared at the words hewn in the stone: "Dane the Defiant, son of Voldar the Vile, grandson of Vlar the Courageous . . ." Lut had been well into his forties when Vlar was just a boy, he remembered. So long ago. Bah! It was not good to think of the past—it made him feel so decrepit. He was soon to be one hundred and four years old, for Odin's sake, and no matter what the ladies might say about the fineness of his beard or the shine in his eyes, the ceaseless aches in his joints told him that death was knocking at his door.

Lut looked out over the village to the waters of the bay beyond. The morning fog was beginning to lift. There were no ships in sight. He turned his gaze to the rutted path that led away from the village to the east—the path Dane and his pals had taken four days ago. *Why must every new generation bring me fresh troubles?* he fumed. As the village wise man he had the burden of worrying about each and every young man and woman, offering guidance that would help them survive into adulthood. And what was his reward? They got married and produced *more* children who robbed him of sleep!

"Shouldn't you begin beseeching the gods?" William asked.

"Of course, of course," Lut said. "O mighty and benevolent gods, hear my plea. . . ." Lut went on, working up a ripping good appeal to the heavenly powers. When he gave it his all, he was pretty good at this beseeching business, even though he sometimes doubted the gods were paying attention. For a big ending, he thrust his hands to the skies and raised his voice, saying, "O lenient and merciful powers! Spare our four sons! They are each good and courageous souls—foolish, sure, as all humans may be—"

"Lut, listen!" William blurted.

Lut stopped and heard a dull thunder, building in intensity. Could it be? They both turned to look down the hill, to the rutted path. Four horses and riders emerged from the trees, riding as swiftly as if Thor were throwing lightning bolts at their backsides.

Dane's horse, slick with sweat, was tethered outside Lut's hut when Lut and William arrived breathlessly on foot. They entered and saw that Dane had helped himself to some bread and cheese. He gave them a boyish grin and said, "What's the matter—think I wouldn't make it back?"

"Never doubted it," William said. Then they laughed and vigorously greeted each other warrior style, grasping each other by the forearms.

"Where are the others?" Lut asked.

"We were starving," Dane said between bites. "We rode all night without stopping. Jarl, Drott, and Fulnir went home to eat, but I came directly here with that." He nodded to the table where something was wrapped up in his cloak. Something large.

"A present for me?" Lut inquired.

Dane went to the table and gently unwrapped it. "I found it beneath Yggdrasil."

Lut came forward and with growing awe gazed at the massive book, covered in leather that looked as old as the gods themselves. "Are you mad, boy?" he gasped, once he had regained his powers of speech.

William's eyes popped. "Yggdrasil? You took a book from the Norns?"

"Not *a* book," Lut said. "*The* book."

Lut had beheld many incredible sights in all his years, but nothing quite like this, nothing that filled him with such curiosity and dread. Dane had stolen the Norns' Book of Fate! And it was here in his hut, right in front of him.

Dane quickly spilled out the whole story, ending with how he'd returned to earth with the book concealed in his cloak. He had found Mist and his friends where he had left them. She had exploded in fury and, wasting no time, had mounted her sky horse and flown off, cursing the human race—and particularly Dane—for all the trouble they caused.

The old man ran his fingers lightly over the book's cover, worn smooth by centuries of handling. All his adult life he had been a famed seer, a reader of the mystical runes, interpreting the divine messages or, as he called them, the "whispers of the gods." Rarely were messages as clear as "Don't marry Bjorn Thorgilsson," or "If you go fishing today, you'll drown." Often they were confusing, and it would take a runemaster like Lut to make sense of it. Sometimes even *he* could not deduce the meaning of it, such were the perplexities and mysteries of his craft, and in these few cases he would cheerfully refund his fee.

But now before him lay the future straight from the Fates themselves. How curious he was about the secrets it held. Nearing the end of his life's thread, he still yearned to know what surprises lay ahead. He could feel his feeble heart thumping.

"They'll pay plenty to get this back," Dane said.

"And your price is Astrid's freedom," Lut concluded. "The Norns may not take kindly to bartering with a trifling human."

"Maybe it's time we stood up to them," Dane said. "They make our lives miserable and we're supposed to pray to them so they won't make our lives *more* miserable? Well, now *I* have the upper hand, and they either give me what I want or . . ." Dane hesitated, weighing a dreadful option.

"Or what?" Lut asked.

"Or I'll burn the book."

Lut rose, aghast. "*Burn* it? You'll do no such thing!"

"It would break their control over us!"

"We don't *know* what it would do," Lut said. "Destroying the book could destroy the future of humankind. I want Astrid back as much as you do, but I will not allow you to take such a risk."

"All right," Dane said, adopting a more reasonable tone. "But if we don't make the Norns *believe* we'll destroy it, they won't take us seriously."

The young man had a point. No doubt the Norns would threaten to rain down scorpions and fill their insides with putrid fish guts unless the book was returned. But if they held firm and made the Norns truly *believe* that their power over humans was threatened, there was a slim chance the ploy would work. Of course, once Astrid was returned and the Norns got their book back, they could easily do the scorpion-and-fish-guts trick anyway.

"Can I finally take a look inside that thing?" Jarl said, entering. He came to the book and Dane put his hand on the cover so Jarl couldn't open it.

Dane turned to Lut. "I told the others we shouldn't look inside without talking with you first."

"That was wise," Lut said. "No one should look."

"I just want to see my fate," Jarl said. "What's wrong with *that*?"

"You may see that your story ends badly," Lut said.

"Badly?" Jarl said, bristling. "Like I don't die bravely? Impossible."

"Even brave men die by accident," Lut said. "Remember Erling the Lucky? No better warrior in the village. He choked to death on a pork rib."

"That's right," Dane said. "And his son, Erling the Not-So-Lucky, was struck by one of Thor's lightning bolts."

"If those two knew *how* they were to die," Lut said, "do you think they'd ever want to eat pork or go outside ever again?"

"But if the book says *how* you die, it must say when, too," Jarl said. "If they knew the day——"

"That's even worse," interrupted Lut. "If you know it's your fate to be crushed by a falling tree in five years—you won't be crushed just once, but a thousand times in your dreams. You'll become a sniveling, mad husk of a man, praying for the actual day to come so your misery will finally end." Jarl looked askance at the book as if it were filled with poison. "But if you're really that curious . . ." Lut made a move to open the book.

"No!" Jarl exclaimed. "I mean . . . why should I read of my death . . . when, in my heart I *know* it will come bravely?"

Lut gave him a reassuring pat on the shoulder. "I'm sure it will, son, I'm sure it will. Now, leave me alone to think. I'll hide the book where it is safe."

"Why should *you* hide it?" Dane asked. "I'm the one who stole it."

"And when the Norns come," Lut said, "it's best you don't know where it is."

"Their threats won't sway me," Dane said.

"But perhaps their enticements will," Lut said. "Remember, in the godly realm the Fates are the cleverest of all. Go and rest now." Dane hesitated, eyeing the book uncertainly.

"It is safe with me," Lut assured him.

As he, William, and Jarl moved to leave, Dane paused at the door. "If the Norns are so clever, why would they leave the book unguarded?"

Lut ruminated. "I can think of only one reason. They thought it inconceivable that anyone would be so bravely audacious or spectacularly asinine as to steal it."

"Good of you to clear that up," Dane said.

After the young men had left, Lut sat before the book, staring at it a very long time. How was it possible that the book held the fate of every human being within it? he wondered. The longer he gazed at it, the more the temptation grew. He had always believed that a man could fool his fate, but now he wasn't so sure. If he opened the book and read his fate, would he be able to alter it? Or would the words be as if they were set in stone and unchangeable? What if he read, "Lut the Bent sat in his hut pondering the mysteries of fate when he suddenly fell over dead"? He knew that those words would probably so terrify him that he *would* fall over dead. It would be a self-fulfilling prophecy, hatched by the clever Norns themselves.

Why *had* the Norns left the book unguarded? Was it as Lut had said, that they never suspected it would be stolen? Or was there something more devious afoot?

Lut stared at the book in a kind of delicious agony. If he opened it, his questions would be answered. As a master seer, he reasoned, he above all was equipped to deal with such knowledge. The whispers of the gods had passed through him countless times; the book before him was just a more detailed version of those godly pronouncements. So what was the harm in taking a peek? He knew full well what the harm would be. And yet . . .

With a trembling hand he reached for the book—and all at once its cover flew open and a sudden wind blew up, howling and whipping at the pages, turning them from front to back. Staring agape, Lut was further amazed to see that the wind seemed to be blowing only over the book and nowhere else in the room. His own robe, so close to the funnel of wind, was completely unruffled. Then the pages abruptly stopped turning and the book lay open before him, beckoning, a shaft of golden light shining on a certain spot in the center of the right-side page. Drawing a breath, Lut moved nearer and peered down at the book . . . and what he saw so astonished him, he nearly fell over dead.

His mother had gone on a visit to a neighboring village, so Dane found his own house empty and quiet, and after stoking the hearth fire, he fell deeply asleep, the perilous events of the past few days having physically and mentally drained him.

When next he awoke, the room was bathed in light. He turned over and was thrilled to see Astrid floating there above the floor, her body luminescent, her hair and feathered cloak rippling in a breeze that Dane could not feel. "It was you who took the book, wasn't it, Dane?" Her voice was eerily flat, emotionless, and for a moment Dane thought he was dreaming. "Where is the book, Dane? You must give it to me."

"First you must be freed from your oath. That's why I took it—so the Norns would change your fate."

He saw her face flash in anger, but just as quickly she softened. "If you give me the book, I will return it. This will so please the Norns, I'm sure they will free me from my oath."

"Do you still love me?"

"Dane, there will be time later for all that," she said with impatience. "If you love *me*, you will do as I ask."

"Astrid, why aren't you wearing the locket?"

Her hand shot to her neck, feeling it missing. "I . . . am not permitted to wear such ornaments—"

"You were wearing it in Asgard."

Her eyes narrowed into slits. "Do you know how I will suffer if the book is not returned?" A thick black worm, squirming and glistening with slime, coiled around her ghostly-white neck. "Niflheim is the lair of all that is corrupt and foul. And you will dwell there with me!" A writhing mass of the beslimed worms coiled around her arms and legs, her face erupting in boils, bursting with pus.

Dane bolted for the door, but the floor gave way and suddenly he was sunk knee-deep in sand—and it was moving, for a hole had opened beneath Astrid and the sand was being sucked down into it as if his house was the top half of an hourglass. "Our time is running out, Dane!" the figure screeched, her mouth a gaping hole of black, rotten stumps. "Give me the book!"

Dane desperately clawed against the moving tide of sand, fighting to keep from getting pulled under. "Never! You are *not* Astrid!"

There was a splintering crash. He looked up to see Jarl and Lut standing in the open doorway. Jarl held the book and Lut held a lighted oil lamp. "Enough trickery, Skuld!" Lut thundered. "Dane will not submit!" Jarl dropped the book and Lut stood over it, ready to pour oil from the lamp onto it. "Stop or the book burns."

"You wouldn't dare!" she screeched.

Lut let drop a trickle of oil onto the cover, lowering the flame to it. "Reveal yourself now!" In an instant the sand was gone and the earthen hut floor had reappeared. Looking again at her, Dane was shocked to find the horrific, suppurating creature had become a regal-looking woman, garbed in flowing robes and wearing a crimson headdress. Hovering in the air, frowning, she then deigned to lower herself to stand upon the floor with the mere mortals.

"Was all that really necessary, your worship?" Lut said.

"It's all you humans understand," she said with contempt.

"Allow me to introduce the goddess Skuld," Lut said to Dane and Jarl, "so named for 'that which shall be.'"

Skuld jabbed a finger at Jarl. "You—Jarl the Fair." Her

voice dripped with scorn. "Your fate is worst of all." Jarl was too shocked to speak. "You will never sup at Odin's table. No! For you are to die in bed of old age." Jarl grabbed his chest as if stricken. She cackled with glee and turned to face Dane. "Your theft of my property was all for naught—for you will never see your beloved Astrid again."

"Don't listen to her," Lut said. "She bluffs."

Skuld looked at Lut with a haughty air. "Truth is not a bluff."

"You left the book unguarded for a reason," Lut said. "*That* is the truth."

"You know nothing," she said, eyeing a fingernail as if to see if she had broken it during her overblown, shape-shifting performance.

"I do," Lut said, "because I read the book."

For an instant her face showed surprise, but her arrogance returned. "Impossible. Only I can comprehend what is writ."

"Your eminence, it is time to drop the pretense," Lut said. "I know a man can have many fates, for there are many roads his life can take."

For a moment she was silent, and Dane saw anger welling up inside her. "Yes!" she spat, as if Lut had struck at a secret she hated to reveal. "But each road has a distinct and inexorable fate created by me!"

Dane was rocked by this revelation. "So it's up to *us* to *choose* the road?"

"Yes, son," Lut said. "That's why she left the book

unguarded—to see if you would be so . . . audaciously brave as to steal it.

"Well, your eminence, the road you laid out has been chosen," he continued. "And your threats and frightful transmogrifications have been met with courage and cleverness. The test has been passed. Tell them of the task at hand."

Dane threw Lut a questioning look. "Task? My only task is to free Astrid."

"My conditions are that *if* and *when* you are successful," Skuld said airily, "*I* will decide if she warrants freedom."

Dane would not be at the whim of the Fates once more. "No," he insisted. "You will *promise* to free her if I do what you ask. Those are *my* conditions."

"And I'm not dying in bed of old age," Jarl added. "You have to promise I'll die heroically with a sword in my hand, or the deal's off."

"It appears they have you over a barrel, your eminence," Lut said, barely suppressing a grin.

Skuld glared at Dane with such fierceness he could feel the heat. "Very well, I promise to offer her freedom. But if you fail to kill Thidrek the Terrifying, the road for all three of you leads straight to Niflheim."

5

DANE MAKES
A DEAL

"Kill Thidrek?" said Dane. "I thought I already did."

"He seems to have become *un*dead," Skuld said, "courtesy of our distant and despised cousin, the goddess Hel. When we snip a man's thread of life, it should stay snipped—and we severely disapprove of Hel interfering with our work by making the dead walk again. It sets a bad example."

"Do you mean Thidrek has become . . . a draugr?" Lut inquired.

"He has. And he is in league with Niflheim's hag in some sort of nefarious business. He must be stopped."

"Why can't you just snip Thidrek's thread of life again?" Jarl asked.

Skuld looked at Jarl as if that were the stupidest question

she had ever heard, but she answered anyway. "Once a man has met his mortal fate, he is outside of our dominion. That is why Hel uses draugrs—the *un*dead—to sow her mischief on earth."

"So basically, all you want is Thidrek dead for good," Jarl said, interlocking his fingers, casually cracking his knuckles. "You've come to the right man. Because I will *personally* dispatch the draugr Thidrek. Tell me where he is and the deed is all but done."

Again Skuld gave Jarl a withering glare. "Do you have any idea *how* to kill a draugr? Your weapons are useless against the undead. Draugrs are an altogether different animal, and to kill them you must use this." From the folds of her robe Skuld produced a plump and shiny golden yellow apple, holding it aloft in the palm of her hand as if it were something of awesome magic.

"We hit him with fruit?" Jarl asked.

Skuld sighed in exasperation and said to Jarl, "I'm so glad *you're* not the brains of this outfit." She turned to Dane and Lut, continuing. "Ordinary steel will not cut a draugr. Only an enchanted blade of otherworldly strength and sharpness will. There is but one man alive with the wile to craft such a blade. Déttmárr the Smith is his name. He is an aged dwarf who hovers near death. Bring him this apple of youth from Goddess Idunn's tree. Once he eats it, his youth will be restored and he will have strength again to forge your weapon. But you must not delay; his days dwindle."

From Norse myth, Dane knew that Idunn's apples of youth were what kept the gods perpetually young. "Where do we find this Déttmárr?" he asked.

"Go to the Passage of Mystery," she said. Before Dane could say another word, her image shimmered and became blindingly brilliant, forcing them to shield their eyes. An ear-shattering crack of thunder sounded, accompanied by a sudden rush of wind that almost knocked them off their feet. The light faded, and when they looked back she was gone—and so was the Book of Fate. For a moment all of them just stood there, bedazzled by the effects.

"She couldn't just disappear quietly?" said Jarl.

"Gods have to make big exits," Lut explained, "so as to leave us puny humans in awe." Dane looked down and saw he was holding the apple in his hand. Lut crossed to him, reaching for it. "Give it to me."

Dane pulled it back from Lut's grasp. "Why?"

"Because our mission depends on its safe delivery to Déttmárr, and you will have enough on your hands leading us."

"Who says *he's* leading us?" Jarl said.

"*I* do," Dane said. "Because Astrid's fate depends on us killing Thidrek."

"And if we *don't* kill him, I'm doomed to die of old age," Jarl countered. "I have bigger stakes—*I'm* leading."

This was the same argument they'd had since they were boys, vying for dominance, and Dane knew nothing would be solved until they were actually out on the quest and his leadership skills proved superior, as always was the case. So he proposed they share the command and Jarl grudgingly accepted. That settled, Dane said to Lut, "Where is this Passage of Mystery?"

"It is north of here, a week's ride." Lut regarded the apple, and for an instant Dane saw a look of hunger flash across his face. "It would be safer in my custody," Lut repeated.

"She put the apple in *my* hands," Dane said. "Besides, we have to move fast. Which means, I'm afraid, you're not coming, Lut."

"But I'm the only one who knows the way."

"You'll draw us a map," Dane said.

"A map? Hah! You'll need more than directions. You'll need wisdom," Lut said. "And I have more of it in my left buttock than both your brains combined!"

"He has a point," Jarl said.

Lut's wisdom had saved their skins more than a few times. But there was something worrisome about the old man's insistence on coming—like he had some other motive for being on the journey. "All right, Lut. But the first time you slow us up, you're going home."

Lut told Dane and Jarl not to tell their fellow villagers the reason for their impending trip. Everyone in the village hated Thidrek, which meant they all would like a crack at killing him again. The elders would insist on a special meeting to elect who would go—and by the time the nominations and speeches and votes were finished, Déttmárr the Smith would probably be dead.

So it was kept secret, sort of. Two more men were needed to round out the party. The towering twins Rik and Vik Vicious were ideal candidates, but they were off representing the village at the semiannual bear-wrestling matches. Ulf the Whale was also unavailable, still sick from eating a vat of spoiled pickled herring. Although they weren't the first choice, Drott the Dim and Fulnir the Stinking eagerly agreed to come along. Dane figured that if Lut faltered along the way—which Dane thought highly likely—either Drott or Fulnir could make sure the old man returned home safely.

Thus, it would be a party of five, with Dane's pet raven, Klint, scouting the skies. Next morning the horses were saddled and they were set to leave when William appeared on foot, his bow and quiver of arrows slung over his back. Somehow he had discovered their plans. "Thidrek killed my parents and made me a slave. Of all of you, *I'm* the one who's suffered most at his hands. I'm coming—and if you don't agree, I'll steal a horse and follow you anyway."

Knowing that the boy would make good on his threat, Dane gave in.

Right from the start, Lut knew they were in for trouble. He suggested they take the safer trail north that hugged the coast over flat terrain, then veered inland. Dane disagreed, saying, "Skuld insisted we not delay. We'll take the more direct route into the mountains." Lut's warnings about the mountain route proved accurate. The trail was full of hard climbs and steep descents, yet Dane pushed the party on relentlessly.

Each morning he roused everyone before dawn to break camp and take to the trail, where he set a fast pace all day, refusing to stop and make camp until long after the sun had disappeared from view. Jarl did not challenge Dane to slacken the pace. Indeed, he was more insistent to quicken it to reach Déttmárr before the smith expired. And as the trek wore on and Dane drove everyone to the point of exhaustion, tempers began to fray. Even Dane's best friends, Fulnir and Drott, began to question his decisions, and at noon on the sixth day it all came to a head.

They stopped in the shelter of tall pines to water the tired horses and Lut dismounted, saying he felt the call of nature. Though perfectly true—the old man's bladder wasn't what it used to be—it was the burning sensation in his chest that had him worried, and he needed a private place in which to take his potion of powdered willow bark.

His chest pains had been growing ever more acute for days, and now his potion offered only limited relief. On the morning prior, Fulnir had spied Lut taking the bitter powder and out of curiosity asked what it was. "Oh, just something for the usual aches and pains," Lut had assured him nonchalantly. Had Fulnir believed the lie? Lut didn't know. He hoped he had. With so much uncertainty now fraying their group, the last thing they needed was news of Lut's deteriorating health.

Because then Dane would leave him behind. Which would force Lut to reveal what he had read in the book. If he told them the *real* reason they were on this road, would they continue, knowing the horrible place it led? As Skuld had said, a person chooses his road of fate. And Lut had to make sure they kept to the road they were on. Or the world, and everyone they loved in it, would meet a very nasty end.

Once safely out of sight behind a tree, Lut took a pinch of powder from his leather pouch and swallowed it with water. The taste of it was wicked and he choked a bit getting it down. Strange how something so awful could have such power to do good. Thoughts of death stole over him, but he chased them away, forcing into his mind images of all his favorite foods and every woman he had ever loved, including all six of his wives.

Upon his return, he found Dane and Fulnir having heated words.

"We should make camp here," Fulnir said. "The horses need rest—*we* need rest."

"We're going on," Dane said. "I want to reach the smith's by tomorrow."

"Fulnir's right—we should camp here," Drott said. "An extra day won't hurt us."

Dane looked at his friends as if they had suddenly become

his enemies. "An extra day? We delay for one *hour* and by the time we reach Déttmárr he could be dead. And thus any chance we have to bring Astrid back. So if you even care about that—"

"Of course we care," Fulnir snapped. "We care for Astrid as much as you or we wouldn't be with you. But I say we camp here and get an early start in the morning."

"*You* say? Has your stink-breeze gone to your brain?" mocked Dane, poking Fulnir in the chest. "Since when did you assume leadership?"

Lut saw Fulnir's jaw tighten in anger. "Maybe someone else has to, Dane. You'd ride us all over a cliff if it meant easing your guilt over Astrid."

"Guilt—?"

Lut rushed forward and grabbed both of them by the arms before the fists started flying.

"The ache in my hip bone tells me a storm approaches," Lut advised. "Here among the trees would be a fine place to shelter."

Dane looked up at the blue sky, where nary a cloud was seen. "My eyes tell me your aching bones are wrong, old man. If you and the others are too tired to follow, then stay here. I'm going ahead."

"So am I," Jarl said. Without another word they mounted up and set off up the trail. William was gone, too, in a cloud of dust.

"Let them go," Fulnir said. "I'm tired of being ordered

around by Dane anyway."

"If we don't go now, we'll never catch them," Lut said. "Hurry, help me onto my horse."

"Don't you understand? He doesn't *want* you along," Fulnir said. "I think the only reason he asked me and Drott to come . . . was to take care of you."

Of course Fulnir was right. But Lut knew the party *had* to stay together because all their fates were intertwined. Dane *needed* Lut, even if he didn't know it. Lut demanded to be put atop his horse, Fulnir reluctantly complied, and the three went galloping up the trail.

A light breeze from the west suddenly blew up, and as Lut rode on, the ache in his bones worsened, accompanied by a disturbing thought. He had read in the Book of Fate *how* and *when* he was going to die. But what if Skuld wished to punish him for reading his fate? A flick of her quill could easily change everything. He could die tonight, tomorrow, or even in the next moment. He felt a chill of terror at the awful realization that everything he'd thought was certain could now be anything but.

Distant thunder rumbled. *Oh, help me, Odin, for I fear I ride to catastrophe!*

6

SHIP
OF THE DEAD

Grelf the Gratuitous trudged along the mosquito-infested riverbank realizing that he had reached a new low in his career as boot-licking lackey. Once he had been one of the top practitioners of his profession, serving as brownnosing yes-man to the rich and powerful. *Now look at me!* he despaired. Toady to a rotting corpse, the stinking undead, a cursed draugr. He was a disgrace to the Loyal Order of Sycophants. Was there even such an order, he wondered? If not, he made a mental note that he would have to start one.

"How long must we walk?" asked the draugr Thidrek, riding piggyback atop Grelf. "I thought you said the falls were but a mile or two inland."

"I'm sure that dull roar we hear *are* the falls, my lord," Grelf replied, short of breath. "They must be just around the next turn in the river."

A local villager had told Grelf how best to reach the falls. They were to journey along the coastline until they came to a spot where three small islands lay immediately offshore. There they would find a river that flowed through a narrow gap in the mountains and emptied into the sea. Once they had found the river, Grelf and Thidrek left their horses on the beach and set off on foot—rather, on Grelf's two feet—with Grelf carrying a torch to light their way. "Do you suppose we might stop and rest?" Grelf implored.

"When we're so close?" Thidrek said. "Push on—a little faster if you will."

"Of course, my lord," Grelf mewled, plodding along the muddy riverbank through swarms of mosquitoes. He was the only source of blood in the immediate vicinity, so the insects greedily bit him about the face and hands, not even landing on Thidrek, whose veins were as dry as dust. Grelf started to feel faint from the exertion and blood loss. "Is it possible, my lord, that you could walk on your own for a while?"

"And foul my boots in the mud?"

"Right, sire, what was I thinking?"

"You'd just have to lick them clean anyway," joked Thidrek.

"Of course, sir," Grelf said with a forced chuckle, "you're so kind to spare me that."

Back when Thidrek lived his princely life, one of Grelf's

many duties in his castle had been to be sure his master's wardrobe was smart and spotless. "A tyrant must look stylish while terrorizing the populace," Prince Thidrek would say. "One smudge of dirt and my image of invincibility is ruined."

Now that Thidrek was undead, keeping up appearances was proving even more difficult. The main problem was masking the aroma of his slowly rotting body—a stench that even Thidrek could not endure for long. Grelf, being practiced in the alchemic arts—learned while concocting poisons to eliminate Thidrek's rivals—had turned his skills to perfumery. After several tries, he'd hit upon a concoction of conifer resin oil, myrtle, and crushed flowers that was powerful enough to offset the smell of rotting tissue, at least for a while.

"There it is!" Thidrek cried. Ahead in the moonlight Grelf saw a magnificent cascade of water, perhaps a hundred feet high, that thundered down over a mountain cleft into a deep, wide pool. He felt a swat on the back of his head. "Hurry, Grelf!"

Hurry? It wasn't like the dead were going anywhere, Grelf wanted to tell him. But he hastened onward, struggling along the riverbank, and soon, gasping for air, arrived alongside the falls at the base of the mountain. Thidrek climbed down from his back and Grelf fell to his knees, exhausted. "What's wrong, Grelf? A little hard work too much for you?"

"Just a moment—to catch my breath—my lord."

"Now, now, I won't have you slacking—not with us on the brink of success."

They had been "on the brink of success" many times before, trying to find Hel's Ship of the Dead. For a whole week now they had been trudging up the coastline, exploring every river that emptied into the sea. Seven times they had gone upriver and seven times they'd found nothing. Grelf secretly hoped they would fail again; the last thing he wanted to see was more horrific draugrs.

Along the way Grelf had learned all about the legend of the Ship of the Dead. Centuries ago, Thidrek told him, when the gods were warring, Odin had sent a giant wave to destroy Hel's ship. It was said that the wall of water had swept the craft and its draugr crew to shore and all the way up a river, where at last it had sunk beneath or near a waterfall, and there it lay to this day, its magical secrets there for the taking. Grelf no longer believed there was such a ship, and even if there was, it seemed doubtful that they would ever find it.

Thidrek took the torch from Grelf. "We mustn't dawdle." Grelf followed his master, edging toward the falls along the treacherous rocks slick with wet moss.

Thidrek disappeared from view, and Grelf realized he had slipped through a narrow gap between the curtain of water and the vertical rock face. For a moment Grelf considered fleeing, jumping into the river and letting the current take him down to where the horses were tethered. He would gallop away, taking the other horse too, and be free of his rotting lord!

But he hesitated a moment too long, and Thidrek's skeletal hand grabbed his collar and pulled him through the passageway. When his eyes adjusted, he saw he was now *behind* the waterfall, standing at the entrance to a gaping black cave.

"Weren't thinking of escaping, were you, Grelfie?"

"No, my lord! Never would I leave the side of my master."

Still grasping Grelf's coat, Thidrek pulled him close. The stench was overpowering and Grelf almost gagged. "Good. Because if you ever did *leave my side*, you would regret it. *Most* painfully." Thidrek released him and started into the cave. Grelf followed like a slouching, whipped dog.

Entering the chamber, Grelf saw its dimensions were enormous—certainly large enough to accommodate a marooned warship.

"Keep a sharp eye for anything protruding from the sand," Thidrek said. "If the ship is here, most likely it's buried."

Farther into the cave they went, the roar of the waterfall dying behind them. If the ship was here, Grelf thought, the wave carrying it this far inland and this deep into the cavern had to have been truly monumental.

Grelf tripped over something and fell into Thidrek. "Idiot! Watch your—" He froze, his gaze fixed on the floor.

Poking through the sand, illuminated in torchlight, was a long, pointed piece of wood, the very thing Grelf had stumbled over. Thidrek dropped to his knees and brushed away the sand from around it. The carved head of a strange beast began to appear.

"It's the figurehead!" Thidrek shouted. "We've found it!" Thidrek rose to his feet, done with his part of the manual labor. "Start digging, Grelf. Hurry!"

Grelf started scooping away handfuls of sand. Thidrek struck him hard across the ear.

"Faster! Make the sand fly!"

And Grelf did. He not only felt like a whipped dog, he dug like one too.

Soaked by the cold, relentless rains and feeling the ache of death upon him, Lut struggled to keep up with the pack. Though night had fallen, Dane had driven them onward across a vast and treeless plain that fell away from the mountains to the east. When the rains came, as Lut had known they would, they were caught out on the flat and shelterless expanse with no place to hide. On they rode in the punishing rainstorm, the once-dry streambeds now raging torrents that threatened to sweep horse and rider away. The worst, Lut feared, was yet to come. He spied the flashes of lightning in the distance, and with the accompanying booms of thunder growing louder, he knew Thor's fury drew nearer. Their one hope was to reach the far side of the plateau and find refuge before lightning charred them all.

Lut cursed Skuld and her book. He had embarked on this journey expecting to survive it. But now it seemed she was just playing with him—and could snip his thread of life at any moment. He prayed to Thor for mercy. *Stop this storm so I may live the night!*

But mercy was not to be his. As Lut's horse crossed a creek swollen with rushing water, Thor at last found his mark. The night exploded with sudden light and sound, and the flash of lightning struck so near, the force of its heat scorched Lut's face and he lost his sight completely. Beneath him his panicked horse shrieked and reared—and Lut fell backward, still blinded, and his whole body went cold as he plunged into the icy waters of the creek. Caught in the swift current, he tumbled upside down underwater as it swept him on.

When at last he struggled to the surface, gasping for air and coughing up water, he had regained his sight and saw the creek had merged with another, far larger one. He was in a much stronger current, twice as deep, with the banks too far to swim to. Fighting it would be futile. Best save his strength for keeping his head above water as long as he could.

Swallowed by the blackness of the night and the fury of the river, he thought of surrender, of just letting go. Had he not journeyed life's arduous path long enough? He had lived twice as long as most men, and lived it as fully as possible, filling his days with both the bitter and the sweet.

He heard a dull, distant roar. He wondered what the sound was—then remembered that the plain they'd been crossing ended in a precipitous drop to a valley far below. That was where the current was taking him, over a cliff and hundreds of feet down to a violent and painful death. His reaction was one of instant indignation.

By the gods, no! he railed. *Of all the indignities! A man my age does not deserve to die crushed upon rocks!*

Spying the stream bank in a flash of lightning, Lut fought his way toward it. The roar of the water grew louder and the current gained strength as it was funneled toward the precipice. Weakening now, the pain like a knife in his chest, blinded again by the battering rain, Lut fought on, thrashing and splashing, bent on this not being his journey's end.

Another boom of thunder, and the surging river smashed Lut against a rock, his face scraping along it as the current swept him on. He clawed at it trying to find a handhold. But the rain-slick rock gave him no grip and off he slid, rushing toward the cliff. In a frenzy he spied another rock, looming just ahead at the cliff's edge. He came rushing toward it and made a desperate grab. Sliding across the rock, Lut's fingers found a crack in the rock—and miraculously held on. Fearing the fierce current would tear him away, he reached up with his other hand and soon found another handhold. Half submerged in icy water, and having a tenuous hold on the cold rock, he prepared to do the difficult work of pulling himself up and out of the river. But with the little strength he had left, it seemed impossible. He couldn't hold himself here forever; the current would soon take him. Climb he must, or at least die in the trying. He looked up at the rain-slick rock. No, he wouldn't climb just yet. He would rest here awhile. Yes, rest and wait. Perhaps the strength would come to him. Just hold on, Lut, hold on.

The sand became harder packed the deeper Grelf dug. Thidrek had lent him his knife to loosen the soil. Grelf stabbed at the earth, wishing it was Thidrek's face. His nails broken, his fingertips rubbed raw, he scooped out the loosened soil until he had exposed most of the monstrous figurehead on the ship's prow.

All Viking ships bore carved prow heads—often a dog, a dragon, or a wolf—to ward off attackers and to beseech the gods for protection. But this head was unlike anything Grelf had ever seen. It seemed a cross between a serpent and a cat, with a long curved neck and a scaly hide. Although it was ancient, the burial in the sand seemed to have preserved each finely carved detail. The beastly thing had two ears that lay back flat on its head, a long snout, and, protruding from its half-opened jaws, two tusklike fangs. Its eyes, deep set beneath its brow, were shut tight under heavy lids—but though both eyes were closed, Grelf had the eerie feeling that they might pop open at any moment. Just under its lower jaw, clutched in its two taloned paws, was an ornate horn, and the detail of this too seemed carved by an unearthly hand.

Thidrek cried, "Stop!" and Grelf immediately collapsed in the hole he'd made, too drained to climb out, part of him wishing that Thidrek would heap the disturbed soil back on top of him and let him die in peace. He waited. When nothing happened, he turned his head and saw his master was standing above him on the edge of the hole, peering intently at the prow beast. "I suggest you vacate the dig, Grelf—she may be hungry."

Hungry? Grelf did not hesitate to ask what Thidrek meant. He scrambled out of the hole and a good distance away from it. Thidrek stared into the eyes of the prow beast and intoned an incantation.

> *Sound the horn!*
> *Awake the dead!*
> *Bring foulness forth*
> *And to the living dread!*
> *For slaughter and havoc*
> *O'er the earth shall spread!*

There was the sound of wood creaking, like that of a ship at sea. Grelf watched in horror and fascination as the prow beast's brow began to twitch, awakened from her centuries of slumber. The creature's eyes shot open, glowing red. Her head came alive, growling and hissing. Her clawed paws brought the horn to the beast's mouth, and from the horn's bell came a thunderous bellow, a sound of such force it knocked Grelf back and made him cover his ears.

The earth behind the prow creature started to churn. A rusted sword blade thrust up from the sand like an insect's antenna, testing the air. A shrieking figure exploded from out of the sand as if catapulted. The thing sprang up and landed on its feet, facing them. It held the sword in its skeletal hand, a shield in the other, and from its death's-head mouth came a horrifying war cry. More draugrs shot from the earth in rapid succession and within moments had formed a shield wall as if preparing to defend their buried ship against a score of warriors. Grelf, huddling in terror behind the seemingly unruffled Thidrek, saw that their round wooden shields were rotted, some only half intact, and their weapons and armor were corroded and decayed with rust.

The largest of the draugr warriors, wearing a tarnished bronze helmet topped with the figure of an eagle's head, stepped forward and thrust his sword in the air, quieting the chorus of war cries. Grelf suspected this was the undeads' chieftain, since it was apparent that his helmet and armor had once been of superior workmanship.

"Who dares attack my ship?" the chieftain bellowed.

Thidrek regarded the fearsome creature with his usual haughty air. "I am Lord Thidrek the Terrifying. You will address me as such."

"Well, *Lord* Thidrek," the chieftain said mockingly, "if

you are here to fight, bring your men and they shall die."

Thidrek reached behind him and pulled the quivering Grelf into view. "He's not much of a man, but here he is."

"*That's* what you bring to fight me?" the chieftain roared.

"I'm not here to fight," Thidrek said, "but to make an offer."

"You will offer me blood," the chieftain growled. He grabbed a spear from a draugr warrior and let it fly at Thidrek's chest. It passed straight through him without leaving a mark, as if Thidrek's flesh were but misty illusion. The chieftain and his warriors gaped in surprise.

"You fool, can't you see I am of your ilk?" Thidrek said.

The chieftain squinted at Thidrek, sniffing the air. "You don't smell like the undead."

Thidrek patted Grelf's head. "Courtesy of my bootlick and perfumer extraordinaire. What name did we arrive at for your concoction, Grelfie?"

"My lord, we were down to either 'eau de living' or 'rot-not.'"

"Hah!" the chieftain spat. "We are warriors and care not if our odor offends. State your business, one known as Thidrek."

"I represent the goddess Hel," Thidrek announced. "Her orders are that we sail this ship to the underworld. There, the horn that awoke you will summon Hel's army."

The chieftain pondered this, rubbing his exposed chin bone in interest. "For what purpose do we raise the army?"

"What else?" Thidrek sniffed. "So that I may command it to conquer the land of the living."

"So that *you* may command?" roared the chieftain. "This is my ship! I am commander of it!"

"And the goddess Hel commands *you* to turn this ship over to *me*!" Thidrek roared back.

"Well, I don't think so," said the chieftain, crossing his arms on his chest.

"You dare defy the goddess?"

"I don't hand my command to the first undead lord who happens by." The chieftain smirked. "If you even *are* a lord. Bring me Hel's orders in writing—*on* her official stationery *and* affixed with her personal seal—perhaps then I'll think about it."

Grelf squelched a cheer. His festering lordship's plan was hitting a brick wall!

Thidrek's eyes bulged in rage. "Has the rot eaten your brain? Hel does not issue commands like a lowly village functionary. She is the patron goddess of all that is evil!"

The chieftain was not budging. Feet firmly planted, arms still crossed across his chest, he replied, "I am aware of Hel's evil omnipotence. Which makes me doubt she would send a blustering blowhard as her envoy."

This brought snickers from the chieftain's troops. Thidrek, who like all despots hated ridicule above all, glared at them. "You dare to laugh at me? You—who burrow like worms in the ground? Your shields and weapons are as decayed as your valor. I offer you new life! As my liege men you will sail to glory once more. You will have strong shields and weapons of hard steel. You will know again what it is to be brave and feared—for you will cut a wide swath through the living and eat their flesh and drink their blood to your everlasting content!"

To Grelf's fear it appeared that Thidrek's rousing call to arms had piqued the warriors' interest. But he wasn't sure, since it's hard to read the expression of someone whose face is pretty much rotted away.

"You waste your words," the draugr chief barked. "My warriors are bound to me—and I am bound to no one. Go now before I lose patience." The chieftain ordered his warriors back to their graves. As they had sprung from the sand, they all dived back in as if the ground were water. Soon all had disappeared beneath the surface.

"Well, I guess that's that, my lord," Grelf chirped. "You tried your best, you really did, but perhaps this whole raise-an-army-of-the-dead thing wasn't meant to be."

"I never had trouble enlisting henchmen before," Thidrek said in contemplation. "Why, every cutthroat and brigand in the land was more than eager to serve Lord Thidrek the Terrifying. Have I lost my touch?"

"Perish the thought, my lord! You are as terrifying as ever—now even more so in your, um, draugr personage."

"Then why would they rather return to their graves than serve me?"

"The reason for that, my lord, is summed up in one word. Leverage. Before, you had gold to pay men. *And* you had the threat of death over them if they failed to perform to their ruthless best."

"Of course, the undead have less desire for riches. And since they're not living—"

"You have no leverage over their souls," Grelf said.

"You have summed up the problem quite nicely, my friend," Thidrek said, placing his hand on Grelf's shoulder. "What would I ever do without you?"

"You are most kind, my lord." *Now go lie in a ditch. I'll cover you with dirt and be on my way.*

"In all the years you have served me, do you know what I appreciate most about you, Grelf? When times are at their toughest, you always show me how to find the light behind the darkest cloud."

"Light, sire?"

"You know—the times I wanted to give up, but you always managed to talk me out of it?"

"Uh . . . I don't think this is one of those times. In fact, I'm sure of it."

"You're . . . sure of it?" Thidrek's grip tightened on Grelf's shoulder blade, bony fingers digging deeper into his flesh, and Grelf felt the hot gush of his blood under his shirt.

"My lord—please! What are you doing?" Grelf wailed.

"Applying leverage, my dear man. We *will* find a way to prevail, won't we?"

"Yes!" Grelf cried through the excruciating pain. "We will prevail, my liege!"

Thidrek released him and the whimpering Grelf fell to the ground. "I'm so grateful for your support, Grelfie. I don't know what I'd do without you."

7

A YOUNG
STRANGER

Running alongside the rain-swollen creek, Dane heard Klint, his raven, call to him as the bird flew overhead, searching for any traces of Lut. Dane knew the plateau was soon to end, plunging to the valley floor—which meant that if they didn't find Lut soon, chances were he had been swept over.

He heard a loud *crawk!* ahead and rushed forward. The rain had stopped and a trace of moonlight shone through the thinning clouds. There! Just before the plateau ended he spotted Lut the Bent lying still, Klint hopping up and down on a rock beside the body. "He's here!" Dane called to the others, who were on foot behind him upstream. Dane scrambled over the rocks to where Lut lay motionless, his body so thin and frail he looked like little more than a pile of wet rags. Fearing him dead, Dane drew near and tentatively touched Lut's cheek. It was warm! "He's alive!" he cried.

Lut snapped open his watery blue eyes and scowled at Dane as if he'd been awakened from a blissful dream. "What're you doing in my hut?"

"You're not exactly in your hut, Lut."

The old man raised his head and saw his predicament. "I was dreaming that my roof was leaking." Drott and Fulnir arrived in a rush, happy to see Lut among the living.

"Really cut it close, Lut," said Drott. "Another blink and you'd have gone over."

"It was Death who blinked," Lut croaked as Fulnir and Drott helped him up. "Just when he was cocksure he had me, I slipped from his grasp like a wise old trout."

"Good we still have your wisdom to guide us. It seems to be in short supply." As Fulnir said this, Dane caught a sharp look from him. Fulnir and Drott took Lut away and Dane did not move to help. It was clear they did not want his assistance and blamed him for everything that had gone wrong.

The storm having now passed and the skies cleared, a bright moon lit the way as they rejoined the others and continued down the main trail across the plateau. Dane rode in the lead, feeling the growing animosity at his back. The notion of apologizing to them crept into his thoughts. Perhaps he *was* wrong about pressing on across the plateau. But then again, was it really his fault they had been caught in the storm?

Was their faith so thin that one mishap had turned

them against him? Had they forgotten all the previous times Dane had led them successfully through all manner of danger? What should he do? Take a vote every time a difficult decision had to be made? If so, they'd *never* get to Déttmárr's. It was *they* who should apologize, Dane realized. Would their whining help them reach the old smith any quicker with the apple? No! If there was hardship along the way, so be it. Bringing Astrid back was worth any suffering.

The trail descended gently into a valley, and they found a cave where they could shelter for the remainder of the night. After feeding and watering the horses, Drott and William picketed them inside the cave to keep them safe from roving bears and wolves. Jarl built a healthy fire and they all hung their wet clothes to dry on ropes above it. Fulnir passed out portions of dried fish, flatbread, and hard cheese, and the weary travelers sat by the fire eating in grim silence, the air thick with unspoken recriminations.

Dane was off by himself, brooding, wishing someone would start in with accusations about his poor leadership. Then he would show them. He would tell them they could all go spit in their hats and that he would take the golden apple and find Déttmárr on his own. One man could move faster than a group anyway. If they wanted to rest their backsides for a couple of days, then *fine*, they could catch up with him later.

But no one said a word to him, all acting as if he weren't even there. Dane finally gave up waiting for their criticism, took his blankets, and found a place to bed down. When they awoke, he wouldn't be here, he vowed. He'd be far away with no one to worry about but himself. The last things he heard before slipping off to sleep were the faint little mouse farts that Fulnir often made while lying in his bedroll, and Dane was quick to add these to his growing list of things he wouldn't miss.

When Dane awoke later, the others were still snoring away in their blankets, all fast asleep. From the dying embers of the fire, he judged it was perhaps an hour before dawn. He quietly gathered his dried clothes and blankets and stuffed them into his pack. Carrying pack and saddle, he led his bridled horse out of the cave. As Dane saddled his mount under the cold night sky, the horse became suddenly skittish, snorting and pricking its ears as if catching the scent of carnivores. Dane's hand went to the handle of his sword, and then he heard her voice.

"Will you never stop?" Dane whirled and saw Astrid upon her celestial mount descending from above. As soon as the horse's hooves touched ground, Astrid leaped off and stood before Dane, hands on hips, looking very put out. "Can you go *one* week without risking your life or someone else's? Lut almost died!"

"So you've been watching us," Dane said with a grin. "You just can't keep away, can you?"

Her lips pursed in dismay. "What lame scheme are you up to now?"

"It's not *my* scheme, it's Skuld's," Dane said, and he proceeded to tell her the whole story of why they were traveling to Déttmárr's with one of Idunn's apples, and how, once revived, the smith would make a special blade, and lastly, how Dane would use it to kill the draugr Thidrek and thereupon release Astrid from her oath to Odin. Fully expecting Astrid to be so overjoyed by the prospect of rejoining him that she'd leap ecstatically into his arms and cover him with kisses, he was therefore startled to find her staring at him with cold fury.

"I thought I had made it clear to you. I don't want you to risk lives for my sake. Take everyone and go home."

"Home? I have no home if you're not there."

"Oh, stop," she said. "You still think I *want* to return? I don't. I like being a Valkyrie—I like everything about it. I have shared drink with the gods, have seen places your narrow, boyish mind couldn't even imagine. Do you think I'd be satisfied now with a boring life in Voldarstad with you?" And then she laughed—*laughed!*—at his shocked expression of hurt.

"You're not Astrid. Astrid wouldn't say those things!"

Her face hardened. "You're right, Dane. I am no longer the girl you knew. When will you get that through your thick head?"

Dane lunged forward and grabbed her wrist. "Is it you, Skuld? Come to test me again?" Astrid threw off Dane's grasp with such force that he flew backward and landed in the dirt. For a moment he lay there and saw that her hard, mocking expression had changed to one of surprise, as if she too were appalled by her sudden violence against him.

Her hand clutched the Thor's Hammer locket at her neck and ripped the chain free, letting it fall to the ground. "It is over between us," she said tonelessly, "now and forever." She leaped onto her horse and took to the skies. With an overpowering sadness he watched her until her image vanished among the stars.

Next thing he knew, someone was shaking him awake. Dane's eyes snapped open, and he saw before him a very worried-looking William the Brave. "It's Lut!" the boy whispered. "He's gone!" Dane sat up in his bedroll, gathering his senses. The cave was lit with the first rays of morning, and everyone save for William and Lut was still warm in their blankets. Dane realized with welcome relief that the vivid scene with Astrid had merely been a dream. "Dane! We have to find Lut. He went out to pee hours ago."

"Old men take a long time to empty."

"Not *this* long. I think something's happened."

"All right, all right," Dane said gruffly. He pulled on his boots and strapped on his sword, wondering what kind of new fix Lut had gotten himself into. He knew that the old man was too frail for such an arduous journey and never should have come along. He was like a small child now who had to be watched constantly.

Soon they were outside the cave gazing in all directions and calling his name. This brought Fulnir and Drott outside, and William told them Lut was missing.

"Probably went out to relieve himself and saw an interesting butterfly to chase," Dane said mildly, downplaying the matter. "You know how his mind wanders."

"He has bad pain in his chest," Fulnir said. "I saw him take a potion of willow powder for it."

"Pain?" Dane asked, now worried. "Why didn't you tell me of it?"

"Would you have cared?" replied Fulnir.

They glared at one another until William broke in. "Last night, after we found him—he said he was tired of being a burden to us. Tired of being old. You don't suppose he went off to—"

"Lut wouldn't do that," Dane said. But he wasn't at all convinced this was true, for the old one's thoughts were a mystery of late. Jarl appeared from the cave, and everyone split up to search for him. Dane went north, plunging into thick woods, loudly calling his name. He heard the others call too as they spread out in different directions, expecting any moment to hear a cheerful shout that Lut had been found safe and sound. However, as time wore on, no such thing was heard, and the deeper Dane went into the woods, the more he feared that the old one had met a horrible end, self-inflicted or otherwise.

He remembered the many times he had visited Lut's hut to ask for advice or just to hear him tell amusing stories of his distant youth. When Dane had lost his father at

Thidrek's murderous hands, it had been Lut's wisdom and understanding that had helped guide Dane toward manhood. Now, realizing Lut might be gone, Dane was ashamed he had taken the kindly old sage's presence for granted, as if it would always be there.

Seeing it was now full daylight, he again stopped to listen, hoping for a sign that Lut had been found. But the twittering birdsong and the rush of wind in the pines were all that came to his ears. He walked on—then froze of a sudden to the spot. Some distance away a figure with a hooded cloak had appeared through the trees, kneeling on the bank of a small pond. He or she—Dane was too far away to tell—seemed to be staring intently down into the water.

Drawing nearer, Dane came close enough to recognize the garb. It was Lut's! But as Dane began to rush forward to greet his friend, the figure raised his head and threw back his hood, and Dane saw that it wasn't an old man at all but instead a very young one with a full head of jet-black hair. Dane's footstep cracked a twig, but as the man's head jerked round to look, Dane darted behind a tree to hide. A few moments later he peeked out to see that the man had turned away once more and was looking into the water again. The hairs rising on his neck, Dane pulled his sword from its sheath as quietly as he could. Whoever this interloper was, Dane was determined to learn what he had done to Lut.

But what if the stranger was not alone?

What if Lut had stumbled onto a gang of thieves? They

would certainly know that an old man would not be in the wilds alone. Perhaps they had waylaid him, meaning to ransom him back to his compatriots. Or worse—they were planning a sneak attack on the cave, which would be easy since everyone was spread out in the countryside looking for Lut. The thieves would take everything, including the horses.

Dane decided his best strategy lay in surprise. Once he was close enough, he would make his move and cut the man down at the water's edge. His gang would be camped near the water too. If Dane was lucky, he could kill one or two more and get away with Lut. If he found Lut already dead, then he would kill them all. It was risky, and, yes, a tad foolhardy, but this being his best option, he had to take it.

Sword in hand, he crept from tree to tree toward the kneeling man. He stopped to sniff the air. He detected no scent of campfire smoke, heard no other voices. This was strange. Was the man really alone? And why was he gazing so intently into the water as if possessed by his own image? Moving closer still, Dane saw the gleam of a newly sharpened knife lying on the ground within the man's reach, a knife he was sure was Lut's. Dane drew in a deep breath—

—and rushed, sword high. Lightning fast, the stranger grabbed the knife and whirled, his cloak flying up into Dane's face. Dane hacked down, but up came the knife, blocking the blade. Dane slashed with his sword. The man whipped the cloak up again, twisting the cloth around the blade. The man grabbed the sword blade—now wrapped in fabric—and kicked Dane in the groin. Doubled over in pain, Dane instantly lost his grip on the sword handle and fell backward, splashing into the water. He lay like a stunned fish under the surface, looking up through the water at the rippling image of the man on the bank. The man's hand came down at him and Dane knew it held the knife. But he felt the hand grab his shirtfront and pull him up out of the water. He lay facedown on the bank, coughing and cradling his wounded privates.

"Sorry I had to kick you," Dane heard the man say.

Once he was through coughing, Dane said, "What have you done to him?"

"Who?"

"You know who! You have his knife and cloak."

"Ah. The old man. I have done away with him."

Dane saw his sword lying within reach. Despite his pain he made a grab for it, but the man's boot stepped on the blade, pinning it. "I have done a bad thing," the man said, sounding ashamed.

"You've killed my friend and I'm going to kill you!"

"Look at me, Dane." Bent on destroying the man, Dane struggled to pull his sword from under the man's boot but to no avail. "I said *look at me*." Dane angrily lifted his gaze and for the first time took in the young man's face. There was great strength there, a hint of humor, but certainly no cruelty. Far from it. The eyes were a sparkling blue, filled with wisdom and compassion.

Dane knew those eyes; he had looked into them countless times before.

"Lut?"

The man nodded but then broke into a smile, eager to share his secret. "Dane, it was amazing! I was so weary of my frailties and fearing death, I couldn't resist. From the first bite of the apple I felt so alive again, the vitality of youth flowing through me, my aches and pains vanishing. I grew straighter. Taller. My hair grew back. And look, I've got teeth now!" He grinned to show his rows of strong white teeth. "And muscles everywhere!" Lut pulled back his sleeve, showing his arm bulging with hard sinew. He picked up a stone and threw it over the pond out of sight. "I could brain a squirrel from two hundred paces—I could outrun a deer! And fighting? Well, you saw how I handled myself. When you came at me I didn't know it was you at first. And when I saw it *was* you, I had to end it before you were hurt. Again, forgive the kick."

Dane lay stupefied, unable to speak. Lut a young man again? To see him standing before him, broad shouldered and brimming with youth and vitality—it was amazingly . . . *awful*! How could his most trusted friend be so monumentally selfish? How could he eat the apple that was meant for Déttmárr? Unbelievable! "You delight in your youth—but what of Astrid? Now we have nothing to revive the smith with!"

"I didn't eat the *whole* apple. Just a nibble. There should be more than enough for Déttmárr." Lut turned to the pond, gazing with appreciation at his reflection.

"Just what we need, another Jarl," Dane said with venom.

Lut swiveled his gaze to meet Dane's. "How long have I listened to your woes, soothed your troubles? Advised you, consoled you? *Once* I wish to relieve *my* pain—soothe *my* fears—and you have nothing but contempt for me."

Dane jumped to his feet. "Don't try and turn this around and make *me* the selfish one. You had this planned since Skuld gave me the apple. That's why you wanted to carry it!" Lut waved his hand as if replying to this accusation was beneath his dignity. "Show me the apple," Dane ordered.

"Very well," Lut said with a sigh. He patted his cloak and pockets. "I had it somewhere . . ."

"Where is it!"

"It must've fallen out while we were tussling." They looked around on the ground but saw nothing. Then came a rustling in the nearby bush. Dane motioned for silence and crept toward it. Out sprang a hissing badger, the core of the apple clenched in its jaws. The ferocious beast held its ground, not about to relinquish its newfound booty. Hearing Lut cry his name, Dane turned in time to see Lut tossing him his sword. Dane caught the hilt of the sword and turned back to the badger, meaning to make short work of it, but the animal had the good sense to flee, scampering away with the precious fruit in its mouth.

"After him!" Dane cried. They gave chase across the forest floor, the low-slung badger darting to and fro, barely avoiding swipes from Dane's blade. Lut threw his knife and missed. Dane made a desperate throw with his sword but hit a tree. Dane saw the beast move toward its burrow hole and knew if it went underground, the apple was lost. He made a last-ditch dive, grabbing the badger by its hind legs as it plunged into the hole.

Dane yanked the beast out and it attacked with its legendary fury, biting and slashing him with its razor-sharp claws and teeth. In its rage the animal dropped the apple, and Dane grabbed it and rolled it away. A well-aimed rock thrown by Lut struck the beast a glancing blow. It hissed and snarled, but then, deciding the prize wasn't worth the fight, the badger whipped round and disappeared down its burrow hole.

His face scratched, his hand bleeding from the badger's vicious bites, Dane examined the apple, wiping off the badger spit. All that was left was the core and a little part near the stem. "There's not enough here to revive an elderly dung beetle," Dane bemoaned.

"But the core is most potent," Lut said. "Besides, Déttmárr, being of diminutive stature, will require less."

Dane fixed Lut with an accusatory eye. "How much exactly did *you* eat?"

"As I said, a nibble."

"And the badger ate the rest," Dane said skeptically.

"No wonder he was so ferocious," Lut reasoned.

"As opposed to other badgers that are shy and meek," said Dane. He heard footsteps, turned, and saw Jarl, Fulnir, and Drott approaching. They stopped a few feet away and warily eyed the black-haired stranger.

"Who is that?" Jarl asked Dane.

"Someone I thought I knew," Dane said, walking away.

A moment later he heard Drott exclaim, "Lut! Is that you? You're—you're un-bent!"

Dane returned to the cave, cursing this new complication. As he approached, he saw something glinting in the grass. He stopped and reached down for it and saw the Thor's Hammer locket upon the broken chain. His heart began to pound. Could it be true? His dream of Astrid hadn't been a dream at all.

8

DWARFED
BY A MYSTERY

Dane was glad to be on the move again. The air was warm, the skies were bright with promise, and an encouraging wind blew at their backs as they headed to their rendezvous with the ancient swordsmith.

Lut was elated. So excited was he to be once again in the full flower of youth, Lut could not stop talking. The man had the vigor of a roaring river as he jogged alongside the horses, insisting he felt too good to ride. Lut's memory had returned to him as well, and he hooted with glee, remembering the name of the first girl he'd ever kissed—Hlífey the Quiet—and the favorite insult of his older brother, Freybjörn the Foulmouth: "You dog-livered dung heap!"

For his entire life, Dane had only known Lut to be gray of hair and bent of frame, his voice a thin rasp. And now there he was, erect, feisty, his voice booming with the command of an energetic man of twenty, and Dane still felt it strange to see.

At midmorning, reaching the northern edge of the plain, Dane gazed down into the dry, rock-strewn valley below and halted everyone. He heard the murmurs of his friends as they too now sighted what he had seen cut into the cliffside on the far side of the valley floor: a narrow black crevice, cut like a long jagged scar from the ground to the sky.

"Well, there it is," said Lut. "The Passage of Mystery."

"Doesn't look too mysterious to me," Jarl said. "Sure this is it, Lut?"

"In my sixty-fifth year," Lut said, "my third wife and I journeyed past here on the way to her home village. I remember it clearly."

"How can you remember forty years back when you're only in your twenties now?" Jarl shook his head in disbelief. "Am I the only one boggled by that?"

"Just because I *appear* young like you," Lut said, "does not mean I am equally brainless. My wisdom is intact. Perhaps, if you stop being so damned sure of yourself—impulsively leaping into every fight without a thought—you may live long enough to acquire some." Dane laughed and Lut turned on him. "That goes for you, too." He looked back at Drott, Fulnir, and William. "*And* you." Lut moved off down the trail.

"He may look young, but he's still a cranky old fart," Jarl said. No one disagreed.

Soon they had crossed the valley floor and now stood at the doorstep of the crevice. The rock walls soared up in a V shape, and the trail at the bottom was so narrow that they had to picket the horses and proceed single file on foot. An eerie, moaning wind blew through the crevice, and the deeper into it they went, the more dread Dane felt. The looks of unease on his friends' faces told him they shared his fears. Klint also seemed to be spooked. Riding atop Dane's shoulder, he took wing, flying back toward where they had left the horses. Lut, though, seemed not to have a care in the world, and he led them at a good clip, whistling merrily.

They came to where the passage forked into two deep, tight channels. Without hesitation, Lut took the right one and everyone dutifully followed. Then they came to another fork, then another, and each time without so much as a pause, Lut chose which way to go. Dane started to sense that they were going in circles, first north, then west, then south, going *back* the way they had started. It was as if they were caught in a high-walled maze, an endless loop they would never escape. They came to where the trail forked off into another channel again, and Dane ordered everyone to halt.

"We've already come past here," Dane said. "We're lost, Lut, admit it."

Lut sighed in exasperation, like a parent growing weary of his complaining children. "Would you doubt me if I still looked like the old Lut?"

"That's just it. You're not the old Lut," Dane said. "And

now *you're* the one who's so damn sure of himself. In case you haven't noticed, we've been walking in circles."

"Do you see that?" Lut pointed to a spot on the rock wall, two feet from the ground.

Dane looked; there was nothing but bare rock. "What?"

"If you were familiar with dwarfish symbology, you would see a sign that directs us to Déttmárr's lair."

Dane and Jarl bent down and saw faint scratchings in the rock. Jarl asked, "Why is it so low to the—oh, right. Dwarves are short."

"Any more questions?" Lut asked. "Or can we continue— quiet!" Lut tensed, listening. There was a tinkling sound. They looked up and saw a few pebbles cascading down the rock wall. The pebbles showered down, a few of them bouncing painfully off heads, coming to rest on the ground. The round little stones unfurled like sow bugs and scurried away on tiny legs.

"What in Odin's name is that?" Fulnir exclaimed.

"An unknown species of hard-shelled insect, I'd say," replied Lut. "I'd like to grab one for my collection."

A high, shrieking cackle echoed throughout the crevice. It seemed to come from above. Dane glimpsed a tiny, wrinkled face fringed with a wild fuzz of hair peering down at them from atop the crevice.

Then *boom—boom—boom!* came another cascade of spherical rocks. These were much larger, maybe half the size of a Viking shield—capable of crushing a human head. "Run!"

Lut cried. They did, dashing for their lives up the tight passageway as the hail of deadly stones crashed down upon them, and only by sheer luck were they saved. Dane looked back and saw the "rocks" unfurl like the pebbles had and scurry away down the crevice floor, disappearing around a turn.

Another shrieking cackle came from above. "Care for another round of my roly-polies?" They could now see the wrinkled visage of an ancient she-dwarf leaning over the edge.

Lut cupped his hands and yelled up, "We come in peace to see Déttmárr the Smith!"

"He is close to death and will see no one. Go away!" Another of the "roly-polies" careened down, barely missing Dane, who leaped out of the way.

"I'm tired of these things!" Jarl said, drawing his sword. He hacked at its shell, but his blade just bounced off, and the mammoth insect unfurled and scurried away.

"If he is near death, let us pay our respects," Lut yelled up. "We bring a special gift."

"A gift? Is it gold?" said the she-dwarf eagerly, her interest piqued.

"Yes! We bring gold!" Lut lied. "Lots of it!"

"Well, why didn't you say that before? Come forward!"

They hurried up the crevice, and before long they came to where it dead-ended at an ancient, massive door. Jarl pounded on it with the pommel of his sword. A small hatch opened at knee height and the she-dwarf barked from it, "Show me the gold!"

"I'll be happy to if you open the door," Lut said.

The she-dwarf paused like she was thinking it over. "This better not be a trick." They heard a scrape. Slowly the door opened, revealing the face of the very tiny and very weathered old woman.

"Well? Produce the gold!" she rasped. Lut pushed in past her, as did everyone else, entering a low-ceilinged rock chamber lit by torches. It was a cozy-size living area about half the size of Dane's own hut. It had pictures on the rock walls, a hearth fire, a table and chairs—albeit tiny ones—and ancient wooden shelves holding dozens of soapstone pots and jars filled with what Dane surmised were herbs and root vegetables and dried flowers and such. The place had a rather ripe odor, and looking around for the source of the smell, Dane saw a dozen or more roly-polies of various sizes penned off in an adjoining room.

"Trespass! Trespass!" she screeched. "Who gave you permission to enter?"

"Madam, we mean you no harm," Lut said. "We must see Déttmárr immediately."

"Not until I see the gold you have brought!"

"Very well," said Lut. "But what we bring is infinitely more valuable than the shiny metal you seek." He nodded to Dane, who then brought out the apple core, showing it to her lying in the palm of his hand as if it were a precious jewel.

She gazed at it, her wrinkled brow becoming even more wrinkled, which Dane had thought impossible. "You have to be joking."

"Madam, I assure you I am not," Lut said. "If you'll just lead us to—"

The she-dwarf grabbed a fireplace poker and smacked Lut in the shin. He let out a yell, hopping in pain. She then smacked Dane with it, and the apple core flew from his hand into the fire. Screeching at the top of her voice, she chased Jarl, Drott, Fulnir, and William around the room. They tried to hide behind the furniture, but it was so tiny it didn't afford much cover. Meanwhile, Dane crawled to the fireplace and grabbed the apple core off a burning log, singeing his hand.

Amid the pandemonium, a voice sharper and deeper than the others in the room pierced the din like a knife.

"Give me *SILENCE*!" Everyone froze, falling quiet. "Can a dying man not have *peace*!"

"Oh, be quiet, you old fool," the she-dwarf cried. She sighed in exaggerated defeat, then shot a look at Dane. "Well, go on! What are you waiting for, an invitation from Odin? You came for him—there he is!" She pointed behind him. Dane turned and saw a beaded curtain hung against the wall. Stepping closer, he drew the curtain aside to find that behind it was the narrowest of passageways leading up a steep, curving stairway.

With Dane in the lead, Lut and Jarl climbed the stairway. Soon they reached what Dane took to be a bedchamber, a conclusion he drew from the fact that there was a giant bed in the room. It was nothing but a straw-stuffed dirty mattress covered with a thick woolen blanket. The room itself was covered floor to ceiling with handmade wooden shelves holding hundreds of shining trinkets, and there were half a dozen lighted candles surrounding the bed. As Dane's eyes adjusted to the candlelight, he saw that a body lay beneath the blanket, its head propped on a pillow. A bare twig of a man, it was a dwarf not much larger than the old she-dwarf. The candlelight glimmered off the dome of his round, bald head and lit the outline of his ginger-colored beard that grew like a bush long past his knees.

"Have you come to watch me die?" said the diminutive figure, his voice deep and sonorous despite his obvious illness. For such a small man, he had a very big voice. Feeling more welcome now, they drew nearer to the bed. The sight of the smith's centuries-old face nearly took Dane's breath away. So shriveled and shrunken was he, his pale skin mottled with age spots and falling in folds from his face and arms, it seemed he was more a dried-up piece of fruit than a man. His head was large for his body, and tufts of white hair grew from his protruding ears. Beneath an unruly thatch of eyebrows were his deep-set eyes, one green and the other blue. Though their sparkle was near spent, they were the kindest eyes Dane had ever seen.

"Déttmárr," Lut softly said. "We have come to help save you."

"Big words, for one so young," said Déttmárr.

"We have come from the village of Voldarstad to ask you a favor," Lut said.

Déttmárr waved his hand weakly in the air. "I'm six hundred and nineteen years old. Give or take. Too old to be doing any favors."

"But it's gravely important that you make us a weapon," Dane said. He told him of Skuld and how they had been dispatched to kill the draugr Thidrek the Terrifying.

"A draugr-killing blade, you say? Try another smith. I am but a wasted shell waiting to die."

The old dwarf gave a pained groan. He lay there motionless. For a moment Dane feared he might be dead. He shook him lightly by the shoulders. "Please! Skuld said you alone are the one to make our blade!"

Déttmárr's eyes snapped open. "Did you not *hear* me? I'm too old and tired!"

"But that's why we're here," Lut said. "I, too, was ancient. Death was on my doorstep. But I ate a magic apple that restored me to—"

Jarl broke in. "We don't have time for this."

"*You* don't have time?" said the dwarf. "*I'm* the one who's dying."

"But that's what I'm trying to tell you—we have a remedy!"

"Hah! There is no remedy for old age. Potions! Lotions! Spells! Bewitchments! I've tried them all. I even fasted on nothing but berry juice and ox vomit for an entire month.

Nothing works! Nothing stops the ravages of time—neither man nor dwarf nor gods above."

"Listen, dwarf, if you don't make the weapon and we don't kill Thidrek," Jarl explained, "then I'm doomed to die in bed like you. And that's *not* going to happen. Give him the apple, Dane."

Jarl had a way of getting to the point. Dane held up what was left of the apple core, the last remnants of the partially blackened golden skin around the top and bottom gleaming in the candlelight. "An apple from the tree of Idunn. Or what's *left* of it," said Dane, glancing then at Lut.

Déttmárr stared intently at the apple core, his eyes shining brighter. "It is told," he whispered with new gravity, "that Idunn's apple holds the power to restore life. And if a man were to eat one, he would be magically rejuvenated in mind and body, perhaps even made young again."

Lut said, "So what are you waiting for? Look at me! I went from a man over a century old to one of merely twenty!"

"That may be so," said the dwarf, soberly absorbing Lut's words. "But with so little of it left to eat, I doubt it would have much effect on one as old as me."

"But you're a dwarf!" said Dane. "You won't need as much. We have to try!"

"I don't *have* to do anything," Déttmárr snapped. "It is my life. I will choose whether to eat of it or not to eat of it."

"But why wouldn't you?"

"Because I'm done with life, that's why. The wars, the

treachery, the cruelty, the tears. Do you know how many times someone has come and told me that the world was ending and I just *had* to forge a weapon to kill a demon or draugr or some other denizen of the underworld? Too many times, that's how many!"

Dane tried to comment, but Déttmárr barreled on.

"And did you get a look at that she-witch of a wife I have downstairs? Answer me truthfully. Would you really want to live even a *day* with that woman? Can you imagine how I feel? Six hundred *years* I've been with her. I can't imagine another day with that creature, much less another ten years."

"I heard that!" came the woman's voice from below.

"And I *meant* for you to hear it!" cried Déttmárr. And exploding in a fit of coughing, he collapsed back on the bed. "Go now. Let me die in peace."

"No," Dane insisted. "I'm not leaving without that weapon. Eat!" Dane took the dwarf's hand and placed the apple core in it.

The dwarf stared down at the core in his palm, then up at Dane and his friends. "You're not leaving till I try this, right?"

Dane nodded firmly. Déttmárr lifted the apple core to his nose and sniffed, making a face.

"It's just a little badger spit you're smelling—perfectly harmless," said Lut.

"Go on," said Dane. "Eat it."

Déttmárr gave it a long look, then put it in his mouth

and nibbled off a tiny piece of the golden peel. He chewed and swallowed, waiting for it to take effect. Nothing happened.

He took another bite. Still nothing.

"So much for your magic apple," said Déttmárr. Dane saw the disappointment on the faces of Lut and Jarl, but he refused to give up. He gave a hard stare to the dwarf and watched as this time Déttmárr opened wide and bit off the whole top half of the apple core, stem and all. He chewed it all up and swallowed. Again they waited. Nothing. Dane felt his vitals go cold. Was this really the end of it? A failure before they even started? Déttmárr opened his mouth to eat the rest of the core—and suddenly froze. The core fell from his fingers to the bed, his mouth still stuck wide open.

The dwarf began changing right before their eyes. His white pallor disappeared and a new glow came into his cheeks, his skin turning rosy pink. The deep creases and wrinkles on his face and arms began to disappear as his flesh took on new firmness. The snow-white eyebrows turned dark gray, and fine shafts of new hair began to sprout atop his head. His eyes burned brighter and his beard too took on new color and shine. Dane couldn't find his tongue; what he was seeing was truly an act of the gods.

"*Now* do you believe me?" Lut asked the dwarf.

Déttmárr looked up in wonderment. "By Odin, I can feel it!" he cried, throwing off his blanket and jumping to his feet on the floor, gazing at his newly revitalized limbs. "I'm young again! I can breathe! I can walk! I can dance!"

Déttmárr danced about the room, hooting and shouting with glee and flinging his beard back and forth in front of him as if it were a dance partner.

"Quiet up there!" his wife shouted from below. "You're upsetting my roly-polies!"

This made Déttmárr laugh all the more. He suddenly patted the top of his head, elated to feel he was no longer bald. "Hair! I've *hair* again! Whoo-hoo!" Sent into new squeals of laughter, Déttmárr leaped into Dane's arms and planted a big wet kiss on his cheek. He then jumped to the floor and went scrambling down the stairs.

"Where's he going?" Jarl asked.

"Probably out to find a younger wife," Lut said.

9

A BURNING
DESIRE

Déttmárr was itching to get to work again. Leaving Drott, Fulnir, and William behind with the she-dwarf, Dane, Lut, and Jarl followed Déttmárr down a passageway deeper into the subterranean depths until at last it opened into a vast, cavernous pit spanned by a crude suspension bridge. On the edge of the precipice was a sign that ominously read PIT OF NO RETURN.

"Um, Déttmárr? What's this sign mean?" Jarl asked.

The dwarf pointed down into the seemingly bottomless chasm. *"That's* the pit. And if you fall into it—"

"There's *'no return'*?" asked Jarl, grimacing.

The dwarf nodded and continued across the bridge. With this frightening thought in mind, Dane and his friends now followed him, stepping carefully on the wobbly wooden planks, edging around the gaps where some were missing.

Adding to Dane's anxiety was the fact that the suspension ropes holding up the whole thing seemed to be frayed in places. It wasn't until they were halfway across it that he dared to look down.

His insides went cold. He was staring into a bottomless abyss, a blackness so dark and limitless, it made him feel dizzy. *Don't look down—you'll be all right,* he told himself. He took a deep breath, steadied himself, and continued on.

Crossing the chasm seemed to take forever, but when at last they reached the far side and were on solid footing again, Dane found himself breathing easily once more.

"Glad that's over with," he heard Jarl say.

Déttmárr then led them to a gigantic iron door that he quickly unlatched and pushed open. "Behold," said Déttmárr, "the Smithy of Yore."

The spacious three-sided room had a smoke hole in the ceiling, and rising from the center of a stone floor was a round forge pit. On the walls hung various tools of the smith's trade—hammers, pokers, pincers, tongs—all black-ened with soot and showing centuries of use. Shelves were jammed with jars and lidded pots filled with various clays, powders, and brightly colored metallic nuggets. Three anvils sat atop small stone platforms, and the air was thick with the smell of leather and smoke and exotic odors both pleas-ing and unpleasant. On the far wall was the stoking furnace itself, its large iron doors darkened with age.

The little man found a piece of chalk and squatted in front

of them. "A draugr-killing blade must be of special design,"
he said as he began drawing on the floor. "The undead are
a unique breed of hellion. They're no easy prey. They're fast
and ferociously strong. You'll need something with a long
handle and a good-size killing surface. Something like this."
He pointed to the chalk drawing he'd finished..

"What is it?" asked Jarl.

"A double-sided crescent axe," said Déttmárr. "Heavier
than the usual war axes, but far deadlier if you know how
to use it. The long handle lets you swing it around like this
so you can put the power of your whole body behind it. And
the elongated blade increases the chances for decapitation in
just one stroke. Remember, a draugr is wicked quick. You'll
have one chance to cut off his head. Miss him and you're
likely to lose your own head in the bargain."

Lut and Jarl swung the mold stone out of the now hot
furnace and down onto the floor beside the forge pit. The
mold was in the shape of a large, double-bladed crescent axe,
and there within it lay the liquefied steel, gleaming bright
orange, still a-bubble and smoking and destined to deliver
death to the undead.

Déttmárr stood over the molten metal, dropping items
one by one into it. "The wing feather of a sparrow hawk for
speed . . . wolverine claws for ferocity . . . a bear's belly hair
for strength . . . the eye of an eaglet for true aim . . . ." As
each item hit the bubbling liquid and was incinerated, it

gave a hiss and sent up a tiny puff of smoke, its essence fusing with the molten mixture.

"And ten droplets of elk's milk for . . . for . . . oh, I forget what it's for but I know it's necessary for some reason." Déttmárr uncorked a tiny blue glass vial and dribbled out ten drops of pale liquid into the mold. Although he had never tasted any himself, Dane had heard tales of trollfolk curatives that called for the milk of a mother elk, and so the sight of it here only made him marvel at the mysteries of life even more.

"And now for the real magic," Déttmárr said, and hopping up onto the rim of the forge pit hole, he yelled down into it. "Gregor! I've a blade for your fire!"

The sound they heard chilled Dane's blood. It was a cross between an angry grumble and a beastly roar, and it shook the very ground on which they stood.

"Wha-what's that?" Jarl asked.

"That's Gregor, my fire giant," said Déttmárr with a sly smile. "My secret to forging magic weapons. Gregor was a gift from Odin for my crafting Gungnir, his spear that never misses. This was, oh, three, four hundred years ago, if memory serves."

"*Fire* giant?" said Dane, sounding only slightly less nervous than Jarl. "Dangerous, aren't they?"

"Not if you do as you're told—*exactly* as you're told. Now, who is going down to feed him?"

✳

Dane followed Lut down the stone steps into the dimly lighted chamber. He caught sight of the giant and he felt the hairs on his neck stand on end. The thing was ghastly to behold, and for a moment all Dane could do was stand and stare, letting his eyes adjust to the light. The fire giant had been curled up in the corner, but now he stood and stretched and stared down at them with a mixture of curiosity and vexation.

The height of two grown men, the creature had long hairy arms that ended with hands nearly as large as his head, and his whole body was dusted in soot. His squarish head seemed to be set right into his shoulders with no neck whatsoever, and his large, heavily lidded eyes took a long moment to focus. He was thickset around the middle, but all of it muscle, and the tattered animal skins that were tied around his waist did little to cover his sinewy thighs and haunches.

The giant opened his mouth to yawn, and out between his thick, rubbery lips oozed a stream of black drool that dribbled down into the dark hair on his chin, and when the creature lifted his arm to wipe it away, Dane saw a black smear appear on the back of the fire giant's hand. It was then he noticed that certain parts of the giant's skin were translucent—you could see tiny bursts of flame shoot through his limbs and flare up in his belly, then vanish as fast as they appeared.

The sight of it thrilled him but frightened him too. Dane had seen frost giants before—had fought them and been fascinated by the sight of behemoths made entirely of ice. But this was entirely new to him—a creature made of flesh that ate and breathed fire? Déttmárr had told them that the giant's fiery breath could produce a flame three times hotter than that of any earthbound fire, and that it was this magic potency that would imbue the blade with its killing power.

Above, there came a cry from Déttmárr. "Start feeding him! But not too much at a time!"

"Hungry, big boy?" Lut asked the giant, grinning with ease and showing no fear. The giant gave a growl and eagerly watched as Lut went to the grate in the wall. He yanked open the metal door, and out spilled hot coals. The sight of the glowing embers excited the fire giant, and he lunged forward, straining against the chains that bound his arms and legs.

Getting down on his haunches, Gregor pushed his head toward them as far as it would go and opened his mouth, showing his blackened and half-broken teeth, the black drool again dripping. It was spit filled with soot and ash, Dane realized, no doubt due to his diet, and as disgusting as it was to look at, Dane knew to the giant it was as natural as oats to a horse.

Lut lifted a shovelful of glowing coals and, stepping closer to the giant's open maw, flung it upward into his mouth. The giant snapped his jaws shut, chewing with obvious delight, wisps of smoke escaping his lips as he crunched loudly on the coals and moaned in pleasure. He gulped down the whole mouthful in one swallow, and Dane was amazed to see a faint orange glow under his skin as the coals slid down his throat and into his belly. The giant licked his lips and again opened his mouth wide, eager for more. Lut tossed up another shovelful, and again the giant ate and swallowed, a small fire growing more visible in his belly.

Dane took a shovel, and he too began to feed the fire giant, marveling at the speed with which the giant could chew and swallow and even more amazed by the simple fact that it didn't burn his mouth! The more he ate, the brighter the glow from his innards, and tendrils of black smoke were now pouring from his mouth and his nostrils. Five, six, seven shovelfuls of coal he consumed and *still* the fire giant wanted more.

Dane gave him an eighth, and the giant patted his belly to see if he was hot enough yet. Deciding he was, Gregor tilted back his head and blew a great fireball of flame straight up the flue.

"Yes, Gregor!" Dane heard Déttmárr cry from above. "Keep it coming!" Again and again the giant roared, and up shot more columns of flame, each one higher and hotter than the last. And with each flame he blew, the giant's eyes bulged a bit bigger and turned a brighter shade of orange and the smoke poured from him in greater abundance. The room was so hot, Dane was sweating from every pore. Beside himself, Lut hooted and hollered, cheering the giant on, and when the creature finally stopped blowing fire, it was Lut who called to Gregor and instantly offered him another shovelful of coals, as if daring him to continue just for Lut's own entertainment.

Déttmárr yelled down to stop feeding him—that the blade had reached its desired heat and it was time to go—but Dane and Lut were no longer listening. They were locked in a contest to see who could shovel faster and who could endure the heat longer. Coughing on the sooty smoke that filled the room, his arms tiring in the overpowering heat, Dane was having trouble keeping up, but Lut seemed driven to dominate, determined to prove himself the better man, and his cocksureness was starting to irritate Dane.

And then it happened.

While trying to swallow, the giant choked and grabbed his throat. He issued a strangled cry of pain and all the hair on his face and head ignited, flaring up in a flash. His eyeballs too burst into flame, and at this the giant flew into a rage, stamping his feet on the stone floor. He roared in anger and shot a column of flame straight at Lut and Dane, which they just managed to duck. But this flame, Dane was disturbed to notice, was nearly all white with a tinge of yellow round the edges, and Dane sensed this was trouble.

The next thing he and Lut knew, by accident the fire giant blew the searing-white flame at the rusted iron chain that held his right arm. The iron instantly melted, soft as butter, the flame being so unearthly hot, and in a blink the giant had yanked the chain off his wrist. Puzzled by the sight of his arm now free, he stared at it, unsure of what to do. But soon, his reason got hold of him, and quick as lightning he reared back and blew fire over the chain on his left wrist. That too melted away. With both arms free, he turned to Dane and Lut with a terrifying look that said: *I want to kill you.*

10

THE BLACK
ABYSS

Astrid walked with Mist through the grove of gold-leafed trees in Asgard. She told her sister of her meeting with Dane and of his mission to kill the draugr Thidrek and free her from her Valkyrie servitude. "Pigheaded fool!" she said. "He is risking the lives of all his friends by going on."

"His friends are risking their *own* lives," Mist said, "for they love you too, and want you returned to the fold."

"All right," admitted Astrid, "it's a group effort in insanity. Damn that Skuld! First she conspires to make me join the sisterhood. Then she barters my freedom to get my village kin to do her bidding! I should register a complaint with Odin."

"You'll do no such thing!" Mist gasped. "Our job is to ferry the dead, not mix ourselves in godly affairs. If Skuld learned you were going to the gods behind her back, she'd make you pay dearly. You'd be lucky to be a serving wench in Odin's hall."

"What am I to do, then? I can't just look the other way while Dane and the others traipse into mortal danger."

"Whatever you do, you must be careful," Mist said. "If it were known you still loved a mortal—"

"I do *not* love him," Astrid said with determination, as if trying to convince herself. But she saw that Mist knew the truth. Astrid sighed. "When I became a Valkyrie, why didn't they take away my feelings for him?"

"Even the gods can't do that."

"They give us a horse that flies yet can't free us from loving someone?" Astrid complained. "Where's the logic in that?" They walked for a while, thinking of the predicament. A light breeze ruffled the golden leaves, making a sound much like music. Then Astrid halted, seized with an idea.

"I'll kill Thidrek myself!" she blurted.

Mist looked at Astrid as if her sister's winged helmet had somehow cut off circulation to her brain. "Kill Thidrek? *You?*"

"Once Dane has the draugr-killing blade, I'll steal it and behead Thidrek. Then Dane and the others will *have* to return home!"

"Should I tell you *again* what our job is?" Mist said. "We ferry dead; we don't *make* the dead! We're Shield Maidens, not killers."

"But I'm not killing someone who's alive," Astrid explained. "He's half alive, or half dead, or undead, whatever you call it. Besides, doesn't Skuld *herself* want Thidrek eliminated?"

Mist thought for a moment. "You're not dragging me into this."

"I know. I'm doing this on my own."

"Your own? Killing a draugr is a two-Valkyrie job."

"Well, if you'd *like* to come along . . . ," Astrid said, "I won't stop you." They walked from the grove, Mist grumbling that when this was over *both* of them would most likely be lowered in rank to serving wench.

Dane and Lut threw down their shovels and ran in panic up the stone steps to the smith's forge. Dane glanced back and saw Gregor had already melted one leg chain and was working on the other.

Entering the forge, they saw that the dwarf and Jarl had already fled out the iron door that led to the bridge. As Dane and Lut emerged outside, the dwarf and Jarl were hurrying across it. Jarl carried the newly forged crescent axe.

Wasting no time, Dane and Lut hastened to follow them. As they looked back, they saw the giant had burst through the smithy doorway and now stood at the edge of the bridge, his translucent skin glowing a bright orange. The giant roared and tentatively placed one foot on the bridge, testing if it would hold him.

"No! Gregor, go back!" Dane yelled. "It won't hold you!"

The giant wasn't listening or didn't understand. His other foot stepped onto the bridge, causing one of the frayed suspension ropes to snap. The bridge swayed violently, and everyone was thrown off their feet. The handle of the draugr-killing axe slipped from Jarl's hands, falling onto the wooden planks. As Jarl grabbed for it, the giant took another step, jarring the bridge again. The handle of the blade fell through a gap between the planks. It hung there just by the edge of the blade. If the blade turned an inch, the axe would be gone.

Dane and Lut crawled on their hands and knees across the planks. Behind them, the giant kept coming. He was only three or four steps away. The bridge gave another shudder. Dane heard a grunt, looked back, and saw Gregor's foot had broken through the planks and was stuck. He bellowed in rage. Flames shot from his mouth into the suspension ropes.

Which immediately burst into flames.

The flames spread rapidly upward, as if the ropes were but dry grass. Dane and Lut gained their footing, moving as fast as they could—but again they were thrown off their feet and nearly over the side as the bridge shook and swayed from the giant's violent actions trying to free his trapped foot.

Ahead of him, Dane saw Jarl crawling toward the axe, one point of its blade caught on the edge of a plank, trying to reach it before it fell between the planks and was gone.

Gregor growled in frustration, flames shooting from his

mouth, lighting the wooden planks between him and Dane on fire. The flames quickly ignited the rope holds on both sides of the bridge. Finally the giant jerked his foot free and was on the move again across the fiery planks.

Dane looked back and saw the giant coming on. "He's gaining!" he cried to Lut, who was crawling in front of him. Then one of the rope holds gave way and the bridge flipped completely over.

Everyone hung precariously in midair, including the giant, their hands grasping the remaining intact rope. Ahead of Dane and Lut, Jarl was hanging by one hand; in the other he held the crescent axe. Déttmárr had already made it to solid ground on the other side of the bridge.

"Don't drop the axe!" Dane yelled.

"Easy for you to say," Jarl yelled back. "I can't hang here forever!"

"Throw me the axe!" the dwarf shouted.

"It's too far—I can't make it."

"Do you want to die in bed an old man?" Dane yelled.

"You know I don't!"

"Then throw the axe!" Dane cried.

Jarl let the axe fly. It tumbled end over end; Déttmárr reached out as far as he could, his toes at the edge of the abyss. He caught the handle—then lost his balance, teetering on the edge. He pirouetted, desperately grabbing for a handhold. He fell backward and was going over when a tiny, gnarled hand grabbed a hank of his beard.

His ancient wife pulled him up to safety. "You're not leaving me!" she spat. "I don't care *how* young you are!"

Drott, Fulnir, and William now appeared on the other side, cheering their friends on. Dane and Lut pulled themselves along, hand over hand, trying to escape the flames that were rapidly spreading their way. With both hands free, Jarl did likewise.

Dane glanced back and saw the giant swinging hand over hand, gobbling up space between them—and on his face was that murderous look he had given them before. The look that said, *If I am to die, I am taking you with me.*

Dane did the only thing he could do. He took one hand off the rope above and grabbed his knife from his belt. It was a pitiful weapon against a fire giant, but it was all he had. Gregor closed in and made a grab for Dane, who plunged his knife deep into the giant's hand. Gregor jerked his hand back and gave Dane an angry look. Dane knew a fireball from the giant's mouth would incinerate him in the next instant.

The bridge broke in two. Suddenly Dane felt weightless. He was falling . . . falling into the Pit of No Return. How long before he hit bottom? If there *was* a bottom. Then—surprise—his body jerked to a sudden stop, and he hung there in midair, watching a fireball below him go spinning down into the blackness of the abyss. It was Gregor, he realized. The firelight grew dimmer and dimmer until it was but a barely visible cinder . . . and then all was black.

Dane now noticed he was hanging upside down. His leg was caught in the bridge rigging. This was what had saved him. The bridge hung limply, its end still attached to the edge of the chasm above. Above him he saw Lut hanging on—and above Lut he saw Jarl crawling up the rope ladder to the top.

"The lesson to be learned here," Lut said, "is *never* overfeed a fire giant."

"I'll remember that," Dane said.

Back in the smith's living quarters, Déttmárr sat laying the double-sided axe blade against a spinning whetstone, sharpening her up, or, as Déttmárr called it, "giving the lady her teeth."

In an adjoining room, Lut consulted the runes. Now that they had the draugr-killing blade, they needed to know the location of the draugr they wished to kill. Lut drew out a leather pouch and upended the many runes—flat, coin-size pieces of bone—into his hand. On one side of each piece was scratched a different symbol of the runic alphabet. Dane and the others watched in silence as Lut closed his eyes and began to chant the names of his forefathers. He threw the runes into the air and let them fall to the floor. No one spoke. Some pieces fell rune side up, some rune side down. Lut studied the arrangement, trying to make sense of the message. Dane had seen Lut do this on countless occasions—but from Lut's quizzical expression, it seemed that this time he was stumped.

"What's the matter?" Dane asked. "Forgotten how to read the runes?"

"I've not forgotten," Lut snapped. "One doesn't forget what's in his bones. The runes are the whispers of the gods. Maybe if you'd hush up I could *hear* them." As Lut continued to peer at the rune pieces, trying to penetrate the mystery, Dane wondered if youth had perhaps robbed him of his venerable god sight. A long moment later, Lut's face lit up. "Aha. 'Three brothers.'"

"'Three brothers'?" Dane asked. "What's that mean?" Lut's eyes returned to the runes, peering at them with the same pained expression he got when constipated.

"Three . . . brothers . . ."

"You *said* that. What's it mean?"

Lut studied the pieces and shook his head. "It's not coming to me yet."

"Well, weren't you the one boasting you had more wisdom in your left buttock than all of us combined? Oh— wait. That was *before* you traded in those hundred-year-old buttocks for new ones."

"And these new ones still have more wisdom than you," Lut said.

"I *know* what it means," Drott said, trying to be heard, but they ignored him.

"Then tell me what *three brothers* means, Lut Wisebottom," Dane said.

"The secrets of the runes cannot be rushed," Lut said with annoyance.

"You never took this long before."

"Will you two *listen* to me!" Drott shouted, springing to his feet. All eyes then turned to him. "Can't you remember I was the one who told you the earth revolves around the sun, and the square root of sixty-four is eight, and a humming-bird beats his wings eighty times a second?"

"Sure, we remember," Jarl said. "You drank the water from the Well of Knowledge and got smart for about half a day."

"Yes," Drott said, "and when the effects wore off, I became dim again."

"We *know*, Drott. What's your point?" Jarl said.

"My point . . ." Drott got a faraway look, as if his mind had run aground in thick fog. His eyes latched onto Lut's runes strewn on the floor and he grinned, for he was about to say something smart. "Three Brothers aren't people. They're a place."

"Oh, really?" said Jarl. "And what makes you so sure?"

"Because my grandfather told me," said Drott. His grand-father, he explained, had told him a story about how once he'd been piloting a ship through a passage known as the Three Brothers—three small rocky islets close to a northern shore. His grandfather, who went by the name Skapti the Capable, had misread a navigation chart and run the ship aground, sending all hands, save himself, to their deaths. After that he was known as Skapti the Confused, and thus the family tradition of idiocy was born.

Déttmárr entered, carrying the gleaming blade over

his shoulder. "The job is done," he said, and brought the axe down, setting its wooden handle end on the floor, the little man clearly relieved to be free of its weight. "Every weapon I craft must have a name. This one I call the Blade of Oblivion. Strike down the draugr and that is where you'll send him—to the cursed depths of the demon realm. Now, who do I give this to?"

Jarl jumped up and went to take the axe, but Déttmárr swung it behind his back. "First," said Déttmárr, "we must determine who among you is most worthy."

"I am," Lut said. "For I am wise enough to carry it responsibly and carry out the killing too."

"But I'm the best bladesman," Jarl argued. "Ask anyone! Swordsmanship is my stock-in-trade."

"But," said Dane, "you already fought and lost to Thidrek the last time we met him in battle."

"All the more reason I be given another chance now!"

"Oh, forget it," said the dwarf. "Here," he said, and he threw the axe up into the air. For the briefest moment the double-sided blade seemed to float there above their heads, a sheen of firelight shimmering along its crescent arc, there for the taking. As if driven by some divine purpose, Dane pushed past the others, jumped atop a table, and grabbed the handle before anyone else could. Lut and Jarl grumbled in protest, but Dane had been the quickest and thus the blade was his.

"My job is done," said Déttmárr. "Good luck and fare ye well."

"With Gregor gone, what'll you do?" Dane asked.

"The magic-weapon trade isn't what it used to be," said the dwarf. "I can make more turning out horseshoes or fireplace pokers." He lifted the poker his wife had used on their shins. "See my work? Good, huh?"

"Yes, your dear wife gave us a demonstration," Lut said.

"And now that I'm young and spry, I want to enjoy life more," Déttmárr said. "My wife and I are off on a holiday."

"We are?" she said, not altogether sure what he meant.

"Yes, Inga, my dear." He handed her the last remaining scrap of the apple. "I saved this for you. Idunn's apple. What would you say to a second honeymoon?"

The smile that spread across her little dwarf face lit up the room.

"If it's anything like our first one, I might not recover," she said with a wink.

Good-byes were said, and soon Dane and his cohorts were walking once again down the Passage of Mystery back to their horses. Dane carried the Blade of Oblivion over his shoulder, the weight of it giving him pause. It was real now. He could feel it, the urge for revenge, rising inside him. He had the weapon, he would kill with it—and end Thidrek's existence once and for all.

11

A GHOSTLY
VISIT

Teased by the aromas wafting from his brew pot, Grelf let his fantasies grow ever more grandiose. Rich beyond his wildest dreams! That's what he would be! If his perfumery could mask the off-putting stench of a rotting draugr like his master, oh, what fortunes lay within his grasp.

Having traveled far and wide in his youth, indentured to a spice merchant, he had seen firsthand the kingly sums the rich would gladly pay to cloak themselves in pleasing scents. And if his concoction was strong enough to make the rotting undead smell like a meadow of lilacs, the sales potential of his creation was unlimited. First, he would set up shop in a village somewhere, preferably one near a well-traveled seaport where the merchant ships could supply him with ingredients. Then, with his savings, he would build a perfumery, hire a staff of traders, and send them calling on all the royal courts in every corner of the known world. The orders would no doubt pour in and he'd soon be swimming in riches. And then *he* would be a lord with servants of his own. His own personal lackeys. Imagine that!

There was just one thorny little problem: how to get free of his master?

Grelf sprinkled another handful of crushed flowers into the simmering pot and stole a look at Thidrek. His master lay motionless nearby, eyes closed, chest unmoving, a man completely at rest, looking like a corpse in sore need of a burial. It wasn't exactly sleep that Thidrek was after; it was what he called the "dream of the dead," a peaceful kind of trance he would fall into during which visions of violent acts he had committed—and those he was yet to do—would come to him, presenting themselves for his entertainment as it were.

Grelf eyed his knife and, for one delicious moment, envisioned using it on his undead master. But remembering how useless the chieftain's spear had proven—and how easily Thidrek could read his very thoughts—he quickly chased the notion from his mind. He must be careful. Yes. He seemed to remember, deep in the Norse lore of his past, that to do away with a draugr one must sever its head from its body. But if no normal blade could cut draugr flesh, how was it possible? Was there some magic secret that he was yet unprivy to?

His ruminations were abruptly cut short when, hearing a sound, he looked up to spy a white steed descending from the sky and coming straight for him. He dove away, nearly getting a hoof in his head as the horse flew over him and touched earth.

Rolling over, Grelf found himself looking up at an astonishingly beautiful maiden astride the mount. She was clad in a white robe, breast armor, and a feathered cloak, and atop her fiery-red mane was a golden-winged helmet. Grelf could do nothing but stand and stare, mouth agape in surprise, since, as a lowly man-in-waiting, he'd never conceived he would ever lay eyes on a real live Valkyrie. Her kind only dealt with the well-muscled heroic types who made their living by the sword, not lackeys like him who polished their lord's chain mail.

"Can you speak," she asked of him, "or are you as witless as you appear?" He nodded, mumbling unintelligibly. "Which is it? Are you witless or capable of speech? It is the draugr Thidrek the Terrifying whom I seek."

"Greetings, corpse maiden," said Thidrek, now coming forward, having been roused by the ruckus. "Don't tell me Odin has sent *you* to rectify his mistake."

"Mistake? You mean his order that you be expelled from Valhalla?" she said with a mocking sneer. "No, he has not changed his mind on that."

Thidrek glared back at her. "I'll have my revenge. Fly back and tell him *that*."

"I'm not here to ferry threats, draugr. But to tell you this: the one known as Dane the Defiant comes to kill you."

"That halfling?" Thidrek roared. "He could bring an army and not harm a worm on my head! Go tell him my whereabouts so it may hasten his arrival. He's *another* on whom I seek revenge."

The Valkyrie huffed. "I'm quite sure your revenge list is lengthy—once a wealthy prince who now walks the earth a wretched draugr. That halfling you scorn has a bewitched weapon to end your days."

This brought Grelf to his senses. "A weapon to kill the undead?" he said with an optimistic lilt in his voice, as if it were too good to be true that such a thing existed. Catching a glare from Thidrek, he quickly adjusted. "Uh, I mean, we must find this weapon and destroy it!"

"Why the warning?" Thidrek asked. "Odin seeks to do me no favors."

"Odin is a drunken fool."

"Trouble in paradise?" smirked Thidrek.

"I ferry more dead than anyone. Month after month my numbers are at the top of the chart. But does he notice or care? I can't work that way. So . . . I decided to realign my allegiance."

Thidrek appeared intrigued. "You mean you're working with Hel?"

"She's offered me a chance for advancement. And my own staff of demons in the underworld. This, of course, is just between the two of us; Odin must know nothing of my plan."

Thidrek grinned. "Well, good to have you among my ranks, dearie."

Her eyes turned cold. "I am Aurora, maggot breath. And, make no mistake, you are among *my* ranks." Thidrek bowed in obeisance, agreeing to be under Aurora's command. But Grelf knew that his wily master was never subservient to anyone for long.

The Valkyrie and Thidrek conferred for a while, planning how they might ambush Dane the Defiant and his band. After Thidrek's humiliating defeat last year at the hands of the boy, Grelf knew he was desperately eager to even the score.

The Valkyrie departed on her steed. Thidrek, previously despondent over his failure to recruit the draugr warriors from the Ship of the Dead, was now brimming with optimism. "A draugr-killing blade! Good fortune has shone upon us, Grelfie."

"Good fortune, my liege? This weapon threatens your very existence."

"Think strategically, man! As you have wisely opined, to entice the undead to join my ranks, I need leverage. And what better leverage than to possess the one weapon a draugr fears? The Ship of the Dead will soon be mine!" Thidrek erupted in cackling laughter, and Grelf obediently joined in, braying like a mirthful donkey. Thidrek slapped him on the back—it felt like a sledgehammer hitting him—and Grelf was knocked to the ground, which only seemed to amuse his master further. His cackles echoed through the night, and Grelf, though in pain, laughed even harder, knowing he must get his hands on the draugr-killing blade and behead this monster so he could become perfumer to kings.

Trusting that Drott knew where the Three Brothers lay, the party set off on a northwesterly route toward the sea. William, riding behind Dane in the lead, watched Klint the raven fly along above, pausing here and there to rest on tree limbs and forage for food. In the past Klint would often ride upon Dane's shoulder, but the bird stayed clear of him now, as if frightened of the draugr-killing blade Dane carried.

Since they had set out from the dwarf's lair, William noticed a creeping uneasiness in the group. There was less talk, even from Drott, who normally nattered on like a magpie. Now that they had the blade, their mission was to do one thing—to kill—and the prospect of that put everyone on edge and kept them preoccupied with their own thoughts.

William wondered if *he* could kill Thidrek if given the chance. He had enough hatred for him, having seen him murder his own mother and father. And when he had been a slave in Thidrek's castle, he'd been beaten by him more times than he liked to remember. The hate burned within him . . . but when the time came to kill Thidrek, would his courage fail? The thought that it might made him feel ashamed. How could he ever become a warrior—someone like Dane—if the very thought of killing made him almost sick to his stomach?

He pulled his horse alongside Dane's. He wanted to talk about his fears but didn't know where to start. Their horses walked for a while. Then Dane gave a weary sigh and said, "By Thor, this blade is heavy." Dane shifted the axe handle from one shoulder to the other.

"At least you're not afraid to use it," William said, his eyes downcast.

"Who says I'm not afraid?"

"If Thidrek were standing before you right now, *you* wouldn't hesitate to kill him."

Dane thought for a moment, as if visualizing that scene. "It terrifies me."

"What? *You*, terrified?"

Dane glanced back to see if Lut and Jarl had heard this. They didn't appeared to have. "Not so loud, Will."

William couldn't believe that Dane—the one person he most idolized—was actually . . . *scared*. Then he thought this could all be a ploy. "Are you saying this just to make me feel better?"

"I'm saying it because you're the only one I can talk to." This *did* make William feel better—that Dane saw him as a confidant he could trust.

"You can't talk to Lut?"

"I could before, when he was old. But now if I admit to him how I feel, he'd use it against me. Say I was too weak to lead. I can't even tell whose side Drott and Fulnir are on now."

"Does it really matter *who* leads," William chanced to ask, "as long as the job gets done?"

Dane reflected on that, his face darkening. "It does to me. Thidrek murdered my father."

"Mine, too. *And* my mother."

Dane reached across and grasped William's arm, one warrior to another. "Then you and I have a score to settle, Will. Remember what I said to you once. Courage is acting *despite* your fear."

William nodded, strengthened by Dane's words. "I'll remember that."

The serious look vanished from Dane's face, replaced with a sheepish grin. "I hope *I* do."

That night they camped in a small clearing in the forest. After the grim *náttmál* rations of dried fish, hard bread, and harder cheese, everyone took to their blankets. William lay in his, trying to find sleep. His thoughts of undead creatures lurking in the dark made the ordinary night sounds of the forest take on an eerie tone. Was Thidrek out there waiting to pounce?

William looked over at the sleeping Dane. The Blade of Oblivion lay next to him, wrapped in a blanket. William wished the blade were by his side; he would feel a lot safer.

He was awakened by a sound, a sharp *crack*. He looked around at his friends but saw they were all asleep. Perhaps he'd been dreaming. Then he heard another sound—that of someone or some*thing* moving about in the dark beyond the glow of the dying campfire. Remembering the time a few months prior—when he'd risen in the pitch of night to investigate a strange sound and been nearly snatched by a savage pack of dark dwarves—William decided not to be so foolishly inquisitive. And so he lay, unmoving, in his blankets, waiting for the sound again. Moments later there it was—the soft footsteps of someone approaching. He turned his head ever so slightly to see what or who it might be— but saw no one there! It was as if a ghost were treading the ground beside him. His blood froze as the crunching sound of footsteps passed right by his blankets and he saw the grass flatten beneath invisible footsteps. He shut his eyes, hoping that his mind was playing tricks or that he was dreaming.

He opened his eyes a moment later to see Dane awaken and sit up. Dane pulled on his boots and uncovered the blade. He stood, shouldered it, and crept quietly out of camp and into the woods. As Dane passed, William noticed that his eyes were glassy and his face a blank mask, as if *he* were in a dream. William had the urge to call out a warning but then thought better of it. What if he were mistaken and Dane was merely going off to relieve himself? He'd look foolish if he woke everyone. He lay there, gripped with indecision and fear.

If ghosts or wights or horrible draugrs were about, he'd rather not stumble into their midst. But then again, if they *were* about, Dane was in danger. *Act despite your fear . . . act!* William pulled on his boots, grabbed his bow and quiver of arrows (even though he knew such weapons were no use against beastly specters), and crept from camp, following Dane's path into the woods.

12

WAR OF THE
VALKYRIES

Awhispering voice had invaded Dane's dreams, bidding him to rise from his blankets, take the blade, and follow. Unable to resist its call and still cloaked in sleep, he walked into the darkness of the forest, away from the safety of his mates. Soon, the chill of the night worked to rouse his slumbering senses, and with dawning awareness he asked himself, *What in Odin's beard am I doing out here?*

Again came the honeyed whisper, *You're just dreaming, Dane—keep walking.* He was about to continue when he heard a different whispering voice say, *See? I told you he'd catch on. Your plan won't work.* The first voice said, *Quiet! You didn't have to come along.* Then the other retorted, *Killing draugrs is NOT what we do!*

Killing draugrs? Dane came to a halt, the fog of sleep

lifting at last. He found himself in moon-silvered darkness, faint tracings of frost on the nearby branches of trees. He felt a hard jerk on the handle of the blade. He grasped it tighter and yanked it back. A sharp blow to his midsection nearly knocked him to the ground, but he held on to the handle, refusing to let go. Fighting back, he thrust out an elbow, felt it connect, and heard a cry of pain. He jerked the handle free and—*whoosh!* He swung the blade in a blind attempt to dispatch his enemy.

"Stop!" a voice cried, and a moment later a figure materialized, standing before him a few feet away. It was Mist, the Valkyrie, her form glimmering like a candle flame in the silken darkness.

Dane gaped in shock. "Mist! What are you doing here? You tried to take the blade!"

"She didn't." Another glowing figure appeared on the ground before him, and he saw it was Astrid, holding her cheek where she'd been hit by Dane's elbow. "I did." She stood, her hand dropping from her face, and Dane saw the bruise healing before his eyes. "If not for your lucky blow, I would've had it."

Struck speechless for a moment, Dane's shock soon gave way to anger. "You entered my dreams again!"

"It was *her* idea," Mist said. "She wanted to lure you from camp and take the blade. I only came along hoping to talk her out of it."

"Astrid, why would you do it?" Dane asked. "You know I

must use the blade to kill Thidrek."

"It doesn't matter *who* kills Thidrek—only that the deed is done," Astrid said.

"But that wasn't my bargain with Skuld. *I* must kill him to free you."

"How many times must I say this, Dane? I don't *want* my freedom. Serving Odin is the most exciting and rewarding existence there is."

"She lies," Mist said.

"You stay out of it," Astrid hissed.

"I will not," Mist retorted. "If your treasured sisterhood meant so much, you would not risk banishment from it to save your human kin from harm." Mist turned to Dane. "That is why she wants the blade—to do the job herself so you and the others may return home safely."

"Well, well, well . . ." came another voice. Astrid and Mist froze in dread as a new ethereal light appeared overhead. Looking upward, Dane saw, seated atop a descending celestial steed, a Valkyrie with cherry-red hair flowing from beneath her golden winged helmet. The horse touched earth and the Valkyrie adeptly dismounted, pointing a smug and disdainful stare at the three of them. "What's this? Two of my sisters and a human conspiring to kill a certain draugr?"

"We, uh, thought there was a battle here," Mist said quickly, "but merely found this one wandering in the night." She sniffed the air. "Ooo, fresh blood on the wind. Well, let's be off—heroic dead to ferry and all that." Mist started to walk from the scene, no doubt to retrieve her celestial steed, but Astrid remained rooted.

"She *knows*, Mist," Astrid said. "No use pretending."

"I heard you discussing the plot in the grove," the other Valkyrie said, casually twirling a strand of her red hair around a finger. "And waited until you made your move."

"If you report us to the Council of Sisters, I'll deny everything," Mist said. "You can't prove anything, Aurora. It's our word against yours."

"I've not come to catch you in the act," the one named Aurora said, "but to help you. Thidrek is close by."

Her words electrified Dane. "He's near?"

Eyeing him as if he were nothing but a lowly insect crawling amid a steaming pile of horse manure, Aurora addressed Astrid instead. "We mustn't wait. The draugr Thidrek is ripe for the kill."

"And why would *you* help us?" Astrid asked suspiciously.

"Not out of love for you," Aurora sniffed. "Odin favors you. As do his chosen warriors, the Einherjar. Bat your pretty blue eyes at them and they swoon. But with you returned to earthly form, it's one less competitor in my way."

"I *knew* it," Mist said. "Always with the self-interest."

"Must we continue to stand here?" Aurora snapped. "Delay will only make Thidrek grow suspicious."

"Suspicious? Is he *expecting* us?" Dane asked.

Again Aurora eyed him as if he were a warty form of life unworthy of her attention. It was the same disdainful look he had received from Skuld the night she had appeared in his hut, and it made Dane think how nice it would be if humans could vote on which gods and demigods to put in power. In this way, if they ever got bigheaded and arrogant, humans could oust them for new ones, which might teach them not to be so self-important.

"To lure him out of hiding," she said to Astrid, "I made him believe he and I are in league. What pretensions he has! To think a demigoddess of my class would team with such a foul and cursed creature as he. Now, can we go and let this pitiful human smite the draugr so you may be returned to your filthy village and be out of my gorgeous hair for good?"

Thidrek's camp was but a short flight away, Aurora said. Astrid and Mist gathered their celestial steeds, which were tethered nearby. Carrying the Blade of Oblivion, Dane rode tandem with Astrid, determined to keep his fear of heights in check. Soon they were aloft, flying high above the tree-tops. No words passed between him and Astrid, and he wondered if she really was angry with him for wanting to free her from the sisterhood. Or was it as Mist had said, that she was only concerned for his safety? If that was true, then it meant she still had a spark of love for him in her heart. To be so close to her like this again fired his hopes that soon his dreams of returning her permanently to his side would be a reality.

Headed to once more face the man who had killed his father, Dane steeled himself to show this monster no mercy.

One swipe of the blade and he would send the undead Thidrek to eternal misery in Niflheim's Lake of Fire. And then Skuld would pay him for a task well done and free his beloved. Jarl would be angry he didn't get in on the draugr killing—and maybe Lut and William would complain too. But Dane reasoned that he had dispatched Thidrek before, and it made sense that he be the one to finish the job.

They had been flying for what seemed only moments when Dane, his mind occupied with his upcoming kill, felt a sharp and sudden blow to the head. Next thing he knew, he was falling earthward. Then, from above, down swooped a flash of white—he felt the Blade of Oblivion jerked from his grasp—and he spied a figure with flaming red hair fly off with it. Aurora! An instant later he smacked hard into pine branches, tumbling through the boughs, grabbing in desperation for something to stop his fall. He heard a *crack!*—hoping it was a branch and not his bones breaking—and then *oof!* He slammed to a halt, something like lightning exploding in his head.

Dazed, he heard Astrid cry his name. Then the rustle of hooves. Racing footsteps. Soon she was beside him, cradling his throbbing head in her arms. "W-what happened?" was all he managed to say.

"Aurora knocked you from my horse. She took the blade. Oh, Dane, it's only by the will of the gods you're alive!"

"Get the blade back," Dane croaked.

"Mist is after her now."

"I'm fine. Go!" She stroked his hair, and Dane knew she was hesitant to leave him after his brush with death. "The blade is the only thing that matters, Astrid. Please, you must go."

Astrid tore herself away, hopped onto her steed, kicked his flanks, and soared upward like a flaming arrow. He watched as she joined the battle that was raging high in the night sky above him. The three Valkyries streaked across the heavens, looking like shooting stars—only the stars raced at each other and passed, and then doubled back like luminescent hummingbirds engaged in midair combat. Their battle a wondrous light show to behold, had it not been for the fact that he feared it would be a battle to the death. From such a distance, Dane could not tell which Valkyrie was which, only that two of the glowing stars seemed to be teaming up against the third, Mist and Astrid diving and swooping at Aurora from above and below in a concerted effort to knock her off her mount. But Dane knew Aurora had the blade, and that one swipe of it would kill her pursuers—so even though she was outnumbered, the advantage was hers.

Then Dane's nostrils were assaulted by a most awful odor. He tried getting to his feet when a boot flew up and stomped on his chest, pinning him to the ground. Lifting his eyes, he then beheld a vision that had to come from a nightmare. A ghastly decayed face gazed down at him. At first glance it appeared to be smiling, but then Dane saw that as most of its lips were gone, the curve of the creature's blackened, rotten teeth could be forming a grin as well as a grimace. Dane felt it deep in his vitals—the chilling recognition that this was Thidrek the Terrifying once again in the flesh. Well, flesh such as it was, for Thidrek presented a most horrifying sight.

"My, my," growled Thidrek, "the defiant one! Grown a bit since last we crossed swords." Thidrek leaned close, Dane overwhelmed by his odor. He was further horrified to see a beetle wriggling out of a dried bit of flesh that hung from Thidrek's chin.

"And you're looking better than ever," Dane said with a smile of his own, even though he was terrified.

"I have you to thank for that. We were having such a fair fight, weren't we? Well, as fair as a fight can be between a pup and a prince. And then Thor had to seize me in his whirlwind, taking me and his beastly hammer to Asgard. Yes, imagine that! *Me*—in the Hall of Heroes! Ha!" The sinews in Thidrek's neck—what remained of them—tightened and his blood-specked eyeballs bulged in fury. "But then—showing rank favoritism quite unbecoming a god—Odin, the one-eyed brute, deems me unworthy to stay and has me ostracized! And now I walk the earth, not dead, not alive, but oh so eager to settle the score with the lot of you!"

"Your tale touches my heart," said Dane.

"Soon I'll be *eating* your heart," said Thidrek, and a snakelike thing shot from his mouth, swept back and forth across his teeth, and then withdrew. And Dane realized that what he had seen was Thidrek's tongue.

Dane heard something moving behind Thidrek. "Quit lurking, Grelf," Thidrek barked. "Come and see the prize I've caught."

The toadying attendant slunk forward. Dane was struck by the man's physical deterioration. Back when he had been serving Prince Thidrek in his castle, Grelf had been pink cheeked and ever so plump. He now appeared thin and twitchy, his skin sallow and his eyes baggy, as if sleep were a stranger to him. "I'm sure you remember my man-in-waiting," Thidrek said to Dane. "He has chosen to return to my side."

"Serving a draugr does you no favors, Grelf," Dane said. "You look half dead yourself."

"Your eyes deceive you," Grelf said, summoning an air of dignity. "I am most fortunate and happy to serve my master."

Thidrek held his foot upon Dane's chest and craned his neck back to see the luminescent trails of the Valkyrie combat above. "I have reached into Asgard to pluck one of their own to serve me. She told me of the blade and your pitiful desires to use it on me. But it is *I* who will use the blade. With it I shall raise the Ship of the Dead and unleash Hel's minions upon the earth. Sounds exciting, no?"

Dane's heart nearly stopped. *The dark forces of Hel?* Was this the "mischief" Skuld said the goddess was planning?

"You've no idea what you've wrought," Thidrek said. And

then he pointed to the sky. There was a sudden explosion—a burst of pure white sparkles of light falling in the night sky. "Ha! The blade has struck! My maiden has killed one of yours. See? Her embers fall."

Horrorstruck, Dane saw the shimmering embers wink out one by one as they fell to earth in a death spiral. He gave an anguished cry and sprang free from Thidrek's pinning foot. Dane came at Thidrek with his fists, the monster grabbing Dane round the neck with one hand and holding him there at arm's length. Thidrek brayed in laughter as Dane flailed in vain, landing not a punch. The grip on his neck tightened. Dane gasped and choked and desperately pulled at the skeletal claw, trying to wrench it free. He felt himself lifted up, his feet kicking at the air, his vision blurring, the growl of Thidrek's voice sounding then as if it were coming from the depths of Niflheim itself. "Look how merrily he dances, Grelf! Hah! Like a puppet!"

Then—*wham!*—a sudden blow sent him tumbling backward, and a moment later Dane found himself facedown in the dirt. He heard Thidrek angrily bellowing—there were hands lifting him from the ground and he felt horseflesh beneath him. The beast gave an ear-piercing whinny, and Dane watched the ground recede as Thidrek's shouts died away.

Treetops flew past below, and slowly it came to him that he must be slung over the back of a celestial steed. What seemed just moments later the earth rushed into view again and he felt a jarring bump as the steed's hooves alighted on solid ground. He felt hands pull him off the animal's back and gently lay him on the ground, his back to a tree. Astrid's face hovered close to his. "You're alive!" he gasped.

"Mist is dead, she's gone!" she said, choking back sobs. "Aurora killed her with the blade. And then, seeing Thidrek had you, I rode fast and rammed my steed into him, knocking you free." She hugged Dane tightly, unable to hold back the tears any longer. "Mist was my only friend—she died because of *me*!"

"Aurora's treachery killed Mist," said Dane, "not you."

Astrid abruptly released him and looked to the skies as if hearing some faraway call. "A sister has died and I'm called to return home. I must go." She hurriedly mounted her steed.

"Wait! What of the blade?" Dane said, wobbling to his feet.

"Your efforts to free me have only brought more torment. I beg you, Dane, take the others and go home."

"But we can't! Thidrek has the blade now—and he says he intends to use it to raise the Ship of the Dead—" Astrid shot heavenward atop her steed. Dane called to her once more, but she was gone, her luminescent trail streaking away into the night sky.

13

A TWISTED TWIST OF FATE

"You *lost* the blade?" Jarl's face was purple with rage. "How could you *do* that?" The others stood around him, their dagger stares as hurtful as Jarl's insults.

Dane sat in exhaustion before the fire. He had found his way back to camp just before dawn broke, his shouts waking everyone. He excitedly spilled out the whole fantastic tale of the Valkyries, the blade, and the draugr Thidrek. When he was finished, at first they just stared in dumb disbelief. Even his pals Fulnir and Drott appeared shocked and dismayed.

And now he sat there, enduring the wrath of Jarl.

"Whatever possessed you to leave by yourself? Are you really that dumb? I knew you weren't up to this, I just *knew* it! We come all this way—all this way—and you lose my one chance at glory!"

"You were wrong to go out there alone with the blade,"

Fulnir added grimly. "Did you do it just to be the hero?"

Dane started to explain again how Astrid had entered his dreams to summon him—but Jarl was having none of it. He exploded, attacking Dane with punches and kicks and smacking him in the head with the flat of his hand, his anger spilling forth with such force that it took Drott and Fulnir to pull him off.

Lut's voice cut through the boisterous din, Dane expecting to hear him say that now was the time to forget recriminations and band together in brotherhood.

Instead Lut said, "Has anyone seen William?"

For a good hour they combed the woods, calling out his name. But William was nowhere to be found, and Dane grew sick with worry. Klint, who Dane had sent off for aerial surveillance, returned with one of William's arrows held in his beak. Dane bade the bird to take him to William, and off it flew, Dane and his friends following as fast as they could through the forest, the bird stopping every so often to let them catch up. Dane realized, with sickening clarity, that they were headed in the same direction Aurora had led him the night before. Had the boy followed? If so, this was infinitely worse.

They sneaked up on the spot where Thidrek had nearly killed Dane, hoping to catch the draugr by surprise, but the place was deserted. Klint squawked and flew to where William's bow and arrows lay strewn across the ground. After a brief search, they found no other trace of the boy, no blood or evidence of violence, and so it was agreed that, in all likelihood, William had been abducted.

Dane sank to the ground with his head in his hands, crushed by what he had done. Poor William! How terrified he must be! To think he had escaped his master's cruelty once and for all—only to be caught again in the monster's clutches.

"Blade gone. Thidrek gone. William gone." Jarl's voice was hard with scorn. "Where do you lead us now, Dane? The answer is *no*where. Because *I'm* taking command."

"No, you're not," said Fulnir. Ah, Fulnir! What a friend. Even though Dane had mucked up seriously, when push came to shove, Fulnir still was loyal. "Because I nominate Lut to be our leader," said Fulnir. Dane and the others shot surprised looks at Lut, who just stood there, looking calm and confident, as if he had expected the sudden promotion. Jarl was having none of it.

"That's ridiculous," said Jarl. "Sure, he's young and vital now. But how long will he stay that way?"

They all looked to Lut to provide the answer. "To be honest I don't know," he said. "A few days, a week; the apple's enchantment most probably will wear off."

"And then what? We'll be taking orders from a bent-over, decrepit old man!" Jarl railed. He then softened. "Not that there's anything wrong with you being old and bent again, Lut." Lut nodded, showing that he took no offense. Jarl continued his campaigning. "We need someone we can count on all the way through. Someone with the strength and stamina and—fine, I'll say it—courage to do what needs to be done."

"In other words, *you*," said Fulnir.

"Yes. I think everyone agrees that, despite Dane's past exploits, he has shown an appalling lack of good judgment of late, and has lost the confidence of the group." Jarl stopped, waiting for someone to gainsay him, and it hurt Dane to hear that no one disagreed. "So as of this moment, I'm sole leader."

There was a pause. "I say we put it to a vote," Drott said. "Who votes for Lut?" Drott and Fulnir raised their hands. Dane lamented he had lost the trust of the others but felt that if there was to be a new leader, Lut's wisdom beat Jarl's rashness any day. He raised his hand, making three for Lut.

Jarl glowered at them, saying, "You're against me . . . you're *all against me!*" before he stalked away to lick his wounded pride.

For once, Dane found himself feeling sorry for him. Jarl wasn't a bad sort; it was just that he suffered from an excess of self-regard. As for himself, he accepted blame for the loss of the blade and the capture of William. His single-minded drive to gain revenge on Thidrek had pushed him into incredibly poor judgment. But Lut's judgment had been equally poor when he'd chosen to eat the apple, and it seemed rather ironic to Dane that he should be rewarded for such weakness. But this was no time for self-pity, Dane knew, and so he made an effort to rise and walk to Lut and put out his hand in a gesture of fellowship. "I will abide by your decisions," Dane said, trying to sound sincere.

Lut grasped his hand and Dane felt his iron grip. "We have a daunting task ahead."

"I'm afraid more than you know," Dane said. "Thidrek said something about the Ship of the Dead."

Upon hearing this, Lut furrowed his brow in concern. Dane told him of Thidrek's threats of a human holocaust of unspeakable proportions. "'I shall unleash,' he said, 'Hel's minions upon the earth.'"

Lut visibly paled. "Hel's minions . . ."

Dane clapped him on the shoulder. "That's right, O Wise One. The end of the world as we know it. Glad you're in charge *now*?" Dane walked off, a part of him relieved that the fate of mankind was, for now at least, someone else's responsibility.

In a torment of shock and grief, Astrid streaked through the skies toward Asgard atop her steed, Vali, repeating the disastrous scene over and over in her mind. How was it possible that her friend was dead? One moment Mist was right there beside her in the sky—and the next, a swift swing of the blade by Aurora had turned Mist into cinders falling to earth. What a ghastly nightmare. She wished she could just shake herself awake and find her friend beside her once again, her face alive with laughter and high spirits. Yet the bitter certainty that it was impossible felt like a dark hand crushing her heart. And worse, it was her own scheme to steal the blade from Dane that had brought about Mist's demise. Aurora had done the killing, yes, but Astrid had practically put the blade into her hand—and the guilt she bore made her want to join Mist in death.

But if she ended her life now, then no one would know of Aurora's treachery. So despite her agony, Astrid vowed to go to Asgard and testify, for she knew that Mist's murder would already be the cause of great upheaval there. As Mist herself had once explained, the authority and control of the gods operated like that of a spider sitting at the center of a vast web. Events that touched even the farthest-flung points of the web did not go unobserved, for their reverberations quickly traveled up the strands to the godly realm of Asgard. And, unlike the affairs of mortal men, the death of a Valkyrie was cause for panic and, yes, retribution, for it upset the order of things and challenged the sense of control of those in power.

When at last the brilliant arc of the Rainbow Bridge came looming into view, leading the way to Asgard, Astrid felt her insides flutter. Soon she would go before the tribunal. As Mist had warned, her plan to steal the blade from Dane and kill Thidrek went against the Valkyrie edicts of nonintervention in the affairs of man. If Astrid told the truth, she risked severe reprimand. She could be stripped of her flying status and forever made to serve as a mead maid in Odin's corpse hall. But if that was her punishment, so be it. Lugging heavy mead buckets was a small price to pay to see Aurora sent to Niflheim for her heinous act.

Exactly why Aurora had committed such a crime puzzled Astrid. Mist was right when she said Aurora was always guided by selfish reasons—but how could she possible profit by joining forces with such a vile, wretched creature as the draugr Thidrek?

Below, she saw the Valkyrie corps gathered in the grove of gold-leafed trees. Vali, lathered with perspiration from the long journey, glided down. Astrid tied him where the other sky horses were picketed and hurried to the gathering.

Arriving, she saw that many of the maidens were dabbing tears from their eyes. She heard the voice of a sister say, "It breaks my heart to think I will never see her face or hear her kind words again." Astrid pushed to the front of the gathering and saw that the speaker was none other than Aurora, the murderess herself! She stood before the Council of Sisters, five striking beauties dressed in silver robes, presided over by Rain, the queen of the Valkyries. A woman of consummate poise and mystery, Rain, they said, had risen to the rank of queen through equal parts courage, cunning, and wisdom far beyond her years. The fact that Odin found pleasure in her shape had been a boon to her too. Now, bedecked in a golden cowled robe and a dazzling tiara, the queen of the Valkyries peered down at Aurora and bade her speak.

"Please, dear one, tell us what you saw," Rain said.

"Oh, I can't! It's too horrible!" wailed Aurora, putting her hands to her face, wet with false tears.

Astrid could scarcely believe her ears. A fury rose up in her, and before she knew it she had stepped forward into the clearing. "Sisters!" she cried out. "I know the truth of Mist's foul murder!" At the sound of Astrid's voice, Aurora whirled to face her, wearing her own look of fury.

"How dare you return here after what you've done!" Aurora spat. "Yes, she knows the truth of Mist's murder— because she committed it!"

There was a gasp from the assemblage, and for an instant Astrid was rocked by the audacity of Aurora's lie. "That— that is not true!" Astrid sputtered. "It is *her* hand that dealt the killing blow! I was there!"

"More lies by the murderess!" proclaimed Aurora.

"Enough!" Rain commanded. "You shall both have chance to speak."

"I was here first!" Aurora said, stomping her feet like a petulant child.

"Very well, Aurora," Rain sternly said. "Continue."

Aurora spoke her poisonous words, and Astrid had to restrain herself from leaping upon her and strangling her soft, pretty neck. "I saw Mist riding toward me," she said, her voice tremulous with sham emotion. "She was far away, but I knew it was her. She raised her hand to wave a greeting . . . and then I saw Astrid streak toward her from above. She—she had a weapon in her hand, a rather long-bladed axe. I could see it in the moonlight. I screamed to Mist,

'Look up! Look up!'" Overtaken then with sobs, Aurora found it hard to continue. "And then—*sniff, sniff*—the blade came down and she was gone!" This brought more weeping from the gathering and accusing looks aimed at Astrid.

"Astrid, what do you say to this?" Rain demanded.

Astrid gathered her words, trying to remain calm. "My queen, my sisters . . . I have one question for you. Would you kill your dearest friend? When I came to the sisterhood, Mist took me under her wing, taught me your ways with kindness and concern. What possible reason would I have to kill her?" Astrid pointed at Aurora. "Don't let false tears sway you. Ask yourselves: Has she befriended any of you? Can you recall her ever performing a single selfless act—one that didn't serve to feather her own nest?"

More than a few of the sisters nodded, finding truth in Astrid's words.

"I serve Odin," said Aurora dismissively. "My task is to ferry the dead, not fritter my time away making friends."

"But you *do* have time to consort with a draugr," Astrid said. "His name is Thidrek, and Odin himself cast the fiend from Valhalla." This brought murmurs of shock from the throng. "You killed Mist and tried to kill me to hide this damning little fact."

"Is this true, sister?" Rain demanded.

"Me?" Aurora said in a wounded voice. "Consort with a lowly, benighted draugr? Really, sisters, if I only act to 'feather my nest'—as my dear sister claims—then what benefit would I gain by associating with the foul and rot-ting undead?"

Rain's look at Astrid commanded an answer. "I cannot fathom what she would gain," Astrid admitted. "But I know it is true."

"*How* do you know?" asked the queen.

Astrid hesitated, aware that if she answered, she could be dooming herself.

"We're *waiting* for your evidence, sister," Aurora said smugly.

Astrid knew there was no turning back now. "Mist and I visited the human realm to steal a special blade and kill Thidrek. Aurora followed us. She told us where Thidrek was. But as we approached his camp, she waylaid us and stole the blade to protect the draugr from harm. We pursued her, and that's when she used the blade to kill Mist."

Rain stared at Astrid, puzzled. "Sister, are you saying your aim was to *kill* Thidrek? That is a strict violation of our primary edict."

"We are not to intervene in earthly matters—yes, I know," Astrid said. "But the lives of my kin were at stake."

"Your *kin*?" Rain thundered. "You have no kin but those around you! You are to relinquish all love for those on earth!"

"Another edict she has broken," Aurora said. "Mist told me Astrid admitted to her that she still loves one known as Dane the Defiant. Our dear sister was on her way to bring this to the council's attention when Astrid silenced her."

"She lies! Mist was my friend!" Astrid insisted.

Aurora crossed her arms over her chest and said, "We'll see who is lying. Do you still love a human, this Dane the Defiant?"

There was dead silence, as if the assemblage were holding its collective breath, waiting for the answer. "*Do* you, sister?" Rain said.

"Yes," Astrid said, bowing her head.

Aurora waited for the shocked outbursts to quiet. "Are we to believe the words of a sister who has broken not one but *two* of our edicts?"

Astrid groped for words that would somehow make them see the truth. "Sisters, hear me!" She waited for them to quiet. "It is true, I have broken the edicts. For that I must be punished. I came here knowing that I must speak the truth—and knowing that if I did, I would suffer punishment. Yet I came. For there was one sister I loved above all, and that was Mist. I would lay myself open to *any* penalty so that her murderer is brought to justice." She stared at Aurora, who glared back defiantly. "Aurora says my motive was to silence Mist—so you would not know I love a human. If that were so, why would I come here *knowing* this fact would be revealed? No! I would've fled!" Astrid's eyes swept the gathering and saw more than a few sisters nod in agreement. "Truly, sisters, I will plead guilty . . . if one of you can step forward and attest that when you heard of

Mist's murder, you had even the *barest* of thoughts that she died by my hand." Astrid waited . . . and no one moved. "I loved Mist, you all know that," she said, her eyes shining with tears, "and I would sooner burn in Niflheim than ever harm her."

"Oh, you will see Niflheim, that I guarantee," Aurora said.

"Silence!" Rain reprimanded. "The council shall decide, not you."

After a contemptuous scowl, Aurora bowed her head in deference. "As you decree, my queen."

"Is there anything else either of you would like to say?" Rain asked.

Astrid shook her head.

"I have one thing," Aurora said. "Take it as you will. Dear Astrid, pray tell the council the name you went by on earth."

Astrid was caught off guard by the question. "I . . . that has no bearing on—"

"Mistress of the Blade," Aurora said. "Axes were her specialty—the very weapon used to murder our sister Mist."

Murmurs of dismay rippled through the gathering. Rain held up her hand to bring silence. "The council will now deliberate. The accused will remain until we return." The Valkyrie queen and her council members left, disappearing among the trees. Astrid knew that the council would gather in the rose garden. After debate, each member would put a single rose petal into a Valkyrie helmet; white for innocent, red for guilty.

Astrid sat by herself as the queen and her council delib-erated. Once her eyes met Aurora's. The lying wench shot her the coldest of smiles, the kind that said, *My cunning trap has caught its prey*. Fuming, Astrid nearly gave in to the urge to go and slap the wicked thing right in the face, but she thought better of it when she saw the council had returned. The queen held up the inverted golden-winged helmet.

"The two sisters will come forward," Rain said. Astrid and Aurora came and stood before her. "Sister Astrid, take the helmet and let the petals of judgment fall." She gave the helmet to Astrid. Her heart pounding, Astrid turned it over. Six rose petals fluttered to the ground.

Red. All of them. Guilty.

Astrid threw the helmet at Aurora's face and ran with all she had.

14

WILLIAM
ENSLAVED

To William's great dismay, he was once again caught in Thidrek's web. And this time it was much worse than before, for now his master was an undead monster whose persistent rot had dissolved whatever small shred of humanity he might once have possessed. Now the slap of Thidrek's hand to his cheek was not just stingingly painful; it also left behind tiny bits of putrid flesh that often were crawling with maggots and a flesh-eating beetle or two.

"Hit me day and night," William said, "but the first chance I get to escape, I'll take it. And then I'll bring the Rune Warriors back to hack you to pieces."

Thidrek stared down at the boy, who was tied to a tree.

"Hack me to pieces? With what? The blade I now possess?"

"That'll do you no good against twenty men. They'll get it from you, and one swipe will send your putrid carcass back to Niflheim."

"Twenty men?"

"Well . . . it could be thirty. I'm not good at counting."

Thidrek slapped him. "Liar. I happen to know there are only five. And they have no idea where we are going, do they?"

William felt an impulse to shout out all he knew but held his tongue.

"Best you forget about your friends, thrall. You'll never see them again."

"I am no thrall!" William cried. "Specially not to some rotting piece of dung like you." He expected another slap— Thidrek raised his hand to deliver one but then paused, struck by a thought.

"Grelf, you claim to be an expert in matters of the law. This boy was my property before. Now that I am undead, do I lose my rights to said property?"

Grelf sat by the fire, roasting a rabbit skewered on a stick. "Let us examine this logically, my liege. By definition, one can have rights only insofar as he can *exercise* those rights. Since this can only be done when one is living, it follows logically that upon one's death he would clearly lose all rights, chief among them the right to own property."

Catching a frown from Thidrek, Grelf quickly continued.

"*But* if one passes from life into an intermediate state of undeadness—in which he is neither alive or dead but somewhere in between, and still able to freely move about—he is still able to exert his will upon the animate world and, therefore, capable of exercising his rights. Thus, he shan't lose them. Therefore, I see no legal precedent to void your rights, sire."

With an air of sublime satisfaction, Thidrek turned back to William. "And there you have it, boy. All legal and proper. You are mine."

Feeling this logic rather tortured, William dared take another tack. "How can something not alive be in control of something that is? It doesn't make sense."

From behind Thidrek's back, Grelf urgently shot William a warning look, shaking his head as if to say, *Go no further, boy.*

Thidrek picked up the Blade of Oblivion, twirling it thoughtfully. "Your lack of gratitude appalls me, boy. Did I not take you under my wing when your parents were killed?"

"*You* killed them."

Thidrek cocked his head, remembering. "So I did! But I did not kill *you*—for I saw a lad who could be made useful. And a slave remains a slave unless his master sells him. You were unjustly taken from me without payment. Just as all the rest of my property was—my kingdom, my land, my castle, my livestock . . . to say nothing of my prized collection of stuffed beavers!" Thidrek swung the axe, the blade embedding halfway into the tree an inch from the top of

William's head. "I aim to regain everything I lost, and more. If you try to run, I can kill you with the axe, whereupon you will wake to find your*self* in Niflheim at the mercy of m'lady Hel herself. Or . . ." Digging in his ear, Thidrek brought forth a tiny black beetle and held it out to William on the tip of his bony finger. "I can kill you with my bare hands and drink your blood. Then *you* will become like me. And those squirmy little things you're so afraid of will be burrowing by the *thousands* through your whole body."

Thidrek laid the beetle on the tip of William's nose. It began to crawl toward his nostril. As his arms were tied to the tree, William furiously blew air up from his mouth to dislodge the horrid thing, but without success.

"And if perchance you *do* slip away, you'll never really be safe. For every night when you shut your eyes to sleep, the terrors will steal upon you, son, for you'll never know if that will be the night I come for you in the dark."

The beetle was just then crawling into the cavity of William's nose. "Do we have an understanding, boy?"

"Yes!" cried William. "I give my word not to run off!"

Thidrek picked up the insect and popped it in to his mouth, crunching it between his teeth and swallowing it down. "Glad we've had this little heart-to-heart."

Astrid's dash from the grove had taken her sisters by surprise, gaining her a good head start. She was a fast runner and got to her steed and into the air before anyone could stop her.

When she looked back, she saw several sisters had jumped on their mounts and had begun pursuit, led by Aurora. As if sensing the dire nature of Astrid's plight, Vali raced swiftly down, boldly plunging into a bank of dense and turbulent storm clouds. They rode, hidden by the clouds, risking their own destruction as lightning flashed all around them. But this seemed to shake the sisters from her tail, and once she was sure they had given up the chase, Astrid brought Vali to the earthly realm to give her exhausted mount time to eat and rest and herself time to think.

As night fell she sat on a rock, utterly alone. First she'd been ripped away from all her loved ones on the earthly plane—Dane, her father, her friends—and now she was a fugitive blamed for the murder of the only friend she had made since. With nowhere to go and no one to turn to for safe haven, she feared she would not be free for long. She knew all too well that the sisters would be hunting her everywhere, and they would stop at nothing to find her and banish her to Hel's merciless underworld. What was she to do?

Before, when just an innocent girl full of her own self-righteous view of the world, she would have raised her fists to the sky and shouted, *Stupid gods! How can you inflict such injustice? Are you really that uncaring?* But having watched them hold court in Asgard, she knew the gods were all too human, wrapped up in their own squabbles and petty rivalries. If she went to Odin and told him the truth, would he intervene? Without proof of her innocence, how could he? He had enough on his hands without taking on the Council of Sisters. Mist had told her that Odin had interfered once in council affairs and the sisters had thereupon refused to perform ferrying duties until he relented. Godly intervention was out.

She gazed again at the sky and saw no luminous trails. At least for tonight she had eluded her sisters' grasp. But it wouldn't last. A horrible fate was closing in, and she realized that perhaps the only one who would help her was the witch who had put this whole catastrophe in motion in the first place.

Skuld.

How fortunate that William had joined their little troupe, Grelf thought. Now he had a potential ally against Thidrek. If Grelf could gain the boy's confidence, convince him that he too despised their odious master, then they could work together to escape. And once they were free? Grelf knew William had spunk and cleverness; the boy would make a fine assistant in the perfume trade, wouldn't he?

Thidrek had insisted the boy be bound to the saddle (riding tandem with Grelf) to prevent escape. Grelf tied him loosely so his bonds wouldn't hurt. And as they rode, he whispered encouragements to the boy, saying not to fret, that his friend Grelf would take care of him.

At midday they stopped at a stream to feed and water

the horses. Thidrek lay down with his back to a tree, one hand still gripping the handle of the Blade of Oblivion. The draugr closed his eyes and became completely still.

"Does he sleep?" William whispered to Grelf.

Grelf gestured for William to follow him farther from his resting master so they could talk without being heard. "Not as we do," Grelf whispered back. "He describes it as a trance he falls into. It takes only a short time to refresh him. But make no mistake—even in this state he is alert as a house cat."

"Where is he taking us, Grelf?"

Grelf told of the Ship of the Dead and its draugr crew, and how Thidrek had plans to bring it back to the goddess Hel and raise an army of the dead to attack the world of the living.

"That's horrible, Grelf! We have to stop him!"

"Shhh!" Just what Grelf didn't need—the boy complicating matters by trying to be a hero. This younger generation was too brave for its own good. "The best way to stop him," Grelf said, "is for us to escape and find help."

"If the runes are right, then help is not far behind," William said. He told Grelf about Lut's runes leading them to the islands named the Three Brothers.

"It's true," Grelf said. "Three small islands lie directly offshore of a river. Two miles inland is a waterfall—behind which the Ship of the Dead is buried."

"Then all we have to do is stop Thidrek before he gets there."

"May I remind you I am not exactly warrior class, and you are a small boy? The best strategy is for you to flee and find your friends. And then you'll all ride back and dispatch our putrescent lordship. World saved."

William's brow furrowed, as if he sensed a strategic flaw in Grelf's plan. "So . . . while I'm escaping, finding my friends and bringing them back—what will you be doing?"

The boy was irritatingly full of questions. "I'll be doing the big job of delaying Thidrek to give you a good head start."

"You're sure he'll come after me?"

"Of course! You're the prized hostage, not me," Grelf said. "The only way Thidrek can check Dane is by putting a knife to your thoat. It's called leverage, son. Without you, Thidrek has nothing to bargain with."

15

A SURPRISE
FLIES IN

That night, William pretended to sleep. He was bound to a tree with his hands tied behind him. Cracking an eyelid, he saw on the other side of the campfire that Thidrek was now lying against another tree with his eyes closed, in his "trance" state.

Time to work.

Grelf had not tied his wrists tightly—which gave his hands some play. He felt around behind him for the sharp piece of flint Grelf had hidden in the dirt. There! He found it. He began cutting away with it at the ropes binding his wrists.

The big question was, Why was Grelf helping him? William had known the rascal before, when Thidrek was a prince and Grelf was his right-hand man. He'd played the fawning toady to Thidrek back then as well, but William suspected that his only allegiance was to himself. Grelf was a rat who would betray anyone to serve his own needs. Could that kind of vermin be trusted? Right now, William did not have the luxury of doubt. They were going to arrive at the Ship of the Dead tomorrow, so his escape *had* to be tonight.

The razor-sharp flint was slicing away the rope strands around his wrists. Once his hands could move about, he'd cut the rope around his chest that tied him to the tree—and he'd be free!

He heard a soft rush of air above him. He then saw to his utter surprise a large raven circling overhead. Klint! Dane and his friends were close! The bird landed in the tree Thidrek was resting against. *Please don't squawk,* William prayed. He was sure Thidrek knew Dane had a pet raven; if he saw the bird, the game would be up.

Klint cocked his head and stared with interest at the draugr below. Thidrek wasn't breathing or moving; he appeared as good as dead. And ravens feast on the dead. *Fly away, Klint! He's not a corpse!* William wanted to shout. He worked feverishly on the rope, trying to cut away the last strands binding his wrists.

Klint flew down and with his beak snatched something off Thidrek's nose—probably a beetle or maggot. The draugr's eyes snapped open; he gave a bellow and swatted at the bird. Klint flew off, squawking angrily. Thidrek jumped to his feet.

"Grelf! Wake up!"

Grelf stirred, yawning, then—as if remembering their plan—immediately came to his senses, blurting out, "The boy! He's escaped—" Grelf's head whipped around and saw that William was, alas, *still* tied to the tree.

"A raven attacked me!" Thidrek exclaimed. "Saddle the horses. We must ride!"

"To escape a raven, my lord?"

"The feathered wretch was Dane the Defiant's pet, I'm sure of it."

"But my lord, how could he have followed us?"

Thidrek picked up the blade, leveling his bloodshot eyes on Grelf. "Perhaps my loyal and trusted servant has been leaving marks along the trail."

"Heavens, no, my lord! Not me. It—it had to be the boy."

Grelf was the rat again, saving his own hide. How William yearned to spill the beans about their escape plot just to see Grelf squirm.

Thidrek came at William wearing a murderous look. He grabbed his knife from his belt and William thought his end had come. *Do they take ten-year-old boys in Valhalla?* he wondered. But Thidrek didn't use the knife on William; instead he cut the rope binding him to the tree and yanked him to his feet.

"If your friends come close," Thidrek growled, "it's you I'll threaten to send to Niflheim."

Thidrek dragged William toward the horses Grelf was saddling. William knew the binding around his wrists had nearly been cut through but didn't know if a strong yank would sever it. He had to wait for the exact right time to try.

"You'll ride with me, boy," Thidrek said. "I want to keep you close."

Thidrek picked him up and flung him into the saddle. *Now!* William yanked hard on the binding. It broke, freeing his hands. He grabbed the reins, kicked the horse's flanks. "Yah!" The horse bolted away like an arrow shot from his bow. He heard angry shouts but didn't look back as the horse galloped away.

Overcome with a manic frenzy to flee, William raced blindly into the black forest, low-hanging branches whipping at him, slashing his face. He didn't know how long he rode or in what direction; he was consumed by his raging need to distance himself from the devil Thidrek. Finally, clear thinking trumped his animal panic and he slowed his mount and listened for pursuing hoofbeats. He heard nothing but the normal night sounds of the forest. Had he eluded his tormentor? Maybe Thidrek had given up, knowing there were enemies about.

Poor Grelf. Still man-in-waiting to an odious draugr. But not for long. William had to find his friends. They were south—but what direction was that? Lut could look at the stars to navigate, a skill William had yet to learn. Then he remembered something Lut *had* taught him: Moss grew more thickly on the north sides of trees.

He dismounted and at a pine tree quickly felt along the

bark for the spongy moss, since it was too dark to actually see it. There! He felt a thick, soft clump of it. Now he knew where south was—the opposite side of the tree pointed to it.

William threw himself into the saddle and gave a hard slap to the horse's rear, and off she galloped, now headed in the right direction. Had Klint flown back to Dane, squawking and cawing in the secret language he and Dane shared, telling him that Thidrek had been found? If so, William's friends were already headed his way. How joyous he'd be when he saw their faces again. How safe he would feel to be sheltered among them. They would hunt Thidrek down, and once cornered, the soulless wretch would fall to his knees and grovel for mercy. And when he was dispatched forever to Niflheim, William would finally know that the man who had murdered his mother and father would never bring pain to anyone again.

He emerged from thick forest into a wide meadow dimly lit by the moon. He knew this place. He, Grelf, and Thidrek had ridden past it that day. All he needed to do was find the rutted trail they had taken, then follow it south to Dane's party. The horse trotted through the tall grass, scattering nesting birds. Halfway across the meadow he saw a dark swath of bare ground ahead. The trail!

Suddenly he felt a shiver, as if an icy hand had gripped the back of his neck. Instinctively he whipped his head around to look behind him—and saw a flash of light at the tree line from where he'd just come. His heart sank, for he was sure the metallic glint was moonlight reflecting off the Blade of Oblivion.

Thidrek exploded from the trees atop the other horse, his right hand thrust high, holding the axe. William's heels dug into his mount's flanks and the horse broke into a sprint. An instant later they were off the grass and onto the trail. Ahead maybe two hundred paces was the curtain of trees on the south side of the meadow. William raced for it, for he knew its dark cover gave him at least a slim chance to elude Thidrek. Out here in the moonlight, he was dead.

He looked back. Thidrek's horse was sprinting, too, but had not made up any ground. William was going to make the trees—he was sure of it! Maybe he would stay on the trail in hopes of running into Dane's party. What a sight to see, Thidrek suddenly turning tail and running from them!

He breached the tree line. Thidrek would surely give up now. He glanced back just in time to see the axe flying sideways toward him, its blade scything the air making a whooshing sound. In a blinding-white shower of sparks, his horse vanished from under him. The ground came up like a hard fist, knocking William senseless. He lay there, unable to move or talk. Seeming then as if in a dream, he saw Thidrek grinning down at him, the grin turning to a look of distress . . . Thidrek flinging the saddle, blanket, and reins into the tall grass beside the trail . . . William felt himself roughly lifted and slung over Thidrek's horse . . . the horse led off the trail and into a thick covering of trees . . . Thidrek was now just standing there, looking off at something . . . William realized what it was! They were hiding from Dane's party, passing along the trail. William tried to call out to tell them—*Dane, help! I'm here!*—but all he managed was strangled sounds. He saw Thidrek turn and scowl at him. And before he could make another sound, Thidrek brought the blade handle down upon William's skull and blackness descended.

16

A NEGOTIATION WITH
THE NORNS

"Wait! I see something," Dane said. The party halted. Dane dismounted and stepped off the trail into the tall grass. He kneeled down and saw a saddle and horse blanket lying there. The blanket was warm and moist, as if it had just come off a lathered horse. Nearby were the reins and mouth bit. He touched the bit and it, too, was warm. "Someone took these off a horse just moments ago."

Lut dismounted, reached down for a pinch of soil, and brought it to his nose. "Ashes. Still warm," Lut said gravely. Immediately they knew the awful significance of this. The Blade of Oblivion had struck. "On guard, everyone!" Lut ordered. "Thidrek has been here."

Everyone's hands grasped the hilts of their weapons. Jarl, Drott, and Fulnir, still mounted, nervously swiveled their heads around—but in the dim moonlight all they saw were grass and the dark shapes of trees. Then Dane saw something else on the ground. He bent down and picked it up. William's shoe. Still warm. Dane felt sick again. Had Thidrek used the blade on the boy? Was William forever beyond his reach now, locked behind the gates of Niflheim? The thought of the innocent boy suffering in Hel's dark realm tore at him.

"Thidrek!" Dane shouted at the night. "Show yourself! This time we settle it for good!" His words faded away across the meadow. Lut put a hand upon his shoulder.

"We don't know for sure William is dead," consoled Lut. Dane looked down at the boy's shoe in his hand and managed a nod, although he feared the odds were slim. "Thidrek may already be gone," Lut added. "If Three Brothers is his destination, then we *must* get there before him." Dane put the shoe in his pocket, hoping that it would find its owner again. He and Lut mounted up and the party headed north.

They followed the trail as it crossed the meadow and plunged into the woods on the other side. Not long afterward a figure abruptly jumped from behind a tree in front of them, waving his arms madly and shouting. In the lead, Dane barely managed to pull up his horse to avoid running him over. It was Grelf.

"Odin be praised!" he rejoiced. "Hail the Rune Warriors! Come to save me from the clutches of my moldering lord."

They just stared at him. "Come to save *you*? Our enemy's loyal man?" said Dane.

"My loyalty ceased when his lordship ceased to breathe."

"So," Dane said, "all that blather about you being 'most fortunate and happy to serve' him was—"

"Blather," Grelf concurred. "I was kidnapped by the foul draugr, pressed into service—just as William was. We were to escape when your bird interrupted our plans." There came a *squawk* from above. Klint had just landed on the branch of a nearby tree.

"But William *did* escape," Lut said.

Grelf told them of the boy galloping off on one of their horses and Thidrek's pursuit atop the other, reins in one hand, blade in the other.

"And he used it," Dane said bitterly. "We found the other horse's blanket and saddle . . . and this." Dane showed William's shoe to Grelf.

"But he would not have killed the boy," Grelf said.

"Why?" said Jarl. "He suddenly too moral to murder?"

"A dead boy serves him no purpose," Grelf explained. "Thidrek means to use him as a hostage to check you."

Dane felt renewed optimism for William's chances. "Where is he taking him?"

Grelf told them of the Ship of the Dead buried in the cave behind the waterfall. "Your runes were correct. There are three islands near the mouth of the river that leads to the cave."

"Ah! Three *islands*," Drott said, sounding a little smug. "And who among us got *that* right?"

Fulnir sighed, tired of Drott harping on this. "Should we stop and throw you a banquet?"

"Maybe later," Drott said, Fulnir's sarcasm lost on him. "Remember, I like mutton."

"Why are we standing around when there's a draugr to kill?" Jarl said. "Let's ride!" Jarl took off up the trail. Grelf panicked, afraid they were abandoning him.

"You can't leave me here alone!" he whined. "Thidrek may still be about! And—and there's forest creatures that would eat me!"

Dane turned to Lut. "He's been to the cave—his knowledge may come in handy." Lut agreed.

"All right, Grelf, you can ride with Drott," Lut said.

"Thank you! Thank you!" Grelf crooned. Drott offered his hand, helping him up. "I shall not be a bother, just drop me at the first village we come to."

"No, Grelf," Lut said. "You're taking us all the way to the Ship of the Dead."

"The—the ship?" Grelf bleated. "But I do not wish to return there."

"You'll take us to the ship or we'll leave you here," Lut said.

Seeing he had no choice, Grelf whimpered, "Will cruelty to me never cease?"

N

The thought of once again facing the Norns made Astrid's skin crawl. The Wyrd Sisters—how they *hated* this apt name—possessed the dazzling beauty of goddesses and the foul temperament of a bucket of vipers. Also known as the Fates, or the Mistresses of Time, they wrote the destinies of gods and humans.

Months before, when Astrid had discovered that they had fated Dane to die, she had gone to them to plead for his life. The scheming witches had agreed to spare him, but only if Astrid left her earthly existence to serve Odin and become a Valkyrie. Thus, Astrid had learned that the Norns made a hard bargain that was always to their advantage. This time, Astrid was determined to not let them get the best of her again.

As she and Vali emerged from the clouds, Yggdrasil, the Tree of Life, loomed before them. The awe-inspiring ash tree dwarfed all living things; its branches spread out to the heavens, disappearing into the mists above, its roots plunged deep into the very center of the earth. Astrid knew that at the base of the tree the Norns dwelled and conspired.

Vali glided down into the lush grass next to a still pool. On her last visit here Astrid had looked into this pool, seeing visions of her past and future that shocked and amazed her. She hopped from Vali's back as her steed instantly started gorging on the sweet grass. Astrid knew she needn't tie his reins to a tree branch to prevent him from wandering; with such rich fodder he'd stay put and eat until his belly was bursting. Despite being a celestial species, when it came to food Vali was just as piggish as his earthly counterpart.

"Greetings, dear sister."

Astrid turned to see Skuld, garbed in a scarlet robe and matching headdress, standing a few yards away, as if she had suddenly appeared there. "It is a pleasure to see you again," she said with a welcoming smile that did not fool Astrid.

"As it is a pleasure to see you, dear Skuld. I trust you and your sisters are well," said Astrid, attempting sincerity. Across a small meadow at the base of Yggdrasil she saw Verdandi and Urdr, Skuld's fate-spinning sisters. Astrid wished a branch would fall and kill them—then revised her wish. Better that Skuld was with them so the branch would wipe them all out. Then humankind would forever be free of their vicious whims.

"To what do we owe your visit?" asked Skuld.

Was she jesting? She knew perfectly well why Astrid had come. But Astrid humored her, spilling out the story of Mist's death at the hands of Aurora and her unjust conviction for the crime.

"It appears you've stumbled into quite a quandary," said Skuld after Astrid had finished.

Astrid wanted to say the "quandary" was all Skuld's doing. If she hadn't sent Dane for the Blade of Oblivion in order to kill the draugr Thidrek, none of it would have happened. But casting blame on a Norn was—as Astrid's father would say—about as futile and foolish as arguing a mother bear out of her cubs. So she said, "You are correct, m'lady. I had hoped you could advise me as to how I can prove myself innocent."

"And exactly *why* should your innocence be my concern?"

Astrid was stumped for a moment. She had to proceed with caution. "Um, well . . . because you are most merciful and desire to see a mistake of justice righted."

The good cheer vanished from Skuld's face, replaced with a look of haughty contempt. "I do not make mistakes."

"I wasn't implying—"

"Do you think it's easy crafting destinies for everyone? You try it. Every day I must create fates and keep things fresh—from cruel to joyous to somewhere in between. Of course, I could take the *easy* way out and make everyone happy, but that would be hack work and I have higher standards."

"M'lady, I am not belittling your craft," Astrid said, soothing her wounded pride. "I must admit the fate you've created for me is most original."

"Of course it is," Skuld said with a self-satisfied air. "I spin the future while my sisters work in the past and present. What skill is there in knowing what has gone before or what is now? They are rank amateurs compared to me. Only *I* have the genius to create what *shall be*."

Skuld sure was laying it on thick. Astrid wondered why a goddess would have to sing her own praises and malign her two sisters. Maybe she was secretly insecure, like most people in power. "M'lady, your sagacity is without question, but I am confused as to why you would have me become a Valkyrie and then so soon after have Aurora's vicious lies send me fleeing from the sisterhood."

"Who are you to question my methods?" Skuld asked, her tone hardening. "How stupid you are. Do you think I work from moment to moment to refashion fate? I was here before the gods walked the earth—and I'll be here when they are but dust in the wind. Your destiny was shaped before your father met your mother. I created the moment when you first laid eyes on Dane the Defiant and then fell in love with him—it has all led up to *this*."

She gestured to the pond. Suddenly flames leaped from the still surface. Astrid gasped in shock as in the pool's reflection she saw her village on fire and under attack by a swarm of howling, half-decayed men. Draugrs! Thidrek led them, swinging the Blade of Oblivion, as the horde swept in, chopping down men, women, and children without mercy. Then she saw her father on his knees begging for his life as Thidrek stood over him, shrieking with laughter. The monster raised his sword, and Astrid cried "No!" covering her eyes before the blade hacked down, ending her father's pleas. "No! You can't!" Astrid cried. "You can't let this happen!"

Skuld looked at the horrible scene without emotion, as if human suffering had no effect on her. "Destiny can be cruel" was all she said.

"It is you who are cruel, to create such a future as this!"

Blind fury took Astrid, and she leaped at Skuld, meaning to wring the goddess's neck. But all her hands grasped was air. A derisive chuckle made her whirl, and she saw all three of the Fates were now standing a short distance away.

"Now, now, a Valkyrie must keep her head," teased Urdr, who was the Fate who kept the past.

"She must not let anger cloud her judgment," mocked Verdandi, who kept the present.

Astrid took a breath, trying to calm herself. She remembered that the last time she had come before them, the Fates had used the same methods: their haughty manner and immunity to human suffering had caused Astrid to lose her head and lash out in anger. It was their way of manipulating her, Astrid realized. This time she would not play their game.

"Thank you for seeing me, sisters," she said calmly. She turned her back on them and started toward her grazing mount.

"Where do you think you're going?" Skuld demanded.

Astrid stopped and turned back to them. "As the Sisters of Fate, I would think you would know that." She continued walking away from them.

"You do not turn your back on us!" screeched Urdr.

"You insolent child!" spat Verdandi. "How dare you!"

Astrid said nothing as she reached Vali. She whispered in her mount's ear. "Now *they* are losing their heads."

"Astrid!"

She turned and saw the Fates standing before her. Their faces were contorted in angry disbelief that a human would show them such defiance. "Your audience with us is not over," fumed Skuld.

"Really? Then why am I leaving?" Astrid boosted herself atop Vali. Seeing that Astrid was calling their bluff, the harpies immediately adopted a sweeter tone.

"Dear child," Verdandi cooed. "You mustn't take offense at our jests."

"We meant no harm," purred Urdr. "It was all in fun."

Astrid jumped down to the ground. "I'm on to you, sisters. You arranged my conviction so I would come here, begging for your help. When all the while you need *my* help."

The Norns shared a conspiring look. Whispers passed between them. It seemed they were in argument, because the whispers started to grow heated in nature. Finally, Skuld made a curt gesture with her hand, ending the argument, and turned to Astrid again.

"The future you saw in the pool is not of my making," Skuld admitted reluctantly.

"Not of your making?" Astrid said. "But . . . I thought you created all destinies."

"Thidrek is the poison in our stewpot," said Urdr. "He is not living, therefore we cannot control *his* fate. And the destinies of all those he touches become corrupted too."

"Does that mean the future I saw in the pool can be

changed?" Astrid said, grasping at hope.

"Yes," said Skuld.

"But how? Tell me what I must do to make it so!"

"There are two labors you must perform," Skuld said. "One easy, one difficult. First, you must steal Odin's horse."

Astrid stood there, not quite sure she had heard this correctly. "Steal Odin's horse?" The Norns nodded. "You want me to break into the Asgard stables and steal the favorite animal of our most powerful god." The three nodded. "Well! At least that's the difficult labor, right?" The three looked at her. Astrid had a sinking feeling. "R-right?"

17

DEATH TO DRAUGRS

Riding along the coastline in the early afternoon, Dane and his party arrived at a small village, a handful of ramshackle huts hunched along the shore. Grelf assured them that the Ship of the Dead lay just three leagues north. They had ridden hard all day, so Lut ordered that they rest and feed their exhausted mounts before setting off on the final leg of their journey.

Grelf hopped down from the horse he shared with Drott and announced, "Having brought you so close to your destination, I have fulfilled my duties as guide. I now bid you good-bye and wish you all very merry draugr hunting." He started to scuttle away when Jarl grabbed his collar, jerking him back.

"Off to find Thidrek and tell him where we are?" Jarl asked.

"In good faith I've led you here—and still you don't trust me?" Grelf asked indignantly.

"I'd sooner trust a Berserker with my sister," Jarl said. "You're coming with us—all the way."

An enterprising villager who came forward with a basket of food to sell to the weary travelers spoke up. "You're hunting draugrs, you say?"

Lut told him they were seeking the fabled Ship of the Dead that was said to be buried nearby with a full complement of draugr warriors. "Another draugr named Thidrek seeks to awake these undead men so the ship may sail again. We have come to destroy it before that can happen."

The food vendor's face darkened in dread. "We have heard of this cursed ship. Come! Our völva will advise you."

Dane knew that a völva was a female shaman known for her *galdra*, or magic abilities. Another name for such a practitioner of the dark arts was witch, and as the food vendor led them to her hut, Dane expected to see some sinister-looking ancient crone with hairy warts, missing teeth, and a hooked nose. Instead, as they were led in, Dane beheld a handsome woman in fine dress who bade them take seats on the furs laid out on the floor. The hut itself was neat and orderly, with lighted candles giving off a pleasing scent. THE BEWITCHERY said a sign above the door, and Dane noticed she had her fees posted on the wall. One price for standard spells, potions, and elixirs, another for what she termed "designer enchantments." She was even running a two-for-one special.

"The Ship of the Dead is no ordinary craft," the völva explained after she had poured them each a cup of herbal tea. "Hel has bewitched it to resist fire and ordinary weapons."

"Then how do we destroy it?" Dane asked.

"You must destroy its crew," she answered. "Without them, the ship cannot sail."

"Kill the draugrs, you mean," Jarl said with a smirking look aimed at Dane. "Like with a special blade we *used* to have?"

"A draugr who is up and about is indeed difficult to destroy," the völva said. "But asleep in its crypt, the creature is greatly weakened. That is when you must strike—not with blades, but with magic." She explained that—by employing her own proprietary blend of ingredients in a recipe known only to her—she could make a special brew that when poured into the mouth of a sleeping draugr would guarantee to turn the undead creature into a fully dead one.

"Perfect," said Lut. "Can you get started right away? We're in a hurry."

"For *right away*," she said, "there's an additional ten-percent right-away charge to my normal fee." Lut tried to negotiate her down, but she said her prices were fixed by the Guild of Völvas & Shaewives, a labor cooperative formed by the many soothsayers in the area. Everyone had to empty their pockets—including an unwilling Grelf—but they managed to scrape together enough, and she immediately began work.

"How many draugrs need killing?" she asked. "My standard recipe serves five."

"I would say there are twenty," Grelf said, "give or take a draugr."

"I'll make an extra-large portion, just to be safe." Dane watched with interest as she began by pouring rainwater into a stewpot over a fire. "The rainwater must be new—not more than a day old," she said, "so it still retains the freshness of the heavenly spring above from which it came." To this she added a pinch of this and a splash of that from the scores of clay jars in her apothecary, careful to conceal from view exactly how much of each ingredient she was using. After the concoction was left to boil a short time, the völva took a spoon and tasted it, smacking her lips. "Mmmm, now *that's* draugr-killing goodness." The brew was poured into a small watertight cask and sealed with a cork. She then gave Lut the kit bag of accessories: a prying tool, a leather funnel, a needle, and a spool of thread. "Pry open the mouth, put the spout of the funnel in, and pour in the brew. Then quickly seal up the mouth by sewing it shut. Then stand back."

"Stand back?" said Lut

"I'd recommend it," said the völva. "Thank you—come again."

Soon after, the party set out north along the coast and by sundown reached the river that flowed into the sea. They tethered their horses on the beach and in darkness crept inland along the river. A hundred yards from the waterfall they took cover behind a large boulder.

Now, just a short walk from where the draugrs were said to dwell, cold dread gripped Dane. It had always spooked him to be near burial grounds. Of course, most graves were filled with the normal type dead who just lay there. What they faced in the cave was far worse—the kind of corpse that could jump up and bite your face off.

Grelf had told them how, after the chieftain draugr had nixed Thidrek's offer, all of them had dived back under the soil to sleep in their graves again. Were they *still* sleeping? Or had Thidrek arrived at the ship already and roused them once more?

"Ready to do this?" Lut asked him.

"Is 'no' an acceptable answer?" Dane gave a grim smile.

"It's the answer we *all* would give," Lut said, smiling back. "But we've come all this way . . ."

"Right," Dane said. "And we paid so much for the draugr-killing brew. Be a shame to waste it."

"You two finished with the clever back-and-forth?" Jarl said, itching to get to the action.

Lut led them out, carrying an unlit torch, its head wrapped in an oilskin cover to protect it from the spray of the waterfall. Grelf had to be prodded with Jarl's sword tip before he fell in line. Fulnir and Drott trailed, carrying the cask of the völva's brew and accessory bag. Before long they were at the base of the mountain beside the falls. They crept along the wet rocks and soon slipped behind the waterfall, finding themselves at the mouth of the pitch-black cave.

Holding his sword at the ready, Dane found his nerves were stretched tight, fearing something was about to spring out from the dark. Beside him, Jarl, too, was armed and on edge.

Lut removed the oilskin cover and lit the torch with his flint. The fire took hold, filling the chamber with light. As Grelf had described it, the cave was enormous. And thankfully, no shield wall of ferocious draugrs faced them. Dane and Jarl relaxed a bit.

Lut brought the torch down to the ground. In the sand could be seen two sets of footsteps leading in and out of the cave. Lut asked Grelf to place his foot over the smaller print. It matched. There were no other footprints, which meant no one had been in the cave since Grelf and Thidrek. If luck was with them, the draugrs would still be slumbering and vulnerable. The little group went deeper into the cave and it grew eerily quiet, the only sound the muffled shuffling of footsteps through the sand.

A monstrous, fanged beast rose up in front of them. Dane gasped and stepped back, as did Jarl. Their swords came up, ready to attack.

"Wait!" Lut said. He held the torch higher, casting more light on the beast, revealing it to be the ship's figurehead, a reptilian catlike thing with long, spiky fangs. In its paw was clutched the horn Grelf had described.

"Almost l-l-looks alive," said Drott between hiccups.

"Grelf, where are the graves?" Dane asked.

Grelf indicated an area that lay within the hull of the buried ship. Dane, Jarl, and Lut hurriedly started digging with shovels purchased at the völva's village. Fulnir and Drott readied the draugr-killing materials.

"I've been thinking," Drott said. "Exterminating draugrs could be a lucrative business."

"That's not a bad idea," Fulnir said. "We could travel round in a wagon with a big sign that says, 'Got Undead?'"

"That's catchy."

"I've found one!" Jarl hollered. "Bring the brew!"

Drott and Fulnir hurried over with the cask and accessories. Dane and Lut stopped their shovel work and watched Jarl clear away the earth from the body he'd exposed. Like Thidrek, the draugr was in a half-decomposed state. Its skeletal hand clutched a rusted sword, and on its chest lay a Viking shield, the limewood now moldy with rot. Dane had seen corpses before, and this thing appeared to be exactly that: a putrid shell devoid of life.

Fulnir and Drott kneeled next to the body. "Prying tool," Fulnir said, holding out his hand. Drott slapped the wedge-like tool into his palm. Fulnir thrust the end between the draugr's teeth, prying open its jaw. "Funnel." Drott gave him the funnel, and Fulnir jammed the spout end into the open mouth. "Dispense brew." Drott now poured a measure of the liquid from the cask into the funnel. There was a gurgling sound as the liquid trickled down the draugr's throat. "You can close," Fulnir said. Drott took the needle and thread and wasted no time sewing the draugr's mouth shut. The job done, they all stared at the draugr, expecting something to happen.

"The völva said we should stand back," Lut said.

They all took a couple of steps back. And waited. The draugr lay there looking no different than before. "Maybe you didn't put in enough," Jarl said.

"Look, we *know* what we're doing," Fulnir said.

"*We're* the draugr-killing experts," said Drott.

Jarl rolled his eyes. "I still think it needs more—"

The draugr exploded, spewing out a vomitous stew of rotten flesh and entrails that splattered against shirtfronts and faces. For a moment they all stood there, stunned, covered by the disgusting gore. Dane spied a lone eyeball perched on Lut's shoulder. He flicked it away with a finger. "A little *less* on the next one, hmm?"

"Greetings!" said a familiar voice behind them. They whirled to see Thidrek standing before the prow beast, holding a bound and gagged William, the Blade of Oblivion pressed to the boy's throat. Beside him was Grelf, wearing the chagrined look of a man who has been forced to change his loyalties once again. "My loyal and trusted servant has done an excellent job leading you into my trap. Good work, Grelf."

Grelf gave a sheepish nod. "I am honored to serve you, my lord."

"He informs me you've been killing my kind in a most unsporting way," Thidrek said.

Dane drew his sword, "Let's make it sporting. You and me." He took a step toward Thidrek, who pressed his blade deeper into William's flesh, causing the boy to stiffen in pain.

"Stay where you are!" Thidrek ordered. Dane stopped. "Fool, have you forgotten your weapons cannot scratch me?"

"Five wolves can kill a bear," Lut said, drawing his sword, as did Jarl, Fulnir, and Drott. "It may take a while, but we'll get the blade."

"Another step, this pup sees Hel," Thidrek warned. "How she'll delight in his cries of pain."

Dane saw fear in William's eyes—but also acceptance of his fate. As if the boy were giving them permission to attack. Dane gave Lut a searching look. What do we do?

In that moment of indecision, Thidrek whispered something in the prow beast's ear. The thing came alive; Dane stared, transfixed, as the beast brought the horn to its mouth. . . .

"Run!" Lut cried.

An earsplitting blast sounded. From out of the holes that Dane and Lut had dug sprang draugr warriors— rusty weapons and rotted shields in hand, their decomposed faces set in a furious death's-head grimace. A score or more of them shot from the sand like fleas leaping from a dog's back.

They gave blood-curdling war cries and attacked.

Almost instantly their shields disintegrated and their corroded weapons were shattered by the strong steel blades wielded by the Rune Warriors. But steel had no effect on the draugrs themselves—the blades seemed to magically pass right through without leaving a mark. The undead warriors bore in, stabbing with their broken blades, backing Dane and his friends toward a cave wall. If they should be cornered there, Dane knew, the draugrs would take their time, wear them down, and kill them.

And then it got worse.

A hulking draugr in a tarnished bronze helmet topped with an eagle's head—the chieftain Grelf had described—shouted out, "Agi! Geilir! Jorkell!" From beneath the sand leaped three monstrous creatures.

Draugrhounds.

Dane's knees went weak. He felt his heart implode and sink into the pit of his stomach. He'd never beheld something as ghastly, as malefic. Each of their bodies, head to tail, appeared to be a suppurating wound, with patches of black fur and bone poking out here and there. Their pointed ears lay flat against their skulls, and the red, crusted flesh around their massive jaws was pulled back in what looked like savage, pitiless leers. Even the draugr warriors appeared terrified of them, for they immediately ceased their attack and stood aside to let the hounds have at the enemy.

Issuing deep, guttural growls, the creatures fanned out and came slowly, heads low, their yellow bloodshot eyes locked on their prey. Jarl made a quick slash with his sword at one—but his blade passed harmlessly through as if the hound were nothing but a reflected image upon water. Dane and his friends were forced back, and soon they could go no farther. Solid rock was behind them, and draugr warriors blocked escape right and left. The faces of the warriors were alight with bloodthirsty anticipation, as if they couldn't wait to witness the slaughter. The hounds paused a few feet away, and Dane saw their haunches tense and he knew the next instant they would spring. In that last instant Dane said a silent prayer that Astrid would find his soul and they would be together once again.

"Call them off!" a voice commanded.

The hounds' ears pricked up. Their growling heads whipped around to see who dared meddle in their blood feast.

Blade over his shoulder, Thidrek came forward with the confident air of a king strolling into his own court.

"If it isn't Lord Thidrek," said the draugr chieftain with scorn. "And how your ranks have grown. Did you think a measly five warriors were enough to seize my ship?"

"They're no warriors of mine. In fact, their deaths would please me to no end."

"Well, then, I'll let my hounds finish them."

The chieftain went to raise his hand to signal his beasts

to attack when Thidrek said, "Please—I'd rather they didn't die now."

The chieftain was losing his patience. "Bah! I'm in no mood for mercy!"

"Neither am I," Thidrek said. "For a quick death here *is* mercy. I have different plans. I am taking your ship and them to Niflheim. Hel has rather ingenious ways to make death anything but merciful."

"Taking *my* ship? This again?" The chieftain gave a sharp laugh. "I'm sure you've brought me signed orders from the goddess?"

"Here are my orders." Thidrek jumped forward, swinging the Blade of Oblivion. And *fzzzt!* The axe caught the chieftain in the left shoulder, slicing diagonally downward, exiting at his right hip. White sparks flew from the wound, and the chieftain had just enough time to register an expression that said, *This can't be good,* before his entire body exploded in white-hot fire. A moment later there was nothing left, just a sprinkling of fine ash that settled to the ground and the echoing, dying shriek of a soul sent packing to the realm of eternal suffering.

So stupefied were the draugr warriors by the abrupt, violent exit of their leader, there were a few whose eyeballs literally popped out of their sockets. A draugrhound, perhaps incensed by his master's demise, ran and leaped at Thidrek. *Fzzzzt!* Thidrek cut off the beast's head in midleap—and an instant later Dane saw its ashes floating to earth. Thidrek glared a warning at the two remaining hounds, and they slouched to the ground in whimpering submission.

Thidrek turned to face the warriors, daring them to raise a hand against him, but they looked so terrified, none of them made a move.

"Your chieftain is now in Hel's realm," said Thidrek. "You may join him or you may join my ranks." Thidrek aimed his gaze at a huge, fearsome-looking brute who carried a massive, double-bladed battle-axe and wore a necklace made of wild boar tusks. "Well?" Thidrek asked him.

"I am Alrick the Most Merciless, m'lord," said the brute. "And speaking for all, we choose to join your command."

"Alrick the *Most* Merciless, eh?"

The warrior pointed to his much shorter cohort. "Not to be confused with the other Alrick. He's Alrick the Least Merciless."

Alrick the Least Merciless hung his head in shame. Thidrek waved a chiding finger at him. "I expect more from you."

"I'll try harder, lord," said the less merciless Alrick.

Alrick the Most Merciless thrust his fist in the air and bellowed. "All hail Lord Thidrek!" His cohorts thrust their fists skyward, chorusing the salute, *"All Hail Lord Thidrek!"*

Thidrek gave his characteristic malevolent grin. "Pleased to have you aboard."

18

BEYOND THE GATES
OF NIFLHEIM

Never had Dane known such exhaustion. Deep
in his bones he felt it, a sharp, stinging, emptiness. The sea spray in his face did little to
refresh his hopes or restore his dreams. The unearthing of
the ship had done them all in—all except for Thidrek, that
is, who stood at the prow of the ship, caressing his blade
as Grelf kneeled beneath him, cleaning the mud from his
boots.

Dane and his cohorts had been forced to dig the Ship
of the Dead from its sandy tomb, working alongside the
reeking draugr warriors. Even Fulnir, who was used to foul
smells, had come close to retching. As the craft had started
to emerge, Dane was astounded by its macabre construction.
The entire hull of the boat from stem to stern had been
formed from an interlocking framework of bones—human

bones—of every size and length, lashed together with strips of animal hide and leathered sinew, and even, in some places, tarred hair. The gunwale, which ran waist high around the whole perimeter of the ship, was formed by row upon row of human skulls all stacked up on top of each other like so many bricks or stones and cemented in place with a kind of mortar he'd never seen before.

After the ship had been dug free of the soil came the backbreaking task of moving it from the cave and into the river. The horses, even the draugrhounds, were harnessed to pull it, but it also took all the combined hands, alive and undead (except Thidrek, who bellowed commands, threatening to kill the first draugr or human who slacked off), to help push it out of the cave. Once in the river the craft had proven strangely watertight, even though there were gaping holes in its hull.

The sail was hoisted, catching the wind, billowing out and snapping the creased material smooth. That was when Dane's mouth went dry—for he saw that the sailcloth was really made of human skin. Several dozen skins, in fact, all tanned and beaten and stitched together to form one giant patchwork sailcloth, as it were. If one looked carefully enough, as Dane unfortunately had done, one could still see fibers of hair and pores and pockmarks and other blemishes on the skin, and scarier still were the remnants of human faces there, each complete with brows, nostrils, and lips, faint but distinct enough to imagine what the person might have looked like when they were alive.

And one of the faces had even spoken to Dane. From its mouth hole—over which was a faint red mustache—it wailed "Ye look upon a floating tomb, as all aboard this ship are doomed!"

Another face near this one—which still had the tracings of a black beard—said, "Oh, don't start with the 'doomed' business. We're out in the fresh sunshine—can't you be happy over *that*?"

The river's current and wind-filled sail had taken the ship downstream and into the sea. Thidrek did not even have to take the wheel; like a homing pigeon the ship seemed to know exactly where it was going.

Now, far from sight of land, Dane sat on deck tied to the mast along with the rest of his weary and despondent friends. His only solace was that William was back with them. When Dane had seen the boy after their capture in the cave, he had noticed the hollow look of terror on the boy's face, and knew that it came from being under Thidrek's rule again. But after he had been reunited with his friends, William's tough spirit had returned. "How bad was it with Thidrek?" Dane whispered to the boy, who was tied to the right of him.

William looked at the prow, where his lordship was berating Grelf for missing a spot of mud on his boots. "You won't believe this," he said, "but Grelf tried to help me. He's not as bad as he thinks he is."

"Not bad?" said Jarl scornfully. "He led us into a trap."

"He didn't *want* to lead us anywhere," Dane reminded him.

"If he were on our side, he'd slip us a knife to cut these ropes." Jarl gave a hard tug on his bonds, trying to free his hands. This motion alerted the draugrhounds. The beasts—stationed as guard dogs nearby—quickly sprang up, growling fiercely.

"Jarl, idea: Don't provoke the hellhounds," whispered Lut.

"Think they fetch?" Jarl whispered. "If I could get one arm free, I could throw a stick overboard."

"They'd probably come back with a whale in their jaws," Fulnir said.

Drott snorted, trying to suppress a giggle. This brought a chorus of more snorts, squeaks, and honks as everyone tried to keep from laughing—which inflamed the snarling hounds all the more. Dane and the others tried to stop, but the harder they tried, the funnier it was.

A shadow fell over Dane. He looked up and saw Thidrek standing between him and the hounds. "What's so amusing?"

"Nothing much," Dane said. "We bothering you?"

"No, no. Laugh away. Get it out of your system. I guarantee frivolity is in short supply where you're heading." Thidrek snapped his fingers and walked off, the growling draugrhounds dutifully following their new master. Being reminded by Thidrek of their destination put an abrupt halt to the Rune Warriors' merriment.

"Ain't he a dead mouse in your ale cup," Jarl groused.

Grelf was terrified. His plans for escape had so far been foiled, and he was panic-stricken that now he would never get the chance. He stood at the prow, shivering from the cold, trying to pretend he wasn't afraid at all. His only chance for escape now was to slip overboard and swim for shore. But he could only do this if they were in sight of land, and so far there was none in view. He casually eyed the horizon, but in the thickening fog it was impossible to see much of anything except the whitecaps of the pitching sea.

"Grelf," said Thidrek, with an air of grandiosity, "we stand on the threshold of a new order. Can you believe it? You will witness one of the greatest moments known to humankind: the forces of darkness let loose upon the world. All of human civilization wiped out in one swift and merciless blow—and the earth put under the dominion of Hel herself. It'll make that Thor's Hammer business look like child's play!"

"Yes, sire, quite exciting indeed."

"Exciting?" said Thidrek, giving Grelf a look. "Is *that* all you can say? I'd say it's a bit more than that. I'd say it's positively thrilling, man!"

"Yes, yes, of course, your lordship," said Grelf, immediately backtracking to save his skin. "I was deliberately understating the importance of it so as not to risk hyperbole, because we all know what a social gaffe it is to overinflate linguistically that which is intrinsically apparent. In other words, 'Never overstate the obvious,' as you yourself taught me, sire, and this is *obviously* so thrillingly exciting it need not be made any more plain than that for fear that I might insult your intelligence." He stopped and held his breath, hoping he had succeeded in convincing Thidrek he was wholly enthusiastic.

A smile split Thidrek's face in half. His skeletal hand came out to pat Grelf on the head. "Ah, Grelf, what would I ever do without you?" he said, his guttural chuckle chilling Grelf to the bone.

Dane watched his pet raven hop about the deck, looking for insects to eat. Disturbingly, Klint had become a favorite of the draugr crew. After the ship had been put in the water and was under way, the bird had suddenly appeared, swooping down and landing on Dane's shoulder. Knowing the place they were bound for, Dane had tried to shoo the bird away. But Klint found he had landed amid a rich insect smorgasbord. Crew members enjoyed holding a maggot or beetle between their fingers and seeing Klint dive down and take it. For some reason Thidrek tolerated the bird's presence. Perhaps it was because he had a sick sense of satisfaction knowing he was taking Odin's favorite feathered animal into the infernal depths of Hel's realm.

Dane then heard his friends bantering about how they were all going to lose their souls and even though Lut had been the leader, it wasn't his fault.

"What exactly *is* a soul, Lut?" asked Drott.

"It's the animating spirit inside us all," said Lut. "The thing that separates us from the fish and fowl, that makes us human."

"Can you *see* someone's soul?" asked Drott.

"You can see it only in the things we do, the thoughts we think, the good deeds we perform. The soul is an essence, a spark. The flame that lights the candle of our life."

"And *everyone* has one?"

"Everyone."

"What about Thidrek?" asked Jarl then. "Does *he* have a soul?"

Lut turned to look at Thidrek at the prow. "I suspect Thidrek lost his soul a long time ago. Sometimes, if someone isn't loved as a child, they grow up unable to love anyone in return, especially themselves. And their craving for the love they never got forms an emptiness inside them, a bottomless hole they try to fill with other things, like an excess of drink or the lust for gold or the glories of war. But such a hole can never be filled, and men like Thidrek end up empty and cold and full of hatred and the worship of death, for it is only in death that they may find the peace they seek. Thus they have no compunction about hurting other people, and anyone who enjoys hurting other people is said to have lost their soul."

This was a lot for Drott and the others to absorb, and for a time they fell quiet.

Then Dane heard Lut say, "I lied about the apple."

Dane looked back to face Lut. "You *did* eat most of it?"

Lut nodded. "I couldn't stop. The surge of strength I felt was too great."

"Anything else you want to come clean on?"

Lut grew thoughtful and Dane sensed he wanted to tell him something important, but then Lut shrugged and said, "I want to hand back leadership to you."

"*Now*? With us headed to Niflheim?" Dane said, not relishing the burden of leadership under such dire conditions. "Thanks for the promotion."

"But it's *my* turn," Jarl said. "You two have had your chance. Time I assumed command."

"Let's vote," Drott said. "All in favor of Dane retaking command, raise hands."

Since everyone's hands were tied behind their backs, Fulnir offered a suggestion, "Or say aye." To which Lut, Drott, and Fulnir said, "Aye."

Jarl glowered. "Great! Fine! Let Dane lead us! I'm sure he has a brilliant plan to save us from Hel's wrath."

"He always has a plan," chirped Drott.

There was silence as they waited for Dane to say something. Truth was, Dane thought they were doomed and nothing could save them. He would never see Astrid again. He would never hold her or kiss her or have a chance to tell her how much he loved her. He would die in Niflheim, and his soul would be trapped in darkness forever.

"What, Dane? Did you say something?" Jarl said. "Speak up and tell us how you're going to get us out of here. You *always* have a plan, Dane. You *never* fail us."

And before Dane could tell them he had no plan whatsoever and was sure their plight was hopeless, a shrieking wind blew up and a storm took them by surprise.

Lut had been in storms before but never one as violent as this. One moment all was calm, and the next the gale struck with sudden fury, the sky blackening, the wind so blinding and relentless, it tore the tops off the waves and threatened to turn over the ship. In a moment of sudden worry his mind went to Klint. The raven would surely be swept away in this terrific storm—but then he saw Dane had the bird cradled next to him inside his shirt. Everyone was still tethered to the mast, so this meant that if the ship succumbed to the storm, they too would go down, tied together.

A sudden blast of wind took a draugr over the side of the ship and into the storm-frothed sea. Thidrek made no move or call to rescue the victim. He looped a rope over his shoulder and around his midsection, securing himself to the mast.

Lut saw the hounds ferociously snarling and snapping at the waves breaching the gunwales, as if the insane creatures thought they could frighten the storm into ceasing. A giant wave washed over the deck, and when it receded, the draugr-hounds were gone. Praise the sea god Aegir!

Above the windy din, Lut heard a chorus of shrieking

cries. Looking up, he saw the faces on the sail, their gaping mouths screaming in panic as if they, too, were terrified of going to their watery doom. "Furl the sail or we'll drown!" the black-bearded one screamed. He was right. With the sail taking the wind, the ship would surely founder. But Thidrek just stood there, a few feet away from them, face turned into the storm, as if he were *waiting* for something to save them.

And the blade in his hand was almost within reach.

Lut tugged furiously on the wet ropes to free his hands. But his strength was ebbing; the apple's magic was wearing off. He had felt the first signs of it while they were in the cave fighting the draugr warriors. How long would it be— days? hours?—before all his youthful vitality was gone? Lut mustered his remaining strength, twisted, and pulled, and his right hand popped free of the bindings!

He *had* to get to the blade. He got up into a crouch. Thidrek was nearly within reach, his back turned; his guard was down. The slash of the rain and the heaving of the ship put Thidrek off balance, moving him closer to Lut. The blade was there, right in front of him! Lut lunged just as another wave slammed into the ship, pitching Thidrek forward. He missed! He was an instant too late, his waning vigor having slowed his reactions.

The cries from the faces on the sail rose in alarm. A wall of water rose high over the mast, and the ship began to spin in place like a top. Higher and higher the water rose all around them, and it was then Lut saw that a gaping hole had opened in the sea beneath them. They were caught in a gigantic vortex, an immense whirlpool that was whipping the ship round in circles, faster and faster, spinning it madly, pulling the Ship of the Dead down, down deeper into the very heart of the sea. Now not only were the faces on the sail screaming in terror, but so were Dane and Jarl and all his friends, as well as the draugrs themselves. All except Thidrek. He was *laughing*, howling with glee, madly euphoric to be heading into the very heart of darkness itself.

And then, as quickly as the storm had blown up, in an instant it was gone.

The roar of the wind ceased and, with a sudden jarring lurch, the ship stopped spinning. Regaining his vision, Dane saw that the ship now rested upon a still, glassy sea enveloped in a thick, bone-chilling fog. The furious whirlpool had been frightening enough—but this sudden, unearthly calm struck a deeper note of dread. Dane felt the freezing tendrils of death and despair reach into his soul—the clawing fingers of dead souls—and he knew the ship had pushed through a membrane from one world to the other. From the uneasy looks on the faces of his friends, he saw they shared his thoughts.

"So this is it?" Drott asked, his voice trembling. "Hel's realm?"

Thidrek gestured grandly into the fog like a lord showing off his estate. "And let me be the first to welcome you!"

"Are we . . . dead?" asked Fulnir.

Everyone did a mental inventory, checking to see if they felt any different.

Drott smelled his armpits. "I don't *smell* dead."

"If smell was an indicator, Fulnir would've been buried three years ago," Jarl said.

Fulnir loudly expelled some gas. "I don't think the dead can pass wind."

Thidrek sighed in annoyance. "So we don't waste *more* time testing dead versus not-dead theories—you are all *still* alive."

"Wait," said the draugr they called Alrick the Most Merciless. "Do you mean us?"

"No!" Thidrek yelled. "This group"—he pointed to Dane, his friends, and Grelf—"not dead." He pointed to the draugrs. "This group—well, you're not dead, either. You're *un*dead. We've come all this way and you didn't *know* that?"

The downcast Alrick, wounded by Thidrek's sarcasm, said, "I just needed some clarity."

Next there came a sound that chilled Dane's blood, a bestial wail eerily echoing through the blinding fog. The ship lurched forward and began gliding across the dead-calm water, the ghastly howl like a beacon calling the ship home.

" 'Tis Garm, the gatekeeper of Niflheim!" wailed the face with the red mustache.

"Must you narrate every moment of our journey?" complained the black-bearded one.

"I'll narrate if I want to," replied Red Mustache. "At least I'm adding aesthetic value to the experience. All you do is make snide remarks."

Black Beard sighed in exasperation. "Of all the mouthy nitwits I had to be stitched to a sail with."

The Ship of the Dead moved onward, and soon a clinking sound was heard, like the dragging of heavy chains. His heart pounding and breath fogging the air, Dane peered into the mist, wondering how much longer he would live. Piercing the pale vapors just ahead, a row of dagger-like spikes appeared, a dozen of them at least, impossibly long and thick and rising upward like the upper jaw of an immense monster that was about to swallow their ship. Jarl and Fulnir uttered an oath. Thidrek, however, said nothing, standing stock-still as they passed under the teeth. Dane expected soon to slide down the beast's gullet—until he looked up and saw that the "teeth" were but long spikes protruding from the bottom of a massive gate, and the gate was rising to let them pass.

"The gates of Niflheim," Red Mustache solemnly intoned.

"Thank you for stating the obvious," said Black Beard.

Once through the gates, Dane next saw the source of the clinking chains, and his heart near stopped. On a ledge alongside the water there stood a monstrous being as tall as the mast of their ship, and with its two massive forearms it was working an ancient chain-and-pulley mechanism that raised the gates with a grinding groan. Slow and lumbering and covered in dark, bristly fur, the thing stood upright on its hind legs. At first glance it appeared to be a giant wolf, but as they drew closer, Dane saw that in fact it was a nightmarish combination of canine and man, its leg joints like those of a wolf and its four-fingered paws more like human hands, although much hairier. Its head had the longish snout of a hound, with yellowed incisors and drool dripping from its half-opened jaws. Turning its head and staring with dull-witted eyes as the ship passed by, the beast gusted steam from its nostrils and unleashed an earsplitting howl that froze Dane to the marrow.

"Garm, gatekeeper of Niflheim," said Black Beard, beating his sail-mate to the explanation. "But I'm sure you already *knew* that."

The ship continued onward through the eerie fog. Dane looked back and saw the beast work the mechanism in reverse to lower the great gate. As the long black spikes descended into the water, Dane had the sick, doomed feeling that there would be no escape from this place.

He and the others were now trapped in Hel's domain forever.

19

A STOLEN
STALLION

Astray thought hit Astrid as she streaked through the night sky on her way to Asgard. It had been only a year since she had walked with Dane in the woods outside their little village and he had given her the Thor's Hammer locket to pledge his love. On that day her life had seemed set. Her destiny, she'd assumed, was to marry Dane and raise a family and forever live in this peaceful village on the bay.

But it was not to be. If only Skuld could write a different future in the book and sweep all of this away. However, the Norns had explained to her that their power did not reach into the unbeating heart of a draugr. The undead were like filth polluting the river of life, changing the destinies of whomever they touched. This, Skuld had explained, was why she had sent Dane to kill Thidrek in the first place.

Her carefully wrought work of conjuring fate was in danger of being rewritten by someone else, which was an author's worst nightmare.

"So it's not that a horde of draugrs may wreak destruction and suffering upon humankind that distresses you," Astrid had said to Skuld. "You're upset because your book faces revisions."

"Exactly," Skuld had said. "And it's up to you to stop such desecration of my creation."

"And *this* is your plan to save the world?" Astrid had said. "I'm to steal Odin's prized steed?"

Skuld gave a dismissive wave of her hand like she was shooing away a fly, and said, "It's not like we're asking you to do the impossible."

So now here she was, a newly christened corpse maiden on her way to the realm of the gods to try and pull off what was likely the most audacious theft of all time. Never mind that the Council of Sisters had already put a death warrant on her head, and if she were caught—the likeliest happenstance—she would be exiled forever to Niflheim's Lake of Fire. Even if she somehow eluded the whole corps of Valkyries bent on capturing her, she *still* had the hopeless task of slipping past the Einherjar, who guarded the animal she was to steal. Invisibility would not help her, since that trick worked only on humans who were *not* dead. Then, if she somehow miraculously escaped with the prize, there was her second and even more foolhardy task—which involved the magical object that now rested inside the canvas satchel slung over her shoulder, the prize Skuld herself had given her.

Astrid broke through the clouds and saw the grove of gold-leafed trees below. Vali started down, accustomed to landing where he always did. But Astrid knew that in the grove she was sure to be seen by her sisters, so she pulled up on the reins, halting Vali's descent, and flew on. She saw Valhalla in the distance, its roof shingled with countless warrior shields that shimmered in the moonlight. The massive mead hall was lit up like a blazing yule tree. Inside, the nightly feasting and drinking would be in full swing. If there was a right time to carry out her desperate plan, Astrid knew this was it.

Horse and rider glided down, alighting on a grassy plain laden with mist. Astrid knew this to be the Fields of Ida, the place where Odin's Einherjar engaged in furious battles every day to keep their warrior skills sharp.

Once or twice Astrid had watched the frenetic battles. Blood would flow and heads and limbs would be lost. When the dinner horn sounded, the warriors would immediately cease combat, find their body parts, and reattach them. Sometimes a combatant would mistakenly reattach a limb that wasn't his, and it would take a while to sort out the severed pieces, but it was all done in good humor. *Pardon me, Svein, but I think you have my left foot affixed to your right leg.* Then they would stride off like brothers for a night of boisterous song, food, and drink. After the nightly festivities, the inebriated heroes would sleep peacefully on their benches strewn with fresh hay. In the morning they would awake, don their coats of mail, strap on their weapons, and march out to the field to go at it again. Fight, eat, and drink. Fight, eat, and drink. Over and over. The heroic dead never seemed to tire of it—and being Vikings who reveled in gore and ale, they had nothing better to do.

She climbed down from Vali's back. "I will miss you, Vali," she said, stroking and hugging his neck. "Time for you to go and for me to go on alone."

He looked at her quizzically, as if he couldn't fathom why his maiden was giving him his leave. Tears welled in her eyes and she kissed the side of his face. "I know, I'll miss you too. . . . You're brave and headstrong and at times cranky . . . but I'll always love you, boy. Now go!" He still refused to move and she had to slap him hard on the rump. With a loud snort he took off in the direction of the Valkyrie stables, which were a long way across the plain and through the woods. She watched his pearly white form disappearing into the misty darkness and felt a pang in her heart, realizing that this was likely the last time she would ever see the willful, courageous beast.

She steeled herself for the task at hand. Through the mist she could see the faint glow of Valhalla far away, high up between two mountain peaks. Odin's precious treasure was housed not up there, but directly below it on the edge of the plain. Using Valhalla's glow to guide her, she set off at a fast clip, running with everything she had. On and on she ran, and it seemed as if she were in a dream, running toward the distant glow but never getting closer to it. The mist thinned; the first light of morning began to show in the east. Astrid started to panic, for soon the first warriors would straggle out for their daily combat. She quickened her pace, knowing she didn't have much time.

All at once there it was, looming in front of her, the length of two longships away, a tall structure made of massive oak logs on the edge of the plain. Astrid spied an Einherjar standing guard outside its main door, and she immediately hit the ground flat, landing on the satchel. The pointy thing inside poked her and she rolled off it into something wet. Lifting her hand, she saw it was coated in blood—and realized she now lay in a pool of drying gore from the prior day's combat. But lying in blood was better than being discovered, so there she remained, motionless, praying she hadn't been seen.

After a moment, she looked again. The guard had vanished. Had the Norns worked some magic to lure him away? No time to puzzle it out. She got to her feet—and just as she began to run, a heavy blow from behind knocked her face-first into the dewy grass. She rolled over to face her enemy and saw the flash of a broadsword whip down. She jerked away just as the tip of the blade buried in the ground an inch from her skull.

"Dirty trick, Thorstein!" said the guard. "Dressing as a maiden to fool me!"

Astrid found her voice. "I—I *am* a maiden."

"Quit with the games, Thorstein. I'd know your voice anywhere."

Astrid made a move and the blade whipped down again, a finger's width from her ear. She froze, deciding not to take any more chances. "Kind and handsome warrior, you are mistaken. I am *Valkyrja*, Chooser of the Slain."

The guard squinted at her through his helmet eyeholes. He removed the helmet to get an unobstructed look at her. He was an ugly brute with beady eyes, a scarred face, and an unruly beard. The typical dim-witted Einherjar who made playful, drunken grabs at her from their ale benches up in Odin's hall. Convinced that the figure before him *was* female—and quite a beauty at that—he now grinned, showing his black teeth. Astrid had always wondered why the chosen dead who were miraculously healed of all the amputations and war wounds received on earth never got dental repair as well. It was like rotten, black teeth were some badge of honor or something.

"So you *are* a maiden!" He offered his hand; she grasped it and was pulled to her feet. "Thorstein and I have a game we play when on guard duty, you see. We each try to sneak up and behead the other. It's good fun."

"Who's winning?" she asked, trying to make conversation.

"Me, of course," he boasted. "I lead nineteen to twelve." The morning sky was brightening. Astrid saw in the distance a few warriors had appeared and were heading down the long path leading from Valhalla to the Fields of Ida. Soon some of her sisters would arrive to watch the combat, and then she'd surely be spotted and captured. "Have you come to watch me in battle, fair maiden?" the guard asked, moving closer to her. "Afterward we shall sup together in Odin's hall."

"Um, yes, yes, that's it," said Astrid, letting his arm wind around her waist. "Your brave deeds! Absolutely, that's what I've come to see. In fact, if you don't mind, I'll give you a kiss for luck." His face lit up, and he stabbed his sword tip first into the ground to hold it there. With both his meaty arms, he drew her into a bearlike embrace. As she kissed his foul mouth, her right hand slipped away and grabbed onto the handle of the sword. She quickly pulled away from his grasp and swung the heavy blade. For a moment he stood there, wearing a stupid, stunned look.

Then his head fell to the ground. It landed faceup, and his blinking eyes found Astrid. "By the gods, that's some kiss," he uttered. The guard's body bent over, blindly groping for his head so he could reattach it, but Astrid snatched it up before he could and, by a hank of his greasy hair, whirled it high into the air. The head landed with a thud in the high grass a good distance away, spewing curses. Still groping around with his hands, the guard's body found his helmet and, mistaking it for its head, placed it on the bleeding stub of its neck. "No, you idiot!" the head bellowed from where it lay in the grass. "I'm over here!" Astrid took off running toward the stables, hoping it would take a while for the guard to put himself together.

Pushing open the main door with some effort and slipping through, Astrid was met by the many familiar stable odors. She had been in stables before, but none like this, for here was housed the most magnificent, magical horse in all creation. A sudden stab of fear seized her. To even *be* here desecrated the sanctity of the gods. She found herself asking Odin for strength, then realized the irony in this since she was here to steal what Odin prized the most, his heavenly steed, Sleipnir. There was *no* god she could beseech for help, which made her feel even more alone and desperate.

She hurried down the wide center aisle of the stable. Hung on the walls on either side were war shields and gleaming weapons of every kind, Odin's personal armory. As the god of war, he liked to keep his fighting skills sharp whenever he found the time. Astrid knew that Odin's most fabled weapon, Gungnir, a spear that never missed its mark, was not kept here; other gods were so covetous of it, the weapon was never far from Odin's grasp.

Rounding a corner, she gaped in awe. She had seen the beast before, but always from a distance. Now, so close up, the sheer size of the animal was shocking to behold. She'd thought Vali was big, but Sleipnir was two, three heads higher, and wider across the chest than an ox. His most impressive attribute, though, was his muscular legs—all *eight* of them—which gave him the speed and power no horse could match.

The gray steed lifted his sleepy head and peered at her imperiously from his stall as if to say, *Who dares awake me so early?* Astrid had no time to speak softly, stroke his mane, or give him a carrot—not that she had one to offer. She had dealt with willful horses before—Vali, for instance—and knew sweet talk wouldn't cut it.

Finding his tack next to his stall, she wasted no time affixing his saddle and bridle. The saddle was incredibly heavy, and it was a strain to throw it across his high, wide back, but on the third try she made it and began buckling the straps. As she bent down, she was terrified he would crush her against the side of the stall—which he quite easily could—but she showed no fear, and this, she realized later, was why Sleipnir let her live.

"You! Maiden!" She looked up. The guard—head now on his shoulders—came quickly toward her up the aisle, brandishing his sword. "That is Odin's sacred steed."

"I'm just taking him for a little ride," Astrid said. Grabbing Sleipnir's mane, she threw herself up and into the saddle. The horse whinnied, his nostrils flared, Astrid kicked his flanks, and Sleipnir shot from his stall. The guard leaped aside as the beast careened toward the stable doors.

Sleipnir burst from the stable with such force, the doors were ripped free and sent cartwheeling into a group of Einherjar who were limbering up for the day's battle. Astrid saw the shocked, bewildered looks of other arriving warriors, who pointed and yelled and grabbed for their weapons. A spear whistled past her head. Sleipnir gave an angry whinny, his instinct to protect his rider kicking in. Like a mad beast, the horse charged into the warriors, knocking some aside, crushing others beneath his hooves. Astrid fought for control, desperately wishing to escape, for a battle now against the many hundreds of Einherjar could not be won.

At last, as if sensing her wishes, Sleipnir turned away and galloped across the plain. Astrid pressed her knees into his sides, and his hooves left the ground and they soared at terrific speed skyward, his eight legs churning the air. Astrid looked down and saw a group of her sisters who had come to the field to watch the day's battle. And gazing up at her in utter stupefaction was none other than Aurora.

20

THE LAKE
OF FIRE

The Ship of the Dead was far past the Niflheim gate, voyaging up a sluggish river that had the consistency of black molasses and the putrid smell of rotten eggs. The fog had thinned enough for the dim outline of another ship to be seen ahead on the starboard side. As they moved closer, the immense size of the craft became apparent. Dane had never seen a ship so vast; it appeared to be the length of ten Viking longships. But this was no warship. Its wide beam showed it to be a merchant craft, a knorr, designed to ferry cargo.

"A fresh shipment for the goddess Hel," murmured Thidrek.

The knorr was docked at the river's edge, and as they floated past, Dane saw that along the gunwales were carved grotesque figures of grinning, laughing demons. And then he saw exactly *what* cargo the ship had brought. A long procession of grim souls—men, women, and even some children—was trudging wordlessly down the gangplank onto the rocky shore and continuing along the river's edge in the same direction the Ship of the Dead was heading. The faces of these souls were as gray and lifeless as a leaden winter sky, and even their clothes were devoid of color.

"There are so many," Dane said, marveling at the shuffling tide.

"Wars, disease, starvation—the gods harvest us all," Lut said.

"And the fortunate few see Valhalla," Jarl said bitterly. "That was to be *my* fate, but then Dane had to go hand over the Blade of Oblivion to Thidrek—and here we are."

Being in Hel's realm was bad enough, thought Dane, but being stuck here with Jarl and his ceaseless blaming was even worse. "How many times should I apologize for what's happened, Jarl?"

"How many times?"

"Give me a round figure so I'll know when you'll be satisfied."

"Well, let's see . . . we'll be in Niflheim forever," Jarl said, "so how about you apologize every day for the rest of eternity. Just for a start."

"Sure that'll be enough?" Dane asked.

"While we're here you can also do my laundry."

"Look!" cried Drott, pointing to one of the souls walking

along the shore. "Isn't that Horvik the Virtuous? From our village?"

"You're right," said Fulnir in surprise. He cupped hands to his mouth and called out, "Horvik the Virtuous! What are *you* doing here?"

Horvik peered back, equally astonished to see his village brethren in Hel's domain. "What am *I* doing here? What are *you* doing here? And why do you get to ride on a ship when I have to walk? My feet are killing me."

"I guess that answers the question about the dead feeling pain," Drott said to his shipmates.

Fulnir gave Horvik the short version of their plight: that they weren't really dead, at least not yet, and then Horvik explained why he was there. "I cheated Anders Thorgillsson at dice and he killed me with an axe." Horvik pointed to the deep wound in his skull where the weapon had been buried.

"You cheated at dice?" Fulnir asked. "For *that* you're sent to Niflheim?"

"I . . . also stole a cask of smoked herring from him," Horvik said. "And, well, his wife and I—"

"We get the picture," said Fulnir. "But I shouldn't think those errant ways would warrant an eternity in Hel's domain."

"That's the problem with having a name like mine," Horvik the Virtuous moaned. "If you're not virtuous every day, *all* day, they really stick it to you in the end."

"Sorry to hear it," Drott said, "but nice seeing you

anyway. You don't look too bad for being dead," he added, trying to brighten Horvik's spirits.

"Kind of you to say," said Horvik, "I think."

The ship continued up the black, sulfurous waterway, leaving the grim tide of newly arriving dead behind. Here and there Dane began to see small spots of fire floating on the river's surface, and soon the spots grew alarmingly larger in size, as big across as the length of the ship. This reminded him of the house-size icebergs that had harassed them on their last adventure, ice floes the whalers had called "growlers" for the sounds they made when they were crunched together by the wind and the tides.

The Ship of the Dead made no effort to avoid these patches of floating fire, cutting right through them, and Dane shared looks of concern with the others, worried the ship's hull would burn and they'd all sink into the ooze.

"Fear not, my fellows," said Thidrek, grinning madly, "where we go is infinitely worse."

And they were soon to see he spoke the truth, for ahead lay the underworld's vast Lake of Fire.

As far as the eye could see in any direction, its vast surface was aglow with a bubbling stew of molten rock and flame, colored in the deepest oranges and reds and spitting up bursts of steam, the whole of it not unlike the embers of an immense campfire. Worse, the Lake gave off a stench of sulfur mixed with the nauseating smell of burning flesh. Burning human flesh, Dane was sickened to realize.

The Ship of the Dead plowed forward through the liquid rock, magically impervious to the torridity and eruptions of flames.

Dane thought he heard a whisper or a cry of some kind, coming straight from the fire below. Ghostly figures of the dead bobbed to the surface, engulfed in flames, their spindly arms reaching up, their mouths open in agonized screams. The figures rose to the surface, then just as suddenly were sucked under again, as if they were being pulled to the depths by the claws of an unseen demon.

"My parents always said I'd wind up here if I wasn't good," Drott said between the hiccups he always got when he was afraid. "I never thought this place was real."

"N-n-neither did I," Fulnir said, his voice quaking. "I thought m-m-my folks were just making stuff up to keep me in line."

Thidrek—clutching the handle of the Blade of Oblivion and standing coolly at the prow as if his dead draugr heart insulated him from the searing heat—gave a chuckle. "Parents are like that, aren't they? My father, Mirvik the Mild, filled my head with similar nonsense. He'd say, 'Thidrek, if you insist on being unduly cruel to others, one day you will find yourself doing the breast stroke in a fiery lake.' Funny, isn't it? How wrong fathers can be about their children's destinies, eh, lad?" he said, looking at Drott.

"Uh, are you sure he was wrong about yours, my lord?" Drott was bold enough to ask.

"As sure as I know *your* father was right about *yours*," Thidrek said with a sublime look. "For all too soon you will be drowning in the molten depths."

"My lord," said Alrick the Most Merciless, "you said *all.* Does that mean we're to be—"

"No! Not *you*!" Thidrek barked in exasperation. "*This* group? Tied to the mast? Our *prisoners* will be swimming in the molten depths! By the gods, why must I keep explaining myself? Is your brain full of maggots?"

"Um . . . yes." Alrick shrugged.

Thidrek sighed in exasperation, turned to Grelf, and was heard to mutter, "Whose idea was it to recruit these dunderheads?"

Grelf had the good sense not to answer.

As the ship continued across the Lake of Fire, a pall of woe descended upon Dane and his friends. They had been in awful fixes before, but nothing like this, nothing so seemingly insurmountable. They all had faced death numerous times. But this was far, far worse, for death was merely a prelude to an eternity of torment.

Dane remembered a time a few short months before when he was held captive with his mother on another ship, commanded by the evil Godrek Whitecloak. They were doomed to die, but his mother had looked into his eyes with steadfast determination and had said, "I will not go like a lamb to slaughter." Her tenacity had helped stiffen his backbone and spurred him to act.

But what could he do now?

Even if they got free from the ropes, they had no weapons against the armed draugrs or the Blade of Oblivion in Thidrek's hands. And they couldn't exactly jump overboard into a fiery lake and swim for shore. Even if they did miraculously make it to shore, they were *still* in Hel's realm, which was guarded by a bestial monster who Dane suspected would not open the gate, wish them luck, and hand them free sandwiches.

"Which souls are sent to the Lake of Fire?" William asked Lut. "Will Horvik be thrown in?"

"I believe the lake is reserved only for those whose crimes were the most heinous on earth," Lut said.

"You mean someone like Thidrek."

"He would fit the profile," Lut said.

"If I may interject," said Red Mustache on the sail, "it is the goddess Hel who decides the punishment for each soul. I believe the minor crimes of said Horvik would spare him from such fiery agony."

"So then maybe she will spare us," William said.

Having overheard this, Thidrek roared with laughter. "*Spare* you? Do you think I've brought you here for Hel's mercy? You'll find none of that! Your souls are the kind she's *most* hungry for."

And with that, the towering black parapets of a fortress hewn from solid rock loomed before them. There were murmurs of awe from the draugrmen and stunned silence from everyone else as the ship drew ever nearer the dark, menacing palace. Even Dane's raven, Klint, reacted in fear, flapping his wings and squawking fiercely about the deck, until Lut took him in his arms and comforted him.

Dane looked hard at Lut, at the bits of gray he saw now streaking his hair and the tiny lines returning to his face. He wanted to tell him that he knew what was happening, that he had sensed it during the storm, could see a weakening of his energies. But he said nothing, for he knew that it was Lut's wisdom he prized most of all. It had gotten them through rough times before, and he was hoping it would once again.

Astrid had done as the Norns had ordered. She had slipped into Asgard, stolen Sleipnir, and made her miraculous getaway down the Bifrost rainbow to the earthly plane. Unfortunately, she had been seen by Aurora, which meant her traitorous sister most likely had deduced where she was heading—because no one would be mad enough to take Odin's prized eight-legged steed unless they desperately needed to get to one place and one place only.

Hel's underworld.

Sleipnir had once taken Odin's son to the underworld on a special mission. The steed knew the way in and out, so Skuld had instructed Astrid that all she needed do was command Sleipnir to take her there and the horse would do the rest. Once there she was to deliver the item in the canvas satchel to Hel and hope it would do the trick.

They had ridden all day and on into the night, Astrid feeling more alive than ever, despite the fear that raced through her. The land had given way to the shining surface of the sea, and still they rode on until the sun returned. And then, quite abruptly, the steed drew to a sudden halt. Below her was nothing but calm seas, and she thought that perhaps Sleipnir had stopped for a much-needed spell of rest.

Then, in the very blink of an eye, a dark cloud appeared on the horizon. A shrieking wind blew in. An angry tempest had them in its sudden grip, the sky around them bursting with lightning and booming with thunder. Surrounded as she was by the fury of it all, Astrid's only thought was that this had to be the work of the gods, a warning to return Sleipnir at once or suffer even more dire consequences.

But just as suddenly the steed bolted downward toward the raging waves. Panicked, she pulled back on the reins but was powerless to stop his steep dive. Down, down, he flew, determined to plunge headfirst into the water, and she shut her eyes and clung to his back as tightly as she could, hoping the force of the impact would not knock her free.

But she felt no splash at all. Opening her eyes, she saw she was enveloped in water yet wasn't the tiniest bit wet. Everything began to spin, and she realized that she and Sleipnir were caught in a gigantic swirling funnel of water. Round and round they went, furiously fast, sucked ever downward, deeper and deeper into darkness until—

Just as suddenly she and her steed burst through a wall of wind into a world of thick fog. She found they were hovering above the calmest of seas and enveloped by a dense white vapor so icy cold that it froze the hairs on her skin. She sat there a moment atop Sleipnir, getting her bearings, each of her exhaled breaths turning to frosted ice particles as it hit the air. So this was it, she thought. The Land of the Dead. She patted the steed's brawny neck for bringing her. "Thank you, mighty Sleipnir." He turned his head and gave her an imperious look as if to say, *Foolish maiden, how could you have doubted me?*

Somewhere off in the fog Astrid heard the sound of a ship cutting across the water. They set off to follow it through the Niflheim gate.

The Ship of the Dead came to rest on the shore of the Lake of Fire at the base of ancient stone steps cut into the rock. The steps zigzagged precariously up the sheer granite face to the pinnacle upon which Hel's dark fortress sat. Even from his vantage point far below, Dane saw that along the outer perimeter of the fortress there looked to be hordes of the doomed perched on scaffolding, laboring to repair walls that had fallen down. Driving them on were large brutes cracking whips over their backs.

Drott craned his neck, gazing up at the crumbling fortress. "This is where Hel lives? What happened to the place?"

"Those spared from the Lake of Fire are put to work on Hel's fortress," said Red Mustache. "But doomed souls are notoriously poor workmen. Every time they repair a wall, it just falls down again."

"Maybe Hel should try paying them better," Drott suggested.

"Paying them *better*?" Jarl said. "What part of eternal

suffering don't you get?"

"I'm just saying a happy worker is a better worker," Drott argued. "Whether you're alive or not, human nature is all the same."

"If that's true," Jarl quipped, "when you're dead you'll be just as brainless."

Drott opened his mouth to protest but had no retort.

"Judgment time is nigh," Thidrek announced, gesturing to the fortress. "The goddess Hel awaits."

Dane took Klint on his arm and stroked his feathers. "Stay, Klinty. Where I go is no place for you." The raven gave a complaining squawk, flew up, and landed on the top of the mast. As Dane was herded off the ship, he turned back to take a last look at his faithful friend. Klint was gone.

It was an arduous journey up the cliff. At several places the steps had crumbled away, exposing gaps that plunged to the rocks far below. One by one Dane and his friends jumped these yawning spaces. The last to jump was a draugrman, Alrick the Least Merciless. He easily bridged the gap, but the step he landed on broke away and he fell, screaming his Berserker cry. His body shattered upon the rocks below like a piece of crockery and his skull caromed off a boulder out over the fiery lake. He landed faceup, and his horrible shriek of pain was awful to hear.

Thidrek watched his head sink below the scalding muck and, with a wry grin, said, "Serves him right for being *least* merciless."

The remaining draugr herded Dane and the others up

the steps, and finally they reached the summit. Before them lay a fortress of such massive size that Dane felt puny and powerless standing before it. He realized that this must be its intended effect: to make all newcomers quiver in terror at their first sight of Hel's lair. Its very size was an expression of her ultimate power in the underworld, just as Odin's equally vast Valhalla was a symbol of his rule in Asgard above.

But, oh, what a difference between the two. While Odin's palace was magnificent to behold, Dane was struck by how grotesquely ugly Hel's was. By design or by accident, all its angles seemed crazily askew, and even its soaring towers leaned haphazardly this way and that, appearing as if at any moment they might topple. And, stranger still, dotting the structure were crude, crumbling statues of misshapen demons that assaulted the eye.

"In a way you were right about human nature, Drott," Dane said.

"I was? *Really?*" Drott said, always eager to know when he had inadvertently said something intelligent. "How?"

Dane gestured to the monstrous structure. "This is what happens when the only reward is fear and punishment."

With a thunderous crash, a section of an outer wall then collapsed, sending the scaffolding and the doomed workmen down with it. The brutish overseers waded in, lashing the poor souls with their whips. Dane saw that instead of leather, the whips consisted of white-hot sizzling bolts of lightning that grooved deep burns across the backs of the laborers. Having to watch such pain inflicted on the defense-less, Dane had a sudden urge to rush one of the huge brutes, but Lut, sensing his rash intentions, grabbed his arm to stop him.

"Don't be a fool, son," Lut whispered to him.

Upon Thidrek's orders, the draugrs prodded them toward the fortress gates. Passing an overseer lashing some poor souls, Jarl whispered to Drott, "Why don't you explain your happy worker–better worker stuff to *him*."

Unaware that Jarl was joking, Drott paused for a moment, tapping the brute on the shoulder. "Uh, sir, if I may have a word—"

The brute whirled. He had the face not of a man, but of something of a more bestial nature, with protruding snout and tusks. He gave a furious roar and lashed out with his lightning whip, missing Drott by a hair. "M-maybe now is not a good time," Drott bleated, backing away. A draugr shoved him forward to rejoin his friends. "Some people just don't want to listen," Drott said, shaking his head.

Turning now to Hel's lair, Dane saw that the entranceway was formed by the face of a hideous three-eyed demon, its mouth open wide to accept them. One by one they began to enter, the funereal silence broken only when Jarl asked Thidrek what the name of this creature was.

"Hyrrmund the Firebreather," said Thidrek. "Demon of the Underworld, one of Hel's minions. Up there, those are the Ice Demons whose touch will freeze your soul. Oh, and over there, just above that scaffolding, those are the Sleep Demons, the creatures that visit you in nightmares."

Then Fulnir leaned over to Dane and muttered, "Don't you find the whole demon theme tiresome? I mean, she's Hel, queen of the underworld. She couldn't have dreamed up a better design scheme than this demon thing?"

Once inside the fortress walls, in the dim light Dane could see they were met by a vast moat. A narrow bridge spanned the moat, leading straight across to the soaring, colossal structure of Hel's hall, the entrance to her inner sanctum. Also, there were four of the demon guards patrolling the moat bridge, each with his own lightning whip.

There was an understandably uncomfortable moment as Dane and his friends stood still. No one—not even the draugrs—wanted to move across the bridge. But all Thidrek did was clear his throat—*ahem!*—and the mere sound of it held such menace that everyone instantly sprang to life and began to follow him one by one across the narrow walkway. Dane kept his eyes on Fulnir, who was walking directly in front of him, not wanting to risk a look at the demon brutes. But soon he began to hear a chorus of voices, whispers that seemed to be emanating from somewhere below. *Who is that? . . . Are they alive? . . . What are they doing here? . . .*

Peering over the side of the bridge, he saw that standing shoulder to shoulder in the moat were thousands upon thousands of doomed souls, tightly packed like a herd of swine on their way to market, their faces gray and eyes empty of light. It made him sick to see them, and then one of the doomed ones called out, "We wait eons for an audience! How can they jump ahead in line?"

In a flash the two nearest demon guards began raining lash upon merciless lash down onto the complaining soul and those around him in the pit below—and the shrieks of pain, the sizzling sound the lightning whips made upon the doomed, once more filled Dane with disgust and anger. Again came the words of his mother: *I will not go like a lamb to slaughter.* Drawing ever nearer the sanctum door, he vowed that neither would he; if Hel was to take his soul, she would have to fight him tooth and nail for it.

That steadfast bravado lasted for only a moment, for as they approached entrance to Hel's hall, the massive doors slowly creaked open and an oppressive wave of heavy, sickly sweet air swept over him. All thoughts of defiance fled, replaced with a debilitating fear that almost buckled his knees. He grabbed Lut's shoulder to steady himself, and Lut tried to return a stiff-lipped nod of courage, but all Dane saw was similar terror in his eyes.

His belly roiling with panic, Dane wanted to turn tail and run, but the draugrmen's spear points prodded him on. Glancing back, he saw that the warriors also wore rabbity looks. *They were afraid, too!* And for good reason. They were all about to come face-to-face with a being who engendered such horrific dread that even the brave gods of Asgard feared and loathed her. Dane tried to steady himself and prayed he wouldn't die from fright before he even laid eyes on her.

21

THE GODDESS OF THE UNDERWORLD

O nce inside the doors to Hel's hall, they were enveloped in darkness. Behind him Dane heard the doors close with a thunderous *clang*, and from its resounding echo he concluded that they must be in a chamber of vast size. Afraid to move and fearing what the next moments would bring, Dane stood listening to the frightened breathing of his friends. And then a sound most chilling came . . . a sibilant hiss and slither, followed by a throaty female voice from some distance away. "Have you . . . brought it?"

"I have, your highness," he heard Thidrek say with pride. "*That*, and more gifts for your amusement."

"My *amusement*?" the female voice purred mockingly. "I am not so easily amused. Approach!"

Dane felt a spearpoint jab his back, and everyone began

moving forward as ordered. Soon his eyes adjusted to the dark enough for him to discern dim shapes. Gigantic columns, as big around as ten men standing fingertip to fingertip, rose from the floor, disappearing into the gloom above. The surfaces of the columns seemed to writhe as if alive—and when Dane passed close to one, he saw it was covered with a wickerwork of winding, slithering vipers that hissed at him and the others. This, he realized, was the strange sound he had heard in the dark.

In the distance was a dim pool of firelight. Approaching it, Dane saw what appeared to be four or five females wearing the colorless garb of the dead. They were attending to an entity seated on a colossal black throne, someone—or some*thing*—whose face and body were blocked from view by the attendants.

Thidrek stopped everyone a respectful distance from the raised throne and waited for the attendants to finish. To Dane they resembled frightened handmaidens hurrying to prepare a royal personage to receive guests.

"Enough! Give me the mirror!" barked the unseen one on the throne.

The attendants stepped back, revealing such a ghastly sight that gasps of shock issued from humans and draugrs alike—except for Thidrek, who oozed fawning charm. "Your majesty, you grow more . . . lovely with each passing day."

Dane could think of many words to describe the goddess Hel, but *lovely* was not one of them. Her hatchet-thin, hollow-cheeked face was pebbled with snakelike scales. Her eyes were deep set and beady, her nose but two thin slits, and below that was a cruel slash of a mouth. Her hands resembled hooked, reptilian claws; in one she clutched a long, ornate wooden staff topped with a milky-white crystal orb. A tattered black gown covered her desiccated body.

"The mirror!" she rasped, banging the end of her staff upon the dank floor. An attendant produced a polished silver hand mirror. Hel grabbed it, gazed at her reflection for a moment, then exploded in anger. "This is *not* what I wanted! Is my hair full and wavy?" She grabbed her lank, greasy hair. "It is not! Are my cheeks rosy and full? No!" Like a petulant, spoiled child she threw the mirror at them. "I bring you into the comfort of my hall—and *this* is how you repay my kindness?" She raised her staff as if to strike them, and they cowered like terrified dogs. "Away with you! Prepare my bath!" she commanded.

"Yes, your majesty," an attendant said. She turned to scurry off with the others when her eyes met Dane's. It was Mist the Valkyrie! Recognizing him, she froze in shock for a moment. Dane wanted to call out to her, but she gave a curt shake of her head to stop him, then swiftly fled.

"It was Mist," Dane whispered to Lut beside him.

"I know," Lut whispered back. "Poor thing, to be enslaved here."

To see Mist like this, drained of life and happiness, was heart wrenching. Dane owed his life to her. Twice he had been near death on earth and she had been assigned to pluck his soul from his body and take him to Valhalla. But each time she had disobeyed orders and had even helped him survive. The second time, he had been trapped in an ice crevasse and she had said crossly to him, "I should let you freeze to death and finally be done with you!"

But instead she had shown pity, keeping him awake long enough to be rescued by his friends. Later, he wondered why she had shown such mercy. Did she love him, or was there another reason? Perhaps she could not bear to part him from Astrid, the one *he* loved. But none of it mattered now. Mist was a doomed soul. And mostly likely Dane would soon be joining her, a permanent resident in Hel's realm.

"Why must I endure such incompetence?" Hel fumed. "I'm sure you'd not find such clumsy servants in Asgard. No! If my father, Odin, desires a new coat of armor or another temple built in his honor, all he need do is snap his fingers and it is cheerfully done!"

"It doesn't seem fair that he revels in opulence and you're forced to make do with so little," Thidrek commiserated.

"He ordered me to run the underworld but never *once* mentioned the poor quality of labor down here. Not once!"

"It's a miracle you manage so well, your majesty. I can't imagine any other goddess doing a better job handling the doomed."

"And they never stop coming!" she wailed. "Shipload after shipload. And I must find room for them—as if we weren't cramped for space already!"

"But your majesty," Thidrek said playfully, "aren't you forgetting you'll soon be moving to *much* bigger quarters? Say, the entire land of the living?"

A gluttonous gleam shone in Hel's beady eyes. Her forked tongue flicked over her lips. Dane took it this was how Hel looked when she was pleased. "We'll see how father Odin likes *that*," she hissed.

"Don't imagine he will," Thidrek said. He gestured to the prisoners. "Nor will he like that you've stolen souls meant for Valhalla. My gift to you, to do with as you wish."

She stared at Dane and the others like a snake appraising her next meal. "They are pure of soul, you say?"

"Oh, the purest," Thidrek said with distaste. He grabbed Dane by the arm and jerked him front and center. "Take this one, for instance. Dane the Defiant. Always doing brave and unselfish acts, saving fair maidens, righting wrongs, protecting the weak. It's enough to make a man gag." Thidrek gestured at the other prisoners. "They're all like that more or less. Even this little pip." Thidrek grabbed William by the arm and flung him to the floor in front of the throne. "They call themselves Rune Warriors. And do they fight for plunder or land or power? No! They're all courageous and forthright, the idiots. Perfect candidates for Odin's corpse hall."

Hel clapped her clawlike hands together in girlish glee. It made a dry, raspy sound like dead leaves rubbing together.

"Stealing souls destined for Valhalla! My father will have a fit!" she cackled. "Oh, this is too, too delicious!"

"I knew you would be pleased, your majesty," Thidrek said, clearly glad that he had made the odious hag so happy.

So this was the reason they had been brought to Niflheim, Dane realized. Hel was warring with Odin, and the Rune Warriors were but pawns in the game, a way Hel could have revenge against a father who had exiled her to the underworld. It was as Jarl had said: Dane had led his friends to their eternal doom. But he could not stand there idly while the sentence was passed.

"He lies, your majesty!" Dane blurted.

Thidrek whirled, backhanding Dane to the face. "Silence, dog!"

Dane held his ground, appealing to the goddess. "You will not spite Odin by taking cowards!"

Thidrek raised the Blade of Oblivion to strike Dane down, but Hel shouted, "Stop!" Thidrek froze, the blade inches from Dane's head.

"I am the only one destined for Odin's hall," Dane declared. "Take me, but release the others. For they are nothing but cowards, truly chickenhearted and yellowbellied."

"*Chicken*hearted? I'm ten times braver than you!" insisted Jarl, unable to stand having his mettle questioned, even though Dane was doing it to save his life.

"They both lie," Lut said, stepping forward. "Without me they all would've run crying to their mothers. I'm the only one fit for Valhalla!"

Now Fulnir and Drott chimed in, insisting they were the only courageous ones in the bunch. Then William declared his heroism second to none and that everyone else should be released because they were about as courageous as a kitten in a thunderstorm. Everyone talked at once and some pushing and shoving broke out, until Hel angrily banged her staff on the floor, silencing them all.

"I want the truth! Each says he is brave and the others are cowards—all except you," she said, pointing the end of her staff at Grelf. "Are you the only one of courage here too?"

"Oh, no, your majesty," Grelf insisted. "I'm a coward for sure. Pigeon-livered through and through."

"He is merely my lackey, your highness," Thidrek said.

"And by his admission of cowardice, I sense he speaks the truth," Hel said. "But what of these others?" she asked Grelf, gesturing to Dane and his friends. "Are they all Rune Warriors fit for Odin's hall as your master has said?"

Dane expected Grelf to quickly parrot what Thidrek wanted him to say, dooming them all. But to his surprise, Grelf hesitated. For a moment he held Dane's look, and Dane saw a brief flicker of compassion in his eyes, an emotion he had thought Grelf incapable of feeling. "They are all fit, your majesty," Grelf finally said. "Except for the boy."

"No," William protested, jumping to his feet. "I'm a Rune Warrior, too! Tell her, Dane!"

Grelf gave Dane a slight nod, which acknowledged that

the best he could do was save the boy—and that he would do all he could to take care of him. "A ten-year-old boy is not worthy of Valhalla," Dane said to Hel. "He lacks courage and is no prize." It pained him to say these words and see the look of hurt in William's eyes. The boy had been a true Rune Warrior, as brave as anyone, but if Dane could save his life by telling a lie, it was a small price to pay.

Thidrek sighed in annoyance. "I don't *care*, your highness. If you don't want him, I'll take him as my thrall."

"He is yours," Hel said with a wave of a claw. "But the others I'll gladly keep."

"For torture and death and everlasting agony in the Lake of Fire?" Thidrek asked cheerfully.

"All of the above," Hel said. Banging her staff on the floor, she called for her guards. Two demons bearing lightning whips appeared from out of the darkness. "Take these live ones to the moat," she ordered. "I'll dally with them later."

"Aren't you forgetting one thing, your highness?" Thidrek interjected as the guards started to take the prisoners away. "My reward for bringing the Ship of the Dead?"

"You mean my promise to make you alive once more," Hel said.

"Precisely," said Thidrek. "And how is that done?"

Lut had read of his earthly fate in the Norns' Book of Fate. But he was not on earth now—he was in a different realm

243

where Skuld had no power to mold fate. So everything he had read was now null and void.

As Hel approached them—gliding as if her feet, unseen beneath her black robe, did not touch the ground—Lut sensed that one of them was about to die.

The goddess stopped before them and handed her staff to Thidrek. "To restore your life, you must subtract it from the living," she said. "Touch the crystal orb to the heart of the one whose years you wish to take."

Thidrek grinned in anticipation. "And the one I touch will die?"

"You will take his remaining years of life," said Hel.

Thidrek perused the faces of the prisoners. "Now let's see . . . who is the likely prospect? Someone brave and strong and bursting with heart. This one?" He playfully made a feint with the staff at Jarl, who jumped back from its reach. "Close, but not my choice. This one?" He jabbed the orb toward Drott, who recoiled. "No, too chubby for my tastes." His eyes settled on Dane standing next to Lut. "Now, *here's* the ideal candidate. And isn't it ironic? A day not so long ago, on a hill outside your village . . . you thought you had seen the end of me. You took my years and now I take yours. How does it feel, knowing you'll be within me? When I go to your village and kill every living soul . . . when I plunge my sword into your *own* mother, it will be your own strength flowing within these hands."

Dane stared back at him. "If I am to be within you, Lord Thidrek, those hands will cut your own throat first."

"Defiant to the last, eh?" Thidrek moved to touch the orb to Dane's chest—when Lut grabbed the end of the staff and jammed it into his own. A rush of scalding-hot pain shot through him, knocking him to the floor. The room spun; he saw the blurred faces of his friends crying out, but their voices were fuzzy and distant. It felt like an animal had clawed open his chest and had his heart in its jaws. *By all the gods in Asgard, make the pain stop!*

Dane girded himself for the touch of the orb. How would it feel to have his life siphoned away? Would it be painful? At the last instant he closed his eyes, hoping it would be over quickly. There was a sharp cry of pain and his eyes snapped open. He saw Lut staggering backward, grabbing at his chest. What had he done? Lut crumpled to the floor, gasping, his body shaking uncontrollably. His rosy skin faded and wrinkled, his hair turned gray, and his tall, muscular frame withered and shrank. All the youth and strength that he had so treasured drained away. And then, abruptly, he stopped shaking and lay silent and lifeless, older and more enfeebled than ever before.

"Lut!" Dane knelt and put his ear to the old one's chest but heard nothing. A gasp escaped Lut's mouth. Dane listened again and heard a faint heartbeat.

"Why did he do that?" Hel asked, sounding genuinely baffled. "Sacrifice himself for you? Does he not cherish his own youth?"

Dane looked down at Lut's ancient face. "He is a Rune

245

Warrior" was all he could think to say.

"Ah. Idiotically courageous and forthright."

"He is, your highness," Dane said.

Hel shrugged as if such human qualities were beyond her understanding. "Take them away," she ordered.

"Wait!" Thidrek ordered. Dane turned and saw that Thidrek had retrieved the hand mirror from the floor and was admiring his restored flesh. He touched and poked his face. What had been rotting, green, and crawling with maggots moments before was now sound and whole. "I wanted *his* years," Thidrek said, pointing at Dane.

"Has not my promise been fulfilled?" Hel said with irritation.

"Yes, it's very good, excellent work, your majesty," Thidrek said, checking out his full set of gleaming white teeth that had been rotted, black stumps before. "But he took my life and I demand his in return."

Hel leveled her reptilian glare upon him. "You . . . *demand*? If I am mistaken, by all means correct me, but I thought a human could not *do* that to a goddess." Her tone was brittle and deadly. Thidrek's swagger vanished, replaced with a grovel worthy of Grelf's best.

"Yes, yes, yes, of course you are correct, your majesty," he mewled. "Quite correctly correct, I beg your forgiveness. I will *never* use the, uh, d-word in your presence again."

22

THE CURIOSITY
OF THE DEAD

Riding atop Sleipnir, Astrid followed the ship past the Niflheim gate, keeping low to the fog-shrouded water to remain unseen. Once through the gate, she and her steed soared high over the ship. Looking down, she saw the decks were crammed with a gray mass of people standing still as statues. But these weren't people—at least not the living kind, she realized. They were the souls of the doomed being ferried to Hel's realm. She kicked Sleipnir's flanks and they flew on, following the waterway until they came to Hel's fortress on the banks of the Lake of Fire.

Poised high in the gloom over the enormous, deformed structure, she saw a shallow ravine behind the fortress that afforded cover. She set down Sleipnir, dismounted, and stepped into the black, sulfurous ooze. "Welcome to the underworld," she said to herself.

"Astrid!"

She saw the dim outline of someone approaching up the ravine through the fog. Astrid thought of leaping back upon Sleipnir and escaping, but the gray figure hurried quickly forward, emerging from the gloom, carrying a bucket. Mist! They both burst into tears and fell into each other's arms. It was a strange sensation, for embracing and being embraced by a soul felt like the caress of the wind.

"I was out gathering mud and saw a white flash streak by above. I prayed it was you," Mist said between sobs.

"Mist, I'm so sorry!" Astrid choked out. "It's because of me you're here."

"No, Aurora's to blame. She's in league with Hel. But I'll get my revenge on that little traitor if it's the last thing I do." Realizing the unintended humor of her words, she gave a bitter laugh. "But I'm *already* doing the last thing I'll ever do," she said, nodding at the bucket that was filled with the odorous mud. "Serving as Hel's handmaiden."

"What's the mud for?" Astrid had to ask.

"Her bath. She simmers in hot, stinking muck as if it will soften her scaly hide. She commands that we make her beautiful. But that's like putting sweet cream on a cow pie. No matter what we do, she's still a big steaming pile of—"

Sleipnir gave a snort as he nosed at the mud he was hoof deep in.

"Odin lent you Sleipnir, so you must be on a special mission."

"He didn't exactly lend him to me. I . . . stole him."

Mist's jaw dropped. "Stole him? You stole *the* most power-ful god's favorite horse? That's insane!"

"I don't disagree, but I had no choice. I had to get here, and he knew the way."

"You've come to rescue Dane and your friends?"

"You've seen them?" Astrid said. "They're alive?"

Mist told her that Thidrek had brought them on his ship and had given them as a gift to Hel. "She especially prizes those who are pure of soul, the kind who fill Odin's Valhalla. She put them in the Moat of Souls."

"Where's that?"

"Inside the fortress walls. It's where the doomed are placed until Hel decides what to do with them."

"Is it guarded?"

Mist nodded grimly. "Even if you get them out of the fortress, once they escape, Hel will order the Niflheim gate closed. And there's no other way out."

"Then we must distract Hel so she won't care if they steal Thidrek's ship and escape." Astrid reached into the canvas satchel and brought out the item Skuld had given her. It was a shining crown of simple design, made of bronze. "You say Hel desires to be beautiful. This will make her *believe* she is. And when she is under its spell, she will think of nothing else."

A dubious Mist took the crown, examining it. "Maybe I haven't clearly described the goddess. Or, as we call her behind her back, Her Grotesqueness."

"It won't *change* her looks," Astrid said, "but merely deceive her into believing she's beautiful. Can you get me an audience with her?"

"An audience? You *are* insane. How would you explain your entrance to the underworld?"

Astrid hadn't considered that. She thought for a long moment. "I'll say I'm an emissary from Odin with a gift of peace."

"That flimsy crown? Hel would take that 'gift' as an insult and throw *you* in the moat. No, the whole thing is impossible. You should leave now before you're discovered."

"I can't, Mist."

"But you must! Or you'll be like me, trapped here forever."

Astrid had to tell her the bigger reason why she had come. "There's more at stake than Dane and my friends. The Norns say that Hel will unleash an army of the dead upon earth, with Thidrek leading them in his ship. I *have* to stop him."

"So the Norns are behind this," Mist said. "I should've known. They play with our lives, but in the end they don't care what happens to us."

"I'm beginning to think they do care. At least they don't want our world destroyed."

"It's *your* world, not mine anymore," Mist said. She started to weep again, then found strength to stifle her tears. "I won't let Hel turn it into a place like this. I'll take the crown to her."

"No," Astrid protested. "Eventually she'll realize she's been deceived. You'll be blamed."

"Good. Then at least the hag will know it was *me* who foiled her." She gave her sly, crooked grin, the same one Astrid knew from when they were best friends, flying the skies together in service to Odin. Then Mist kissed her on the cheek and hurried away up the ravine, quickly disappearing into the gloom.

The dead were extremely curious. They pressed in around the Rune Warriors, their gray hands reaching out to touch them. To Dane their touch felt oddly insubstantial, like the light brush of a feather upon his skin. It even tickled a bit.

"Get away, will you!" an irritated Jarl shouted as they crowded in. "Back off!"

Dane was kneeling over Lut, who was sitting up, having just regained consciousness, although his eyes were glassy and he looked confused. "Where are we?' he croaked.

"We're in Hel's moat," Drott said.

"But at least we're alive," Fulnir said.

"Which is more than I can say for the other inmates," Dane added.

Drott giggled as hands touched him. "Stop! It tickles!"

An ancient-looking soul with a long beard stepped forward and announced that his name was Gudmund. "Please forgive our forward manner. Many of us have not seen a living person for ages. Why are you here?" Dane told them how they had been captured, taken to the underworld, and now become Hel's prisoners. "Well, I'd advise you to abandon all hope," Gudmund said. "Besides, once you settle in, this place isn't all that bad."

"Sure, it's a sunny paradise," Jarl cracked. "When does the mead start flowing?"

"At least we're not in the Lake of Fire," Gudmund said. "You've seen it?"

"Can't really miss it," Jarl said. "See, it's a *lake* that's on *fire*."

"The kind of men who killed me dwell there," Gudmund said, "those who preyed on the weak and killed for plunder or just because they liked killing. I was leader of my village and bribed a raiding party to pass us by. But they murdered me and all my kin."

"So that's why you're here?" Drott asked. "Because you bribed a gang of brigands?"

Gudmund hung his head in shame. "Perhaps had I been brave and fought them off, I would have gone to Valhalla."

There was a sharp cracking sound as a flash of lightning lashed down, sparking the ground right near where Lut was sitting. Twenty feet above them on the bridge was a demon holding the whip handle. He stared down malevolently at Dane and his friends, as if the lash he'd given was just a taste of what was to come.

"You pig-faced goon!" Jarl shouted up to him. "Wait till I get you without that whip in your hand!" The guard whipped down again, missing Jarl but catching Fulnir across the shoulders. Chuckling to himself, the guard moved on.

Drott checked out the burn marks across his friend's flesh. "It's not deep. Does it hurt?"

"Nothing worse than a hundred wasp stings at once," Fulnir said, grimacing.

"You mustn't show defiance," cautioned Gudmund. "It will only bring more lashes."

"What are we to do?" Jarl said. "Just stand here and take it like sheep?"

"We have to," Gudmund said. "We're doomed."

"Who says you're doomed?" Jarl challenged. "You're only doomed 'cause you *think* you are."

"Coming through! Make a path!" said a voice. Horvik the Virtuous pushed up to the front. "What's this about us *not* being doomed?"

"You're a perfect example, Horvik," Jarl said. "You don't deserve eternal whipping by demons for what you did."

"You're right. I imagine maybe a day or two of whipping would take care of my sins," Horvik said.

"What about the female souls here?" asked a stout woman soul. "We're shuttled to Niflheim because we didn't go off to war and die with a sword in our hands. Is that fair?"

"No!" shouted several nearby female souls.

"I was a thrall," volunteered a young male soul, "like many here. We suffered on earth—must we suffer here, too?"

"No!" cried many of his comrades.

Jarl waded into the crowd, egging them on to rise up and

fight. "Even in the underworld our friend is true to form," Lut said weakly to Dane. "Whether souls are living or dead, his only instinct is to rouse them to rebellion."

Dane smiled at the truth in that. He looked into Lut's watery blue eyes that had lost the sparkle of youth. "Why did you do it?"

"Give Thidrek my years?" He heaved a deep sigh, as if mourning what he had sacrificed. "I read of my fate in the book."

"The Book of Fate? You *opened* it? What did it say?"

"It said . . . I would die an old man. So here I am . . . old and ready to die."

Dane's eyes filled with tears. "No, I won't let you."

Lut smiled. "When I said 'ready,' I didn't mean right now."

"Oh . . . good," Dane said, relieved. He heard a *crawk!* He looked up and saw his raven circling in the gloom above.

"It's Klint!" shouted Drott. "He's looking for us. Here, Klinty!" A sizzling lash from above caught Drott across the back and he cried out in pain. The demon guard was back, probably alerted by Jarl's rabble-rousing. He whipped down again; Dane jumped in front of Drott to protect him and took the force of the lash across his raised forearm. The pain was searingly intense. The demon drew back the whip again—when a sharp *shriek* caused him to turn his head. Diving from above, Klint caught him at full speed in the face, his beak like a sword tip plunging deep into the demon's eye. The guard stumbled back, lost his balance, and fell off the bridge into the moat.

"Get him!" cried Jarl. But Fulnir was already on the brute, pummeling his hideous boarlike face. The demon roared and threw Fulnir off. He grabbed for the handle of his whip that had fallen to the ground—but Horvik kicked it away, and it was grabbed by the thrall soul. For an instant the thrall stood there, gazing timidly at the whip in his hand, afraid to act.

Gudmund, of all souls, screamed at him. "Use it!"

The thrall reared back and whipped the lightning lash forward to where it wrapped around the guard's legs, sizzling his hide. He bellowed in pain, falling to the ground. Then Jarl, Fulnir, and Drott attacked, pummeling the bestial thing's face into a bloody pulp.

"Look out!" cried one of the souls, pointing to the bridge above, where another demon guard had appeared with a whip. The guard lashed down, but at the same time, the thrall soul whipped a lightning strike back up at him. The thrall's lash caught the guard around the neck. The thrall gave a hard yank, taking the guard off the bridge and into the moat. He fell headfirst, and when he hit, his skull burst open like a ripe melon, spewing blood and brains.

The souls gazed in silent awe at the lifeless guards, shocked that the demons who had so brutally oppressed them now lay dead at their feet. "See what happens when you fight?" Jarl announced, clearly taking credit for the killing of the two demons. "Those two won't beat you anymore."

"But what do we do about the others who are sure to come?" asked one soul.

"And the fact that we're still stuck in this moat?" said another.

The souls all started chattering among themselves, worried about the repercussions of killing the guards. Some voiced panicked fears they all would be thrown into the Lake of Fire. Gudmund held up his hand, bringing silence. "I'm sure this man did not incite us to fight," he said, gesturing to Jarl, "without a plan that would save us from Hel's wrath. Let him speak."

Ashen faces gazed intently at Jarl. They were not aware—as Dane and the rest of the Rune Warriors were—that Jarl was best at stirring things up and doing the actual fighting. But when it came to any kind of strategic thinking? Forget it.

"Uh . . . well . . . uh," Jarl began, his normal bombastic style of speech deserting him. "Look, I just got here. I can't solve all *your* problems."

"He's doomed us!" cried the thrall soul. It appeared that Jarl was about to be swarmed by the angry dead when above them appeared a heaven-sent vision bathed in a golden glow.

"The gods be praised," an awestruck Gudmund murmured, falling to his knees. "Have you come to take me to Valhalla?"

Horse and rider descended. "What? No, sorry. I've come for the live ones," the Valkyrie said.

23

A MAGIC CROWN

William knew he didn't belong here. He belonged with the rest of the Rune Warriors—not with Grelf, Thidrek, and the monumentally repulsive goddess Hel. It had hurt when Dane had said that he lacked the courage to be a Rune Warrior, though he realized Dane had only said this so Hel would spare him from death. But would death be worse than being thrall to Thidrek? He wasn't rotting and full of maggots now, but his living state had not lessened his capacity for cruelty, William was sure. It helped that Grelf was with him. He thought he could even trust the man a little—but not to the point where Grelf would risk his own skin to save him from harm.

The four of them stood high up on a fortress parapet that afforded a view of the Lake of Fire. Hel raised her staff, pointed the orb end at the Ship of the Dead, which could be seen docked below, and proclaimed, "By my command, summon the cursed damned! Awake those who will venture forth to destroy the world of the living!"

William watched, transfixed, as the carved wooden creature on the prow of the ship came alive once more. The horn was brought to the creature's mouth and a thunderous, deep bellow echoed across the lake. Three such blasts followed the first, and after the last bellow sounded, William saw what looked to be the heads of dragons slowly rise from beneath the fiery muck. There were hundreds of them—no!—thousands spread across the lake! What ungodly horde was Hel unleashing? As the heads continued to rise, William saw they were but the figureheads on the prows of Viking warships, a vast armada, summoned from the cursed depths. The ships rose and settled upon the lake, and to William's horror he saw that at the oars were dead Viking warriors—those whose savage brutality had no doubt condemned them to reside in Hel's worst place of punishment.

Realizing they had been raised and given new purpose, the thousands of ship-bound warrior dead cheered and began to bang their oar shafts in unison against the gunwales, chanting a war chant as their drumming grew ever louder.

"There is your army, Thidrek," Hel intoned. "I free them to make war on the fools who worship Odin. They will follow the Ship of the Dead wherever it doth go. The Niflheim gate is open. Take them and deliver earth to me!"

"Yes, your majesty," Thidrek said. "I shall leave at once."

"Excuse me, your majesty," said another voice. Everyone turned to see that one of Hel's handmaidens had come onto the parapet. "A guard confiscated this from one of the Rune Warriors," she said. "I thought I should bring it to you." She came forward, and in her hand was a metal crown, tarnished and simply made.

Hel gave it a cursory glance. "Why do you bother me with such a crude trinket?"

"The one they took it from swears that he stole it from Skuld herself," the handmaiden said.

This appeared to strike a chord of interest within the goddess. "Skuld, you say?" Hel took the crown in her hands, inspecting it. "That witch of fate has simple tastes. I'd never wear a thing so ugly." She handed it back to the servant. "Away with you!"

The handmaiden started off, then hesitated. "May I keep it, then? The one who stole it says it has magic."

"Magic?" said Hel, raising an eyebrow.

"It is said to enhance the beauty of one who wears it, your majesty. But since your, um, loveliness already has no equal, you would not need such help." The handmaiden hurried away.

"Wait!" commanded Hel, and the handmaiden froze. "Bring it back." She returned and Hel snatched the crown and placed it upon her head. Nothing changed. She was still as homely as a bullfrog's butt. "Fetch the mirror!" she ordered.

"I have it right here, your majesty." The handmaiden produced the mirror and Hel eagerly grabbed it, brought it up to her face—and gasped. Tears glistened in her viperish eyes. "You were right!" she said breathlessly. "I—I am . . . resplendent."

William whispered to Grelf, who stood next to him, "What's *resplendent* mean?"

Grelf whispered back, "It means dazzling." They shared a confused shrug, for either Grelf was wrong about what resplendent meant or Hel had been bewitched to see beauty that wasn't there.

Just then, Alrick the Most Merciless rushed onto the parapet. "My lord, the prisoners have escaped!"

Dane held on tight to Astrid as they soared high into the gloom upon Sleipnir. Below he saw Jarl and the rest of the Rune Warriors running out of the gates of the fortress at the head of a mass tide of the dead, liberated from the moat of souls. Demon guards rushed to stop them, using their lightning whips, but the souls were armed as well with the whips they had taken off the dead guards. Bright flashes of lightning erupted here and there as the crowd of the dead skirmished with the outnumbered guards, overwhelming them and taking their weapons. In the confusion, Dane saw his friends make it to the steps leading down to the Ship of the Dead. Now all he and Astrid had to do was to find William, because he was not leaving without the boy.

When he had first seen his beloved Astrid sitting atop Odin's eight-legged steed hovering above them, his first thought was that it was a mirage spawned by Hel's trickery. But then Astrid had set the gigantic horse down among them, and he saw—as did the dumbfounded others—that it really *was* her. His first instinct was to pull her from the horse into his arms and shower her with kisses. But her sharp command had brought him to his senses.

"Quick!" she had said. "Climb on Sleipnir and I'll take you out of the moat. Drott, Fulnir, you two first!"

"You're leaving us to face Hel's wrath alone?" Gudmund had asked.

"Of course they are," the thrall soul had said bitterly. "Why should the living care about us?"

"Go your merry way," said another. "Give no thought to the suffering that is sure to be inflicted upon us when they discover two dead guards in our midst."

"Which never would've happened if *you* hadn't shown up," said yet another.

"They're really laying on the guilt," Fulnir had said. "Isn't there something we can do?"

Lut had an idea. He pointed to the wall of the fortress that abutted the moat. "If the workmanship is as bad as we've been told, a couple of kicks from the horse should knock that wall down into the moat. Then we can *all* climb out over the blocks."

Astrid flew Sleipnir to the wall. "Stand clear!" she had

shouted. It took only a couple of kicks with his four massively powerful back legs and the wall collapsed. The living and dead gave a loud cheer and immediately started scrambling up the rubble and out of the moat—all except Lut, who was so weak, he had to be carried by Fulnir. Dane joined Astrid atop Sleipnir, and Jarl led everyone else to storm out the fortress gates.

William and Grelf stood at the ramparts, watching the furious battle below between the dead and the demon guards. "What's happening, Grelf?"

"I'd say young Dane and his friends have sparked a rebellion. Look! There they go!" He pointed beyond the fortress walls, where William saw the Rune Warriors escaping through the melee toward the steps that led down to the Ship of the Dead.

William's joy at seeing his friends escape was abruptly tempered by the knowledge that they were leaving him behind. But they *had* to, didn't they? They probably had one chance to save themselves, and that meant they could not come back to rescue him. Those were the hard facts, he knew, but he still felt the ache of abandonment. He wanted to cry, but that was what a little boy did, and he was not so little anymore. In his heart he *knew* he was a Rune Warrior—which meant he must be willing to sacrifice his life for the good of the others.

"There! Thidrek and the draugrs!" shouted Grelf,

pointing. William saw the undead horde and Thidrek, Blade of Oblivion in hand, rush out the fortress gates in pursuit, battering their way through the mass of the dead fighting the demon guards. William looked ahead and saw Drott, the last of his friends, disappear down the steps.

William wished he had done something to stop Thidrek, or at least delay him. But, in truth, what *could* he have done—tackled Thidrek before he rushed out? That would have delayed him for only an instant.

When the draugr Alrick the Most Merciless had arrived and announced the escape, Thidrek had immediately asked Hel to close the Niflheim gate to trap them. But she did not seem to hear him, so beguiled was she by her reflection in the mirror. The transfixed goddess had then floated away into her abode, humming merrily to herself, never taking her eyes off the mirror. Aware that he could not *demand* that Hel act, Thidrek had taken matters in his own hands and rushed out with the draugr warriors.

Now, looking down upon the pandemonium, William said a prayer to Odin, asking him to help his fellow Rune Warriors escape. He felt Grelf's consoling hand on his shoulder. "You'll see your friends again, lad. I'm sure of it."

"So am I," William said with sudden joy, pointing up. A horse was streaking down at them—and on its back were Astrid and Dane!

Grelf's mouth shot open. "By Odin's beard! It's Sleipnir!"

The steed set down next to them. "What did you think?"

asked a grinning Dane. "That I would leave a Rune Warrior behind?" He extended his hand. William jumped up to grasp it and was pulled onto the steed's back between Dane and Astrid.

"Thidrek and the draugrmen are probably to the steps by now," Grelf said. "You must hurry."

"Thank you, Grelf," Dane said. "You're a better man than I thought. Good-bye."

"Wait!" William said. He looked down at Grelf, who stood there, shoulders slumped in despair, a pleading, abandoned-puppy expression on his face. The man was not much good for anything and no one would miss him, but he had done his best to protect William. "There's room for him."

"Oh, thank you! Thank you!" Grelf gushed. "I promise you won't regret taking me with you! Double pinkie promise!"

"*Four* on a horse?" Astrid said.

"He's a big horse. Besides, it's only three and a half," argued William. "I don't weigh that much."

Dane gave a grudging sigh, as if he *knew* he would regret this, but he extended his hand to Grelf, and after a brief struggle to arrange everyone on the steed's back, they were up and away.

They flew over the scene of battle, and Dane was glad to see that the dead were routing the demon guards. He wondered what would happen to the souls after their revolt. Would they have some manner of freedom without Hel's brutal demons to keep them in line? Dane had witnessed the glories of Valhalla and the grimness of Niflheim, and he was convinced there was gross injustice in the afterlife. He hoped that this revolt would show the gods that big changes were in order.

Soon they were flying over the steps. Thidrek and the draugrs were at the top and quickly descending. Dane saw that Jarl and Drott were now halfway down and had leaped across the void where the steps had fallen away. But Fulnir, carrying Lut, was hesitating, afraid his leap would come up short. Dane glanced at the shoreline below to be sure the Ship of the Dead was still there. It was—right where they had left it—but then Dane's eyes beheld a staggering sight. On the lake was poised a vast armada of Viking ships manned by dead warriors!

"Where did those ships come from?" Dane gasped. "And the men?"

"Hel's army of the dead raised from the lake," Grelf said.

"But the good thing is," William added, "the Niflheim gate is open for us."

On the longships, Dane saw, the dead men sat still at the oars, as if waiting for a signal to start rowing. "Will they follow us?" Dane asked.

"Hel said they will follow the Ship of the Dead wherever it goes," William said.

Astrid flew Sleipnir down to where Fulnir and Lut were halted. "Stay there! I'll come back for you!" she shouted to them. "Everyone else get to the ship!" Jarl and Drott raced down the steps. In moments Astrid had deposited Dane, William, and Grelf on the rocky shore next to the Ship of the Dead, and had headed back up to retrieve Fulnir and Lut.

Dane looked up, and his heart sank when he saw that Thidrek had almost reached them. One swipe with the Blade of Oblivion and they'd be dead. Sleipnir soared upward—and an instant before Thidrek was in reach of them, Fulnir, with Lut riding piggyback, leaped onto the steed's back. Thidrek swung the blade, barely missing them. Odin's horse, trained in manners of warfare, angrily kicked with his four back legs, crushing the stone steps Thidrek was standing upon. The steps fell away—and Thidrek would've gone too if Alrick the Most Merciless, standing on the steps above, hadn't grabbed the scruff of his coat. Thidrek dangled over the abyss, bellowing in rage while Astrid took Sleipnir away to the shore below. They landed and Fulnir hopped down with Lut still on his back. The old one was pale and frail looking, but he managed to complain, "Blast that Thidrek! I give him the strength to swing that blade and he nearly kills me with it. Damned unsporting of him!"

Above, Thidrek was already working to bridge the gap in the steps, which was now too wide to jump. He had ordered the draugrs to form a chain using their bodies—one grasping the next one's legs and so on—to form an undead span to the next intact step. Thidrek was climbing down this draugr bridge, holding the handle of the Blade of Oblivion in his teeth, and would soon be across the gap.

"One thing I'll say for him," Fulnir commented. "The bastard never gives up." He took Lut onto the ship, where the others were rapidly preparing to shove off.

Dane turned to Astrid, who sat high upon Sleipnir. "You never gave up either."

She looked at him, her eyes holding the warmth he had known forever. "I never will." She kicked Sleipnir's flanks, the horse shot upward, and she called out, "I'll follow you out the gate!"

Dane gave a quick look up at Thidrek and saw he had climbed over the chain of draugrs and bridged the gap. Suddenly, one of the draugrs seemed to lose a grip on the next one in the chain. He gave a cry, the span broke, and three of the draugrs plummeted—coming right at Dane standing on the rocky shore! He jumped aboard just as the bodies hit and shattered upon the rocks, arms, legs, heads ricocheting everywhere. The head of Alrick the Most Merciless landed in the ship next to Fulnir, who grabbed the thing by its hair and flung it overboard into the lake to join his Least Merciless cohort.

Dane yelled, "Shove off!" Jarl pushed the ship away from the rocks with an oar, and out they floated into the lake. Dane felt a rush of relief—at last they were beyond Thidrek's reach.

"It appears we have new owners," observed Red Mustache on the sail.

"I like them better," Black Beard said. "They don't smell as bad."

Dane heard a splash behind them. He looked back and saw the torso of one of the smashed-apart draugrs floating in the muck halfway between the ship and shore. Thidrek, handle of the Blade of Oblivion between his teeth, leaped onto the torso, balanced there for an instant, and threw *another* torso he was carrying farther toward the ship. *He was using the bodies of the draugrs as stepping stones!* Before anyone could react, Thidrek jumped forward onto the next floating torso, took a big leap from there, grabbed the gunwale, and swung himself aboard.

24

A MAIDEN'S
REVENGE

"Why, Grelf . . . I don't remember giving you your leave." Thidrek stood on the stern of the ship, brandishing the Blade of Oblivion. When he had jumped aboard, everyone had scrambled toward the bow. Dane, Jarl, Fulnir, and Drott held oars they could fight with—but wood didn't stand much chance against the blade.

"Nor you, boy," Thidrek said to William. "Such gratitude. I spare your life and you flee my protection. Not once but twice. That is simply not acceptable."

"Begging your pardon, my lord," Grelf said, "if you'll allow me to explain my situation—"

"Spare me your bleatings," Thidrek growled. "For now I'll believe that you were kidnapped. Get behind me so when I turn them all to ash you'll not be nicked."

Grelf did not move. "My lord, I choose to stand pat. Your barbaric cruelty has forced me to seek employment elsewhere. No hard feelings, I hope." Dane couldn't help being amused. Grelf, of all people, had developed a backbone.

"You choose to die with this rabble rather than serve me?"

"I'm amazed myself," Grelf said with a shrug. "Quite unlike me."

"You'll be last, lickspittle. And I'll make it very, very painful."

Thidrek advanced on them. Jarl and Drott swung their oars at his head and Dane and Fulnir lunged with theirs, but the blade quickly turned them into kindling. Thidrek kept coming, slashing with the weapon, backing everyone into a tight pack in the bow. Further retreat was impossible, for another step back and some of them would fall off the ship into the flaming lake below.

Sleipnir swooped in from above, and one of his hooves hit Thidrek a glancing blow to his head. He staggered back, stunned for an instant. Dane and Jarl went to rush him, but Thidrek regained his senses, thrusting the blade in front of him, forcing them to stop. Blood trickled from a cut on Thidrek's forehead, and he gasped for air, as if he couldn't catch his breath.

Astrid pulled the horse up to above the mast, where they hovered. "Stay away, Astrid!" Dane yelled. "He's ours!"

"Afraid you . . . have . . . that backward," Thidrek said between gulps of air.

"My lord, you are not looking at all well," Grelf said.

Indeed, Dane saw a sudden change come over Thidrek. Deep age lines appeared on his face; his thick, black hair began to whiten and thin, and his tall, muscular frame shriveled before their eyes. Thidrek gazed in horror at the backs of his hands as wrinkles appeared and age spots grew like blotches of mold. "What's . . . what's happening to me?" he said, his voice a hoarse whisper.

Lut tottered forward. "The years you took were but a wisp of time."

Thidrek jabbed a crooked finger at Lut. "But you were young!"

"My youth was an illusion. . . . What you see is my true age. My time ends soon . . . as does yours."

"You tricked me!"

Lut shrugged, then stuck out his tongue and blew a wet, loud raspberry at Thidrek.

"Could *not* have said that any better," Dane said with a laugh. Others were laughing, too, and this made Thidrek furious.

"Bring her about! I will use the orb to take *your* life, as I wanted!" he said to Dane, his voice now a weak rasp.

"We're not going back," William said. "But you're free to."

All of them advanced slowly on a retreating Thidrek. "We're not far from shore," Fulnir said. "Maybe you can swim for it."

"Stay away from me! Stay away!" With every step back

Thidrek seemed to age a little more and a little more. By the time they had backed him into the stern, he was a stooped, withered husk of a man, too frail even to hold the Blade of Oblivion, which fell from his grasp at his feet. "Grelf, help me! Help me!" he wailed, his back to the fiery lake. "Haven't I always been a kind and generous master?"

"My lord, I refuse to answer on the grounds it would most assuredly hurt your feelings." And with that Grelf gave his master a push, and Thidrek tumbled backward over the railing and splashed headfirst into the lake. Thankfully, he was swallowed whole and without a peep by the fiery muck, sparing everyone from hearing his dying cries of agony.

Thidrek was dead—destroyed for good—but there was no time to celebrate. Their oars were gone, and with no wind in the underrealm to fill the sail, they were stuck without means of propulsion.

"What about the horse?" William suggested. "Can't he tow us out?" One end of a rope was quickly tied to Sleipnir and the other end to the bow of the ship. Soon they were under way at a good clip, the massive steed, with Astrid at the reins, flying in front of the ship pulling them along. Klint, riding atop the mast, squawked excitedly.

"Just as I feared," Grelf said, gesturing behind them. They all looked back and saw that the Viking ships raised from the lake were moving at equal speed behind them, the dead warriors pulling at the oars.

"What do they want?" Drott asked. Dane quickly

explained that this was Hel's army of the dead and that Thidrek was to lead them to conquer earth. "This is easily solved," Drott said. He cupped his hands and shouted back at the following ships. "Change of plans! Thidrek is dead! And we have no interest in conquering earth! Go back!" The ships kept coming with no slackening of speed. "They don't follow orders very well," Drott observed.

"Their orders are to follow the Ship of the Dead wherever it goes," William said.

"Which means if we go out the gate, they go out the gate too," Dane said. "And we'll be responsible for unleashing Hel's army upon earth."

Hel's empire was in revolt, the doomed had seized control, but she was blithely unaware of it all. Simmering in her bath of foul, sulfurous mud, humming to herself, the goddess was bewitched by her false reflection in the mirror. Mist was standing close, so if the magical crown slipped off, she would be there to quickly replace it upon Hel's head to keep the illusion going. Her guards had urgently knocked on the door, beseeching the goddess for orders to quell the insurrection, but she had sent them all away, so intoxicated she was by her own image. Eventually Hel would realize that she had been tricked—but Mist hoped that would come after Dane, Astrid, and their friends were far beyond the boundaries of her wrath.

As for herself, Mist had no illusions. When Hel's anger

came, it would erupt like a volcano, incinerating every soul in its path. Mist's only chance lay in the revolt. If enough of the demon guards had been killed, then perhaps Hel's power to inflict torture on the innocent would be over.

The door slammed open and in marched Aurora in full pique. "*What* is going on! The doomed are rioting! Your majesty, you made promises to me that I would be joining a well-run organization—not one in a shambles!" Hel kept merrily humming to herself, eyeing her reflection, deaf to the interruption. "Your majesty!"

"She can't hear you." Mist came out of the shadows and Aurora's jaw dropped in surprise.

"What's wrong, Aurora? Weren't expecting to see me?"

Recovering from her momentary shock, Aurora regained her usual snottiness. "Dear, dear Mist . . . why do you look so drab and unhealthy? Oh, that's right, you're dead."

"You should know—you murdered me."

"And how have things been since then?"

"I'm handmaiden to her highness. I give her beauty treatments."

Aurora glanced over at the ugly hag simmering in mud. "They're not working," she whispered with a snicker.

"No, she's quite happy. Look at her gazing at her reflection. She thinks she's . . . what's the word? Oh, yes—resplendent."

Aurora's eyes narrowed in worry. "What's wrong with her? Is she mad . . . or bewitched?"

"Mad, I'd say. Too bad—your having switched sides just when the ol' girl's gone brainsick."

Aurora's worry lines deepened. She went past Mist and stood before Hel in her tub. "Your majesty, you must quell the rebellion or all will be lost!" The goddess hummed along, having no interest in anything other than her reflection. Aurora stamped her foot. "Your majesty, this is no way to run the underworld!"

Mist knew this was her one chance. Standing behind Aurora, she called out to her. "Dear, dear Aurora. I'm afraid you're finished."

"Finished? Ha! At least I can leave here. You can't." Aurora turned and saw Mist had Hel's staff in her hand with the orb end pointed at her. "What do you think you're going to do with *that*?"

"You took my life. I want it back," said Mist.

"There has to be another way," Jarl insisted.

"There isn't," Dane said. He turned to William. "Tell them again what Hel said."

"She said the ships will follow the Ship of the Dead wherever it goes."

"And if we sink this ship here, now—they'll have *nothing* to follow," Dane said. For a long moment no one spoke, each contemplating the horrible consequences of this. Finally, Jarl broke the silence.

"I have pictured many ways I would meet a glorious end.

But burned to a crisp in a fiery lake was *not* on the list."

"Along with Astrid, there's room on Sleipnir's back for three of us at the most," Lut said. "William, gather the splinters from the oars. I will make the straws to draw. Shortest three out of six will go."

"Six?" Fulnir said. "There's seven of us."

"I'm staying," Lut said. "Death comes soon to me anyway."

"But what about us?" Black Beard said. "Has anyone thought about us?"

"You sink our ship, we go down too," said Red Mustache. "We should have a say about this."

"Look, you're just faces on a sail," Jarl said. "We're live human beings."

"We have souls just as you do," railed Red Mustache. "You can't throw us away like we were nothing!"

"They do have a point," Drott agreed. "Their souls mean just as much as ours."

"Now I've heard it all," Jarl said, throwing his hands up in exasperation. "Why don't we just take the sail down and tie the four corners together to make a gigantic pocket so everyone can fit inside, and have Sleipnir fly us *all* out of here!" In all his sarcasm, Jarl didn't know he'd inadvertently stumbled upon a brilliant solution to save them all. Later, of course, he took credit for the plan, boasting that his brains were just as superior as his brawn.

It didn't take long to free the sail from the mast and securely tie the corners together. There was just enough room for everyone within the pocket—but the weight was too enormous even for Sleipnir to lift. There was much argument as to who would stay behind, Lut insisting it should be him. It looked like they would have to draw straws again, but then a miraculous sight appeared out of the gloom.

Mist, beautiful Mist, her raven hair flowing, her skin glowing with life, arrived riding another celestial steed. How she had gained life again and how she had acquired a Valkyrie's horse were questions that would have to be answered later. Another rope was tethered to Mist's horse—and together the two steeds had more than enough strength to lift everyone.

But before they left the ship, it had to be sunk. Dane took the Blade of Oblivion in his hands, raised it over his head, and with all his might chopped down into the bottom of the hull. Sparks flew and the fiery muck began to flood in. Dane had to scramble quickly to the sail pocket. Before he got in, he threw the blade overboard and watched it disappear beneath the surface. They were lifted off just before the decks were submerged and the ship sank.

Moments later, Dane looked back and the Ship of the Dead was gone. And then he saw an amazing sight. All across the vast lake the Viking ships were doing as Hel had said. They were following the Ship of the Dead and sinking beneath the surface of the lake. Soon, all that could be seen were the dragon heads on the fronts of the ships; then they too disappeared and Hel's army of the dead was gone, returned to the place of punishment where Dane hoped they would dwell forever.

They received quite a fright when they approached the Niflheim gate.

Garm, Hel's gatekeeper, gave a deafening roar and leaped at them as if the sail pouch full of people were a thrown toy he was supposed to retrieve. Dane was sure the gigantic jaws were about to snap closed around them—when the monster's chain played out. The creature jerked to a stop in midair and fell into the river, making a gigantic splash behind them.

They flew out the open gate into the region where the waters were still so thick with fog that Dane could not even see the horses above. Soon, a distant roar was heard. As they flew on, the roar increased in power—and Dane knew they were approaching the enormous whirlpool of water they had traversed before. Suddenly they were inside it, being pulled upward. Dane looked up and saw a wonderful sight framed by the ever-widening circle of water. Blue sky!

As they shot from the water into glorious sunlight, everyone gave a delirious cheer. They were free again, back in the world of the living. Sweet, sweet sea air filled their lungs, and the warmth from the sun maid Sol caressed their faces. Never had Dane felt so happy to be alive and so certain that all he wanted in his days ahead was to be surrounded by those he loved.

25

A PROMISE
KEPT

It was dusk, the sky a deep purple to the west, as
Sleipnir and Mist's sky steed landed them back on
Thor's Hill overlooking Voldarstad. It brought tears
to Dane's eyes to once again see the rooftops of his village.

As they all climbed out of the sail, stretching and talking gleefully about how nice it was to be home and what
an amazing ride it had been, Dane had other things on his
mind. Lut could barely stand, and knowing his friend was
weakening, Dane walked him over to the giant runestone
the villagers had erected the past winter to honor him and
his friends. Lut ran his bony hand along the face of the stone,
patting it affectionately as if greeting an old friend.

"It is good to be here," he said with finality. He suddenly tottered and nearly fell, but Dane caught his arm
and righted him, insisting that he sit and rest awhile. Dane

removed his cloak and laid it on the ground, and with nary a grumble, Lut lay down on it, the light in his eyes a bit fainter than before. Water was fetched and Dane held the goatskin up so Lut could drink.

Dane had lain beside his old friend during the entire trip home, watching him sleep and seeing to his safety, talking to him as if he were awake and could hear every word; Lut had long ago taught him that a man's mind is always working even when asleep. Dane too had slept for a time, and had awoken once to find Lut awake and gazing out at the great red sun dying on the horizon. A faint smile had returned to the old man's eyes, and there was a look of pure peace on his face. Though they spoke not a word, he knew the man so well he could read his thoughts by simply looking at his face. "You're going home," he had said to Lut, and Lut had shut his eyes and nodded, beaming a smile. And now, gazing down upon his friend and feeling the weakness of his grip, Dane feared the end was nearer than he thought.

The various villagers began to arrive on the hill, hugging and kissing Dane, Astrid, and all the others, happy to see them home once again. Casks of ale were hauled out, and the villagers began to drink and toast the Rune Warriors in celebration. Others gathered round Sleipnir, marveling at the sight of his many legs and the glossiness of his hide, and Drott lifted children up onto the horse's back. Then a voice interrupted them.

"Uh, excuse us—"

"Yes, we don't want to be a bother, but . . ."

All heads turned to see it was the faces on the sail that were now speaking. The sail had been removed from Sleipnir and its ropes slung round the runestone, where it snapped and billowed up, filled by the wind off the bay. "Might you perchance give us assistance?" said Red Mustache.

"What is it now?" said Jarl.

"You're all home now, safe and sound," said Red Mustache.

"Now it's our turn," said Black Beard. "We want to be free, too."

"Our spirits yearn to join our ancestors!" wailed Red Mustache.

Jarl and Dane looked at each other in puzzlement.

"What do you suggest we do?" Dane asked.

"Fire will free them," Lut said. Dane was surprised to see him standing somewhat unsteadily beside him now. He pointed to a lighted torch in the hand of a villager. "The purifying power of fire will set them free."

There was a pause as they considered Lut's words.

"Works for me," Black Beard said.

"May our souls rise to the heavenly realm!" cried Red Mustache.

"I'm sure they will," Dane said. He took the torch and lit the edge of the sail. It smoldered for a moment, then caught fire, the flame quickly tearing up the side of the cloth and spreading across it. One by one, as the faces were swallowed in flames, Dane saw large puffs of acrid black smoke issue forth, and then from out of the smoke arose the spirit bodies, transparent against the night sky. They floated there in the air with looks of joy on their faces, the joy of finally being free. Red Mustache and Black Beard and their sail-mates waved good-bye as they drifted slowly up and away until at last they were gone. Dane stood there a long moment, marveling at the magic of it all, until the silence was broken by the feeble voice of Lut the Bent.

"Dane . . ."

Seeing Lut collapsed on the ground, in an instant Dane was down on his knees beside him, rolling him onto his back and taking the old one's hand in his.

"Lut! Lut!" he said, looking into Lut's fading eyes. "Are you all right?"

Others crowded around, offering help, but Dane shushed them into silence.

"It is time, my son," rasped Lut.

"No, it is *not* time," said Dane, fighting back tears. "You've much life left to live!" Dane's heart nearly burst as Lut pursed his lips and slowly shook his head. "But we need you! You can't leave us now! No! No, you can't—" Dane was frantic now, for he knew there was nothing he could do to save his friend. This was the end, as painful as that might seem. Though it had always seemed that Lut the Bent might live forever, Dane had known that someday they would have to say their good-byes.

"I will take him," Mist said solemnly.

Lut's eyes brightened for a moment. "I am to go to Valhalla?"

"You will sup with Odin tonight," she gently assured him.

No longer able to hold back, Dane burst into tears of his own, hugging Lut tightly. "You—you were the best friend I ever had, Lut," he said, choking back sobs. "And—and I'll miss you the rest of my life."

Lut patted the young man's head and said, "But now you'll have Astrid to love and guide you. . . ." Dane looked up at Astrid, and his eyes met the warmth of her smile.

Laboring to form words, Lut whispered, "Remember, the blood of a Rune Warrior runs within you . . . but most of all remember this. . . ." Too weak to speak aloud, he gestured for Dane to draw nearer. Dane bent closer, putting his ear to Lut's lips, the old man's breath warming his cheek. The words Lut whispered he spoke only to him. When Lut had finished, Dane drew back and squeezed Lut's hand. Dane wiped the tears from his eyes and forced out a final good-bye to his friend. Others of the village then said their good-byes as well, murmuring, "We love you, Lut," and "Good-bye, old friend," and "May Odin look upon you with favor."

"Farewell, my Sons of Thor . . . ," said Lut ever so faintly, "till we meet again. . . ."

And as the words escaped the old man's lips, Dane saw his chest heave to a stop and his eyes fall shut. For the briefest instant, Dane sensed a powerful force surrounding him, as if he were being embraced by the moon or some other kind of magic, and the next thing Dane knew, the great Lut the Bent was dead. He had taken his last breath, and Dane felt as if the light had gone out of the world, for indeed it had.

And then Dane was lit by a new glow, and looking up through his tears, he saw it was Mist on Sleipnir rising toward the heavens. And behind her on the other celestial steed sat Lut. No longer old and feeble, he was young and vibrant and waving good-bye. And as the sky horses rose into the star-frosted sky, Dane's heart lifted, knowing that Lut's spirit was to dwell forever in Valhalla, enjoying the rewards of a life well lived.

Astrid's tears were streaming down her cheeks when there next came a blinding flash of light and a new presence was among them. It was Skuld, her crimson robe the color of blood in the torchlight.

"Well, isn't this a cozy little scene," said Skuld, the screech of her voice like a knife that cut through the din of voices and quickly silenced the gathering. "It just warms my heart to see you all safely back home."

"I didn't think you had a heart," said Astrid lightly.

Skuld flicked her a cold look. "A common mistake among your kind. Thinking you know everything about us who look down upon your deeds."

"You look down on our deeds? Well, maybe we look down on yours."

"Rather an unkind remark for a girl your age," Skuld said snidely. "But under the circumstances, I'll overlook it."

Never having seen a real live goddess before, the assembled villagers had all fallen silent and prostrated themselves in a show of awe and respect. All save for Drott, that is, who stood with his eyes closed looking very preoccupied as he scratched at his rear end and grunted.

Skuld looked at him sharply. "You!" Drott's eyes shot open. "They call you Drott, do they not?"

"When they're being nice to me, yes," said Drott.

"Pray tell *what* are you doing?"

A look of panic crossed his face, and then he said, "It's my warts."

"Your warts," said Skuld dryly.

"Yes, three big ugly ones, right on my butt," he went on nervously. "My left buttock, actually, on the bottom part of the cheek. I just woke up one day and there they were. Three big warty warts. Have *no* idea how they got there. They say you can get warts from being kissed by a toad, but I swear I never let any toads kiss me on that particular part of my body. At least none that I know of, and even if I did—"

"*Spare* me the details!" hissed Skuld, waving the air dismissively.

"Goddess Skuld," said Dane now, approaching the Norn sister and still stirred with emotion. "Thidrek is dead—*as* you requested."

"Yes, yes, yes, I *know*, dear boy," said Skuld, annoyed.

"What do you think I'm here to do? Give you a back rub? Yes, you journeyed to the underworld, scuttled the Ship of the Dead, thwarted Hel's evil plan, and did away with that very unpleasant creature Thidrek the Terrifying. Although why he called himself that I'll never know. Wishful thinking, I suppose. He was no more 'terrifying' than a hairy mole on the tip of my nose. Now, I've no time for idle banter. Shall we get to the business at hand?"

"The oath we swore was that she be freed," said Dane, eyeing Astrid with ardor. Skuld gave him a long, imperious stare that could melt lead. "You are mistaken, young man. I did *not* say I would release Astrid from the sisterhood."

Dane exploded. "What? I have witnesses! You, in fact, *did* say—"

"—I would *allow* her to leave the sisterhood. It's her *choice*."

"Her choice?" Dane sighed in relief. "Well, if that's all there is to it, go on, Astrid, tell her." But Astrid just stared at him, openmouthed, not knowing what to say. "Astrid?"

"She is *thinking*, young man," Skuld said. "Of the golden perfection of her life in Asgard. The gods. The games. The feasts. The frolic. The thrill of crossing the heavens on her celestial steed. Age will never take her, nor will her beauty fade. . . . She shall forever be young and strong and worshipped by mortal men. And once a corpse maiden has tasted such a life, it is near impossible to turn away from it." Skuld smiled in satisfaction. "The moment I free her from bondage, all those pleasures will be lost to her forever. *That's why she's thinking, boy!*"

Astrid stood frozen in silence, eyes shining with tears. It was true! All true! She had told him before, hadn't she? About how she liked being a Valkyrie and how she would never again be satisfied with a boring life in their village? But Dane had convinced himself she had said this only to spare him from harm, that deep down she still loved him.

He took her hand in his and looked into her eyes. "I will let you go, Astrid . . . if you will say yes to this: Of all the wonders you know as a maiden . . . are they worth more to you than my love forever?"

Tears streamed down her cheeks. She paused, then said simply, "No."

Dane embraced her and kissed her, and he knew he would never know a more joyous moment in his life than this.

"You're a fool, girl," said Skuld. "When you are old and wrinkled, you will regret this."

"I will not," Astrid said. "As long as he is beside me—old and wrinkled too." Then to Dane she said, "After all we've endured, did you really think I'd leave you again?"

Dane shrugged. "Women can be unpredictable."

Then the indignant Jarl stepped forward. "All right, they got *their* happy ending. What of us? The Rune Warriors. What's *our* destiny to be? Am I to die a hero? Tell me."

"Yes, yes, *fine*," said Skuld, rolling her eyes, anxious to get on with things. "But I haven't the time to go into it all now.

If you like, I'll send you each a glimpse of your future in a dream. That way, if you like what you see, you can take it as truth; if not, you can believe it to be merely a passing fancy. Now—if there are no more *interruptions*—I shall complete the ritual."

She shot a sharp look at Astrid. "Our sister," Skuld announced in authority, "has chosen to return to her kind. It is my solemn duty to grant her wish, however repugnant I may find her choice to be!" She gave Astrid a sour smile and then raised her bony hand on high, stretching her three middle fingers to the sky. "Let it be so from this moment forth that the one known as Astrid, Mistress of the Blade, hereby does relinquish all higher powers once bestowed. And in shunning the sisterhood, she too shall be shunned, nevermore to know or remember her golden time amid Odin's hallowed halls nor her heroic doings among us who live without pity. In the name of Odin and all his domain, I pronounce thee free and unfettered of all bonds to the *Valkyrja* sisterhood, emptied of the silver light and returned to life on the earthly plane. In Odin's name I command it! "

To everyone's shock, a crackle of lightning shot forth from her fingertips and enveloped Astrid in a ragged white light, briefly illuminating the awed faces of all who looked on. Astrid felt her insides jump. Gone was the lightness of spirit she had felt while a Valkyrie, replaced by a flood of something even more wonderful—the love she felt for Dane and her people. And borne aloft by this wave of emotion, she turned to her beloved and kissed him again and again and held him in her arms so tightly, it felt as if they might be welded together as one piece of the same forged steel, never to be parted. And so busy were they receiving cries of congratulations from the gathered villagers that Skuld's departure went entirely unnoticed.

The following afternoon, beneath bright blue skies, scores of Norsefolk from villages near and far gathered onshore to pay solemn respect as Lut the Bent was sent to sea for the last time. As was customary, men and women of stature were often laid to rest on a stately longship that was then set aflame and put to sea. The rising column of smoke and fire a signal to the gods that, though they had taken the dead one's spirit, the body was to remain earthbound and returned to the sea from whence all life came.

Standing at the prow of the ship where Lut's body lay, Dane looked over the vast gathering of mourners on shore and struggled to find the right words. Words that would both honor the departed and heal the hearts of the living. He wanted to pay tribute to all Lut's finest qualities, to tell his whole life story with none of his greatness left unsaid. But despite his desire to inspire, no words came. Only the sounds of the sea lapping at the shore and birds wheeling in the sky. Dane began to panic that he'd lost his tongue altogether, when from out of the crowd a small child ran up the plank and onto the ship. It was a little girl of no more than five, and she ran to Dane and took his hand and simply stood there beside him, looking out at the people, a cherubic smile on her face. And from her smile he found his words.

"Lut the Bent loved children," Dane said in a voice full and strong. "For in children are found the things we adults often lose. Love unconditional. The freedom to dream. And, of course, hope. For it is hope above all things that sustains us. So let us look with hope upon the children to find the strength we seek. Though Lut the Bent was certainly no child, he never lost his childlike sense of wonder nor his belief that one person can work miracles in the lives of others." Dane stopped, finding it difficult to go on. The child then smiled and said, "Good-bye, Lut." And this gave him strength to proclaim, "Long live Lut the Bent, a man wiser than his days and more loving than any heart I've ever known!"

There were cheers from the crowd and the ship was pushed out to sea, and Dane stood in a daze until Astrid came and took his hand and told him he'd done well. They stood together watching the great ship sink into the sea.

"What are you thinking?" Astrid asked him.

"Something Lut said. 'Humor in the face of death is the height of character.' It's something he had until the very end, and something I'll never forget."

"He won't forget you either. Where he's going—where he already is—he still thinks of you, and loves you now more than ever."

The dreams came, just as promised, and in less than a week Dane had heard what each of his friend's fates was to be. Jarl the Fair boasted that he would marry a princess—Princess Kara, no doubt—inherit her kingdom, produce many children, and live grandly until his forty-ninth year, at which point an enemy's sword would pierce his heart and thus he would meet his end with a king's courage. Jarl said that his dream also foretold that he'd continue to prove himself superior in the annual Festival of Games, taking the crown twice as many times as Dane would in the years to come, and that his hairstyle would become so popular it would be copied by other men and even be named "the Jarl."

Fulnir the Stinking reported, somewhat more humbly, that indeed he and Drott would find success as experts in the killing of draugrs, and that each would come to have his own lands rich with grain and game fowl. He would marry as well, Fulnir said, and although his bride would be no princess, she would bear him children and love him truly and never complain about his ripe odor save for the times he complained about her cooking.

Drott the Dim said that he had dreamed he rode a whale out of the sea and up a mountain, and there atop the highest peak he built a home for her, made the whale his wife, and lived out the rest of his days eating heaps of seal meat and salted herring. Dane said that he had heard whales made good wives, but the having-children part might be hard. Jarl snickered and said that maybe the dream meant that he was to wed Ulf the Whale. Amid the laughter, Drott thought for a moment, then told Dane that Skuld had most probably sent him the dream as a practical joke and that Fulnir's dream was meant for him too.

Ulf the Whale's dream foretold that he was to attend what was called a "school" somewhere far to the south and gain great knowledge, and that he was then to lose half his weight and change his name to "Ulf the Narrow," and that this bodily transformation would bring him much fortune and many wives.

Grelf was much relieved to report that indeed he was to find great renown as a perfumer to kings and caliphs, and that, as he had hoped, William the Brave would be his man-in-waiting. When William insisted that, according to *his* dream, he was to be more like an assistant and perhaps eventually a co-owner of the perfumery, Grelf grudgingly gave in on the point.

As to Dane's other friends Vik and Rik the Vicious Brothers, no dreams came. And though downhearted at first, they soon took it as a sign that, because their valor and vigor were of such majestic magnitude, the gods could not reveal their destinies, for they would so greatly outshine the fates of all their friends as to cause excess worship from females of the village.

And as for Dane and Astrid, they were living their dream, spending each day together walking in the woods and fishing in the streams, planning their future together. One day not long after their return, Dane and Astrid lay in the grass atop Thor's Hill, gazing at the clouds and marveling at the shapes they made. One looked like a sheep's behind, Astrid said, and another a liljekonvall, or a lily of the valley. As it scudded cross the sky, the lily bumped into a new cloud, slowly forming a new image—and for one amazing moment Dane swore it looked exactly like Lut the Bent! There he was—his beard, his eyes, his very *smile*—alive in the sky once again, looking down on them with wise benevolence.

"Do you see it, Astrid?"

"Yes, yes, I do," he heard her say, and felt her hand squeeze his.

"It's him!"

Dane's heart soared. For one golden moment Lut was with them again. And then, taken by the wind, piece by piece the clouds drifted apart to form new shapes, and the magic of the moment was gone.

And then came Astrid's voice again. "You know, Dane, there's been something I've been meaning to ask you."

"Yes . . . ?"

"The night Lut died . . . what was it he whispered to you?"

Dane did not answer. Not because he had forgotten Lut's words—far from it; the words he had uttered would be forever etched in his mind with undying clarity. But Dane thought of Lut's last message as a private gift given only to him, and thus he had treasured it as something secret and sacred, something never to be revealed. But Astrid, he now thought—certainly he could tell her. She was the love of his life, his most trusted friend. But try as he might, the words wouldn't come. All that did come was the hot feeling in his throat he always got right before he cried. And catching Astrid's look, he was relieved to see that she knew all that he felt in his heart. She patted his hand and lay back on the ground, gazing up at the clouds.

"Someday, Dane," she said softly. "Someday you'll tell me."

Perhaps he would tell her what Lut had told him. Someday. But for now he was content to lie beside her in the splendor of the afternoon, the sun warm on his face and the scent of lilacs on the breeze, free of worry and full of nothing but the pleasure of her company. Again Lut's words came to him like some god-whispered lullaby. *No god is greater than the voice in your very own heart. . . .* Yes, perhaps he would tell her one day, for who better to hear it? But until that time, Lut's words would be his and his alone, a gift to be cherished and inspired by the rest of his days.

ACKNOWLEDGMENTS

A lthough authors are usually the only ones given credit, a published book is always a team effort. In this case, our team includes our fabulous editors—Warrioresses of the Word—Donna Bray and Ruta Rimas; our very talented art director, Carla "The Artful" Weise; the famed illustrator Greg "I Can Draw Anything" Call—we love the covers, Greg!—and all the other kind and diligent folk at HarperCollins who have worked so hard on our behalf.

We also wish to acknowledge the many personal friends and colleagues whose friendship and support over the years have stoked our creative fires and fed our souls. They include: Jodi Reamer; Amy Schiffman; Sandra Lucchesi; John Thornton Lundgren; Kitty and Tim Miller; Tom and Jane Jennewein; August Jennewein; Thelma Jennewein; Harald and Veshlemoey Zwart; Greg Chappuis; Sally Anderson; Cary

Odes; Kit Stolz; Dale Launer; Dan Ackerman; Rich Cronin; Rich Siegel; Bob Busker; Glen Wormsbaker; Joe Galliani; Babs Mondschein; Seth Greenland; Tod Goldberg; Scott Phillips; Darren Star; Douglas Kinsey; Catherine Palmer; Gerald Graham; Thomas Faiver; Lt. Col. David Fautua; James Walsh; Kevin Donohoe; Mark Stroble; Michael "Boom Boom" Baser; the Guest family; Michael Parker; Christine Dishaw; Laura Parker; Allison Robbins; and Jake Jennewein.

In Memoriam
Geno Foster, Hal Kaufman, Mike Roth, Jeff Rothberg
~ *Fine men, gifted artists, beloved friends* ~
